ANONYMOUS

BY
CHRISTINE
BENEDICT

*To Shelly
Best wishes
for 2016
C. Benedict*

Loconeal Publishing

Loconeal Select
Amherst, OH

ANONYMOUS

Anonymous is a work of fiction. The names, characters, places, and events in this novel are either fictitious or are used fictitiously. Any resemblance to actual events or persons is entirely coincidental.

Published by Loconeal Select. Loconeal Select books can be ordered through booksellers, Handcar Press Distribution or by contacting:
www.loconeal.com
216-772-8380

For information about custom editions, special sales, and premium corporate purchases, please visit www.AuthorChristineBenedict.com

Second edition: 2014

ISBN 978-1-940466-13-2

Printed in the United States of America

DEDICATION

This book is dedicated to my husband Bob, my daughter & son, Becki & Nathan, my sister Lynn Anderson, and to my mom & dad, Frank & Mary Lou Wilson. Thank you for all your support. Thank you for believing in me.

ACKNOWLEDGMENTS

I would like to thank Dr. Neal Chandler, Toni Thayer, Beth Sump, Heidi Corso, Jeannie Wagner, Huda Al-Marashi, Jeremy Proehl, Janet Wells, Jennifer Weinbrecht, Laura Walter, and Alison Widen for your invaluable assistance and encouragement throughout the writing process of Anonymous.

Thank you my dearest friends Stella Trujillo & Judy Yantz for being there through all the ups and downs it took to get Anonymous published. No one has read as many rewrites as the two of you throughout the evolution of this story.

CHAPTER 1

It was 1984; the year Debra turned twenty-one. Debra could see the farmhouse as they drove up the gravel road, the lightning rods rising above the battered roof. The catalpa tree towering over a gingerbread gable and a sunken porch. They had traveled five hundred miles to get here, to this relic, to these fourteen rooms amid fifty acres of pokeweed and thistle and blackberry barbs. This their new home.

A runaway from foster care, she married Greg right out of high school. She thought she loved him, and maybe she did, the best she could ever love anyone.

The car rolled into the driveway, the trailer hitch jangling, as though each were unstoppable carnival cars chinking to the crest of a free-fall. She never wanted to come here, much less buy this house, a haunted-looking monstrosity. But she never came right out and said the word 'no,' a forbidden word from where she'd been, a word worth tasting blood in her mouth. It wasn't that way with Greg though. That's what she liked about him. She would have said no if she wanted to. But she wanted to make him happy. The way family is supposed to be.

". . . got the keys?" Greg jammed the gear in park, the old Pontiac grinding in turn.

She opened the glove compartment. The heavy door slammed open and the keys fell out into her lap. That's when she saw a half-melted Reese's Cup. "Got something just for the occasion," she said, her bid to support him. "Want some?" They took turns biting off a chunk, him licking his fingers, the two of them eyeing their buy. Inside she felt like that child again, the nomad running away from each foster

1

home, her things at first in a brown paper grocery bag she remembered—a bag that tore first off. A black garbage bag replaced that, snagging so badly her things would fall out. After that she stored her things in a cardboard box, the last of which was in the back seat, the logo Exxon Motor Oil bleeding through masking tape.

From the car to the house, she stepped onto the buckled porch and through the century-old doorway into the smell of rotted wood and dead animal stench. Standing there, her shoes sticking to the yellowed floor, she felt a crack in the wall as though it were a bloodline to a pulse. The wall itself seemed to Ouija board-guide her hand over the pitted molding and to the kitchen where she saw the unmistakable gnawing of rats. Barely touching a grimy cupboard knob, she opened the cupboard under the sink. There were no drainpipes, just a bucket-size potato chip tin, all rusted and sticky. Debra moved the tin and choked back a breath when carpenter ants bubbled out like lava.

They would be living here in thirty days which was all they'd paid for to stay in a cheap hotel. Greg could work here on weekends, but only nights during the week. She would come alone on those days, to what masqueraded as a handyman special—a blacklisted house in such ill-repair, she still couldn't understand how they got the loan. It was a recession and banks weren't partial to self-employed contractors like Greg, even if he'd worked construction. Six banks had turned them down; an omen to stop from her point of view, a quest from Greg's. Surprisingly the seventh bank approved the loan, mandating twenty-percent down, charging thirteen-percent interest—a bank with a reputation for mortgaging and repossessing that dated back to the depression. Between points, closing costs, and scant building supplies, their savings was near about nothing.

"I can't believe this is finally ours," Greg said, a beacon of smiles.

"I can't believe it either . . ." she said, a game face of wonderment.

Crowbar in hand he pried a kitchen cabinet off the wall, unfazed by the ants scattering to the corners of the floor.

Debra took it all in, the chill in the air, the spooky aura, and her husband who was oblivious to all of it. She did not believe in things such as haunted houses, although it was tempting right now.

"I'm not sure where to start," Debra said, her eyes following a crack in the wall.

"How 'bout here," he said, tossing down bits of rotted wood. "Drag whatever you can outside."

Weary of ants and whatever else might crawl out, she stacked as much as she could carry in a trashcan, hauled it outside, and emptied it in a dumpster, one chunk at a time. What did it matter where they lived? She thought to herself. He was the only real family she'd ever had. And he was good to her, a gentle man, not like her stepfather, the man her mother killed. Really, she told herself, that's all that matters, not this place. They would fix up their new home and be happy here. She would make sure of it.

Debra and Greg worked steady for six days to prepare the walls for drywall, having agreed on fixing five rooms for now, enough to live in. Listening to the sound of his hammer against the ceiling, she watched him, his focus only on plasterboard held in place by his head from the top of a ladder. She'd never seen him so quiet, different somehow. But Debra wouldn't make anything of it. Anyone would be anxious on a project like this, she thought to herself.

Alone today for the first time Debra trudged up the quarry-stone steps.

Greg was working on a job, a paying job, and couldn't be with her—something she'd have to get used to. She looked in the window as if everything could have magically changed, and felt cheated somehow because nothing had. Inside she opened the bucket of white mud, the finishing goop that sealed seams and imbedded nails in the drywall. Which dried like chalk, which she sanded by hand.

Her hands were small, delicate, the kind of hands that could fit inside a mayonnaise jar. She'd bitten her fingernails down to the quick; so she'd picked at her cuticles and bit them, too, tearing fine strips of skin. She wanted so badly to stop. It was ugly. It hurt. But she would bite them anyway.

She scooped a glob into a finishing trowel and she spread it over a sunken nail head. The old water pump kicked on. The cracked windows whistled, each in their own haunting pitch. 'So what if you're alone,' she told herself. 'You've been on your own before.' Smoothing her strokes against the drywall, she tried to imagine it completely done, all painted, the molding varnished. The smell of new carpet. A place where friends would come. She wanted so badly to have a friend here. At least someone to tell her how silly it was to get the spooks.

The water pump kicked off, and she was startled by a heavy-fisted, 'thump.' Eyes wide, she stood erect. She scanned the long vertical window, the cracked glass, her reflection in the glare; and thought to open it, but knew the window frame was painted shut like all the rest.

Hesitant, she picked up the trowel again.

Another sound startled her, a heavy 'tap, tap, tap.' The scrape of fingernails inside the wall. A shadow flashed in the window. That's all she needed to push her outside, onto the porch where she stood, searching for all that was holy to explain it. "Hello?" she called out. She waited. No one replied.

'It was just a bird,' she told herself. 'A bird must have flown smack dab into the window pane. Dumb thing.' She would stay out here a little while longer, just till the scared was gone.

She watched two cats dart across the yard. Then a third; a black silhouette of a cat rubbed up against the catalpa tree. She called out, "kitty, kitty," thinking she'd name it Midnight. But instead of lingering, it turned to the field. Wanting to be outside she followed its hurried gait to the end of the property line where an old barn was barely standing. She could see the farmhouse from here, an acre distant, at the very back, where people must have moved in and out as often as they dropped off unwanted cats. She saw a tabby cat climb through a hole in the bug-eaten barn, and looked inside. Another cat, too big to be a kitten, nudged the tabby until the tabby let it suckle on a teat. A dozen or more cats were crouched on a tree branch that had fallen through the barn's roof. And something up high hung from a rafter, a mangled mess of fur. A mutilated cat. A noose around its neck. She stared at it like in a dream or in a nightmare, where you don't want to believe, but there it is, right in front of you.

She wrenched barn siding off in pieces and crumbs, and squeezed inside, the structure creaking as it swayed. Amid great piles of ceiling and roof and branches, she prayed for the poor wretched animal. But try as she might to reach it she couldn't. Maybe it was best not to disturb it for when the police would come.

She'd been waiting an hour, and then an hour more, for the Lorain County Sheriff. Evidently the township had no police. All the while scooping and spreading white mud on nail heads. The longer she waited the harder she slapped the trowel on the wall. She scooped another glob and venomously ground it into the drywall as if she were punishing this place for bringing her here. Who was she kidding, she thought, no one would come. That's the way it always was. No one ever came until it was too late.

A silent rant to empty walls was suddenly diverted when she heard floorboards creak. She stood very still. The sound of floorboards, footsteps, came from upstairs. She went outside again more mad and scared, and stopped short on the porch, nothing but fields wherever she looked. "Breathe-breathe-breathe-breathe," she said in succession, cupping her mouth in her hands. She watched the sky, her breaths shallow, not knowing what to think. A great flock of geese flew overhead, their distant honking like the sound of city street traffic. She knew it was an odd way to look at it, and maybe no one else would have seen it that way—no one else—except maybe her mother. A terribly disturbing thought. Her mother heard things— things that weren't there.

Her mother was a paranoid schizophrenic, a manic-depressive— a hereditary trait. That's what doctors had said. No one suspected the things her mother had done, not until the authorities came. One of the reasons for foster care, a supposedly safe haven for Debra.

Debra knew she wasn't hearing things. She couldn't be. She would fight the odds of heredity. She went back inside and looked up the stairs from the bottom. Something or someone was making that noise. Maybe a raccoon got inside, or maybe . . . . She gripped a pointing trowel from Greg's toolbox, as sharp as any knife, and crept up the stairs the same way she tip-toed when her stepfather was drunk. His face ablaze, she would feel his eyes upon her and would fold her arms against the soft swell of her bosoms, having been ashamed of how they lifted her blouse.

At the top of the stairs, she looked down the long narrow hallway toward the first bedroom door, and turned the glass knob. The opening door swayed a net of cobwebs. A 1920s bedroom set triggered her to see people who had slept on it decades ago, people who were probably dead by now. This was her bed now, her bedroom. An eerie quiet stilled the cobwebs, the dust on a sunray. A fresh chill in the making, she backed out of the bedroom and despairingly approached another bedroom door, the second of five.

Suddenly a door slammed, jolting her very core, an angry-handed slam. She inched out of the room, out of the hallway, and ran down the stairs, all the way to the front door. Her hand on the knob, the door opened all by itself, and she stood face to face with Greg.

"You scared me half to death!" She held her chest.

"I came home early so I could work on the plumbing."

"I'm so glad you're here. I swear someone's upstairs. Either this house is haunted or . . . . Someone slammed a door up there."

"That was no door. I tossed some plywood out of the truck."

"It wasn't plywood. I heard the floorboards creaking at first. Look upstairs. See if there's something up there."

"I know what it was." His face lit up. "It's that knurly tree branch," he said, as if they were embarking on some sort of funhouse ride. "It scrapes the window up there when the wind hits it just right." He settled his hands on her shoulders, carefree, content for all times.

"No. That wasn't it . . ."

"Trust me. It's just a tree branch." He ran his hand down her back. He pulled her into himself, hugging her like an overzealous lover, in affection for all he knew. And pinned her there.

"Don't! Stop!" she yelled.

"Don't stop?" he said, his breath warm on her neck. He hugged her so tightly she couldn't move within the smell of tar and chimney soot, trapped in the sweat of a working man. The memory flashed of how she would hear her bedroom door click-lock in the night, of hearing her stepfather pull off his belt in the dark. Her body squirming struggling against Greg's, she hated him right now. She hated how he touched her.

"I mean it." She could have hurt him just then, she could have jerked up her knee or bit him hard but she swiped her nubbin fingernails under his shirt, one dull pass, one nail sharp enough to draw blood.

"Hey." He pulled back. "What cha do that for? I wasn't hurting you."

"Why do you have to be such an ape? Why do you have to be all over me?"

"Look what you did." He looked confused, hurt, wiping blood on his tar-stained shirt. "I got up at six o'clock this morning to fit everything in today. I was just playing around."

Guilt suddenly washed over her. The whole thing started with a hug; all of it under a minute. He'd been doing so much, working so hard. "I can't believe I did that." Her hand outstretched, he stepped back, redirecting himself to the chalk-dusted sandpaper.

She knew she'd acted on impulse—maybe over reacted—yes, something ingrained to survive. But he was all she wanted right now, the man who pillow-whispered to her in the night, for that ease to fall over her, like when the dentist says you're done and you finally unclench your fists. "Greg. Listen to me. Someone killed a cat out in that barn. I just wanted you to look upstairs."

"You should have told me that."

"I need a gun. I'll take the rifle if I have to."

"Oh come on. You don't need a gun."

"I mean it . . ." she suddenly heard floorboards creaking, slow and deliberate. "There it is again," she said, her eyes on the ceiling. "You can't tell me that's a tree."

His face blank, he was listening for it, she could tell. Watching him gnaw on it as though she'd asked him to pull a grape flavor out of timothy weed.

"Are you kidding me?"

". . . I don't hear anything."

She leaned into him, his chin whiskers catching her fine hair, and spoke softly, "Where's the rifle?"

CHAPTER 2

Debra kept secrets from the time she was nine, pretending to have a normal life. Having been an only child, she longed for someone her age or older or younger, a friend to share her secrets with. She made friends easily, but her mother condemned them. Fakes, she would say, nobody smiles at you unless they want something. They lie to get what they want from you. Debra and her mother moved often, sometimes driving for days, running from evil people who do evil things—people who didn't exist. Debra didn't want a doll or toys when she was little, not as much as she wanted a friend.

Painting from the top of a ladder, Debra heard a fistful of knocks at the front door. She could see the top of someone's head through the door's high diamond-shaped window. Whoever it was, they must have been standing on their toes to see inside by the way their eyes disappeared and appeared.

I've got company now? It had almost been a month since Debra first came there. The house wasn't ready for guests. There were bare light bulbs overhead—no light fixtures yet. The yellowed floor had been scrubbed clean—no new carpeting either. No working windows. No electricity upstairs. For every 'no this' or 'no that,' her only comfort was that 'no one' had actually been upstairs when the floorboards creaked. As far as she could tell.

Debra towel-dried her painted fingers, close enough to the door to hear them talking.

"I can't wait to see the suckers who bought this dinosaur," a man's voice said. "They should have just torn it down."

"Be nice," a woman's voice said.

She was angry, hurt—him looking down on them, on her. Who were these people? Her neighbors? There were only two other houses on the gravel road. Beyond that, freshly tilled farmland as far as the eye could see.

Debra opened the door politely. "Can I help you?"

The man held a plate of cookies. The woman held a casserole, her face awash in smiles. "Hi. I'm Julie. We heard someone bought this place. Been meaning to stop by. This is my husband, Kyle."

Kyle nodded in agreement without so much as a smile. His serious manner and his perfectly groomed hair reminded Debra of a banker, except for his jeans and a flannel shirt. He was tall and thin, sunburned crow's feet around his eyes. He shook Debra's hand so loosely, she wondered why he even bothered. His hands felt rough and callused; then she noticed that he was babying a scabbed-over cut between his thumb and forefinger.

"I'm Debra. Nice to meet you," she said to the man, feigning a smile. Julie handed Debra the casserole. "I've been dying to see what you're doing in here."

Debra took the meal, and noticed calluses on Julie's small freckled hands. Then she noticed the same freckles around the laugh lines of her Irish-like face. "This is really nice of you," Debra said. "Thank you."

"The cookies are from Sam and Marie. They live right over there." Julie pointed to a house that Debra couldn't see. "They wanted to come and meet you but he has a touch of Alzheimer's; it's acting up today. You'll like them." Julie had a friendly way about her, like

11

she'd known you all your life. Her dark hair curled in spirals to her shoulders in hues of red, so different from Debra's long straight hair, a pecan kind of brown. Debra liked her, the lilt in her voice; it was the sort of voice you'd heard at Girl Scout camp in the middle of the night when your bunk-mate giggle-whispered.

"I have to thank them for myself. Just a couple of days till we move in. Tell me. Are there any stories going on about this place?" she said half-kidding.

"Don't all old houses come with old stories? Believe me, I've heard them. Don't pay them any mind. Just kids trying to scare each other." Julie stepped inside, glancing around. "You've really been working here. I'd love to have a big house like this. How many rooms does it have?" Kyle came in behind her, set cookies down on a sawhorse, and just stood there rattling his pocket change, an unnerving thing about him.

"It's got fourteen rooms and two stairways. This'll be the living room," Debra said, suddenly troubled when she saw the rifle at the foot of the stairs. Out in plain sight, here all these weeks amid paint cans and varnish, dusted in sawdust and splattered in paint, it seemed to have blended in with the scenery. She would say that Greg put it there haphazardly moving in their stuff. She would act put out, downright appalled, that he could be so careless as to leave it there. But there was no need. She directed them elsewhere. "We're keeping this old front door. My husband says it brings character to the house," she addressed both guests. "We have to replace the window in front. We'll do the rest of them later."

"This is going to be nice when you're all done. I love the arched doorways," Julie said.

"Greg arched them himself. This one goes to the kitchen, and the doorway to the dining room is over there. There's a corridor in the dining room that leads to the basement. And that's the bathroom, of course. We're only doing five rooms, enough to move in. You should have seen it when we first bought it."

"It must have been pretty bad. Every time I drove by, I saw one of you guys throwing a cartload in the dumpster. Look at your hands."

Debra lifted her hands where Band-Aids had taken an art form. There were splinters and blisters, in addition to biting her fingernails and cuticles.

Kyle interjected. "Come on Julie. We've got to go." He held the door open.

"You've got to work up to getting calluses. I have some Udder Balm. If you can get past the smell, it'll really help." Julie seemed to ignore the husband.

"Hey, it was nice meeting you. Come on Julie." Kyle snatched the back of her collar and tugged.

Julie jerked away, shooting him a dirty look. "Go on if you're in such a hurry. I'll be there in a minute."

Kyle left, not so much in a huff, as it seemed indifference.

"I know how it is," Debra said. "Thank you for bringing dinner. It was nice meeting you."

"Don't mind him. He thought your husband might be here. I'll get some of that salve for you. I'm right down the road, just across the way." Julie pointed in the direction of her house. "You can see it from halfway up your driveway. I better go. He needs me to iron his dress-shirt. Some sort of meeting tonight. If I don't hurry I won't catch him in the shower."

Debra grinned in anticipation like when you know the end of a joke and you want to hear it anyway because it's just plain funny.

"Whenever he gets pissy, I wait till he's in the shower and turn the washing machine on. A load that takes all the hot water," Julie said, her eyes gleaming. "He gets pissy so often he thinks we need a new hot water heater." She scooted out the door and took off jogging. ". . . see you soon."

Debra yelled, 'bye,' and waved from the porch, content, really content for the first time since she'd been here. Someone like this, she thought. Way out here. Someone who gets it.

Having to pee, Debra unzipped her jeans in the bathroom before remembering that Greg had turned off the water.

"Geez-oh-Pete." At this point the gas station was too far. She traipsed down the corridor that led to the basement. A quick flip-of-the-switch was all she wanted, just enough water to flush. The stairwell was dark and steep; the light-bulb's pull-chain at the bottom. She clicked on the flashlight from Greg's toolbox, and holding her pants up, cautiously stepped down the narrow stairs. Every inch she eked past spider webs meshed in between the cracks of hand-hewn quarry-stone walls. She stopped at the bottom step where she could finally reach the light, not wanting to take the last step onto the broken cement, muddied from the last rain. It smelled like the bottom of a creek bed, like earthworms and sludge. Spider webs were draped from the ceiling to the walls, and hung like shelves in every corner.

The quarry-stone walls dating back to the 1800s were pitted blocks of sandstone—every bit her idea of a dungeon. From where she stood, Debra scanned the walls, trying to see the water valve. But she didn't know where to look. A wolf spider the size of a quarter sat very still at the bottom step, then scurried across the floor. She shuddered right down to the bone. Another spider sat like a brooch on a jacket that Greg had hung on a hook. And in that moment before the light flickered off when all she could hear was her own heart, she swore that something was crawling up her leg. She let out a piercing yell, kicking wildly. She kicked off her shoes. She kicked off her jeans and dashed up the stairs in her panties, wanting to nail the door shut right then and there. At the top of the steps she eyed a yard stick that she'd used to stir paint, and picked it up. Then she made a mad dash to the basement and flogged her jeans to death right there in the sludge. Holding them at arm's length, she brought them upstairs and looked them over. She begrudgingly pulled them on, and ran outside to the back field. The sun shining off the white of her derrière, she squatted behind a briar bush where no one could see.

At least that's what she thought.

CHAPTER 3

Greg had worked from the time he was twelve, cleaning stalls at first and then chopping wood. Having been one of ten children nothing came free, not the Moped he'd seen for sale in someone's yard, not even candy, which his mother condemned. Candy produced sickly kids, she would say, sickly kids couldn't milk cows. He'd bought Hershey candy bars and Hostess everything with that first pay. He'd thrown it all up, too. By the time he was fourteen he was tearing off roofs, having donuts and Almond Joy candy bars for breakfast, all for a Honda Dream. At sixteen he started saving for a Harley. By the time he was twenty-one he had worked his way into almost every aspect of construction, his hands were entirely callused and Dick's Bakery knew him by name.

Tending to the old house's demands, Greg was shoveling dirt along a trench that ran from the house to a creek which was twenty feet away from the house. He took off his baseball cap and swatted a deerfly, thinking about what to eat, and second-guessing himself all day, wondering if he should have used a solid pipe instead of a corrugated one.

A black Ford Ranger advertising 'Zore Masonry' pulled in the driveway. A man shot up his hand, getting out. "Hi," he yelled from the driveway, approaching Greg. ". . . stopped by with my wife the other day. I see you're all moved in. How're you guys coming along?"

Greg reached up to shift his baseball cap—the one he usually wore. He was twenty-two years old and already losing his hair. He extended his hand. "I'm Greg. Good to meet a neighbor."

"Kyle." The two wrangled a handshake.

"Tell your wife thanks for dinner the other night," Greg said, throwing a glance at the broken ground and back at Kyle. "It's coming along. It'll take a while. But we're doing all right."

"Saw you working a backhoe yesterday. What're you doing here?"

"I replaced the drain tiles to stop the basement from flooding. Some moron, from who knows when, slopped cement over the drain in the basement that goes to that creek. I've got to level the floor with cement—might take a couple loads. I think I can get it down through the coal-chute."

"I wouldn't mind helping you." Kyle gestured toward his truck. "We can work something out. Say, would you like to go in on some freezer meat? I fatten a calf every summer, but this year my boys took over my stalls. They're entering their own steers in the Lorain County Fair, counting on the money for college. There's a lot of grazing in back of your place. We can build a lean-to." Kyle rattled lose change in his pockets all the while. Greg had known men with this nervous tic—a sign of insecurity that could make a man humble or make a man mean.

"I'd like to, but . . ." Greg shifted his gaze to a mound of dirt. How could he tell a stranger who had more change in his pocket than he knew what to do with, that he-himself was broke? He was embarrassed to say their kitchen curtains came from a garage sale and they rummaged through flea markets for mixing bowls and such. "I'm kind of cash-strapped these days, what-with the house and all."

"It won't cost you anything, except to have it butchered. I can get a calf, three maybe four months old, cheap, and by the end of the summer we'll have freezer meat. We can get him as soon as tonight. This is the time of the year to do it."

CHAPTER 4

With one more box to unpack, Debra slid her finger over a chip on the edge of the plate, watching the motion of her own hand. He would tie it up, he said, it would eat grass. She would just have to bring it water. "Think about the money we'll save," were his exact words. "Steak by the end of the summer."

'Great. A big-horned creature—right in back,' she thought to herself. 'Great. A do-it-yourself *Running of the Bulls.*'

Debra knelt next to the cardboard box, tattered as it was, the logo Exxon Motor Oil bleeding through masking tape. Maybe it was time to get rid of it, things she carried too long—memory scraps, some good, mostly not. She peeled off the masking tape and leafed through old report cards from grade school, letters from Greg, a goofy hat from King's Island Amusement Park—keepsakes all. Lastly she unfolded a ninth grade English assignment where she had written a poem.

The wind tarried through the sun sprinkled trees
A chant of yesterday, today will seize . . . .

She mindlessly tugged at her lashes, staring at the poem, wishing she hadn't found it; the reminder of when her father was killed, of the sound of him dying.

Debra was thirteen when the courts awarded her father custody, the man her mother had stolen her from. She'd known little of him and less of his big-bellied wife. It was a happy time though. Her stepmother would say, 'Here, come feel the baby move,' and guide Debra's hand to the ripple of a sweeping foot. Debra liked to think the baby looked something like her, maybe her eyes or her nose or her hair. Anything to make a half-sister whole.

Her room was apart from the rest of the house, a screened in porch turned into a bedroom. It felt a little like camping. Plastic fastened over the screens kept the rain from blowing inside. She fell asleep to the wind whistling through the screens, puffing the plastic in and out— her father and new mother upstairs.

In the warmth of a patchwork quilt, Debra's eyes opened when she heard a rifle-shot and breaking glass. Disoriented at first, she thought she was waking up from a dream. Then she heard a woman shouting outside.

"How could you do this? I thought you loved me," the woman yelled. Debra heard another shot. She heard an explosion rumble the house. Thick smoke came quickly, smoke she could feel hot in each breath.

She sunk to the floor where the breathing was easier and crept to the living room, and tried to yell 'get out, get out,' coughing, tearing, instead. She heard her father, her stepmother, coughing and choking upstairs.

The curtains flamed wildly, the couch, the chairs. Something fiery fell from the ceiling. Debra bellied up to the nearest door and opened it, knowing somehow no one else would get this far. In the open door she saw Aida cock the rifle again.

"Mom?" Debra felt her body buckle, her limbs give way. She could see her own self as though she were watching from above.

Aida disarmed, and ran to Debra, and dragged her to the curb. Fire and smoke billowed through the doors and the windows, black, dense. Sirens in the distance, Aida rocked Debra's body, clutching, holding it close.

"See what happens when you don't listen to me. I told you, but you just didn't listen." Aida sat suddenly still, a cellophane glaze in her eyes. "You said you loved me. How could you do this to me? I'm your mother . . . not her."

Amid the flames under the stars, a mother rocked a lifeless child. Blocking out the sound of sirens, the smell of smoke. "You just don't listen. Look what you made me do."

A fire truck and an ambulance drove up to the curb, and a medic rushed over to Debra. "I've got her now," a uniform said, reaching for her.

Aida kicked at him, reality distorted. "No. You can't have her. Take someone else's child."

"Ma'am please. She's in distress. It doesn't look like she's breathing."

Aida tightened her grip, her jaw clenched, hate in her eyes. The medic waved police onto the scene, telling her, "Ma'am, we can't help her if you don't let us take her." The man's voice was soft and sweet, something that fueled the ire in Aida.

"I know what you do to young girls," she yelled, squeezing the child in her arms. It took three men to subdue her for all the kicking and clawing and spitting she did. Finally handcuffed inside a police car, Aida watched them hover over Debra, their chest compressions jarring the small body. "This is all your fault," she said, "look what you made me do."

Debra remembered it as though she'd watched the whole thing as an observer. With one deep breath her body reclaimed her soul. They said her heart had stopped. She knew she had died, for however long. Her unborn sister told her so.

The doctors called Aida's episode a relapse. She had stopped taking her medication for one reason or another. Aida didn't remember any of it—shooting out the basement windows, the bullet hitting the gas line—an accident, maybe, but what did that matter? The judge ordered six months of in-house psych, and then released her because she was doing well on a new medication. Doing everything right, going to work on time, getting a place to live, Aida was awarded custody of Debra again. But as usual, not for long.

Debra had been mindlessly tugging her eyelashes as she'd played the scenes in her head. Uprooting a tight bunch of them, eyelashes came out in her hand. She rubbed her fist in her eye, stopping herself from pulling out any more. She wasn't going to start that again, not when it had taken so long to grow them back.

The catalpa tree scraped a window upstairs, sounding so much like a phantom rocking chair. She went outside, and as she sat down on a quarry-stone step, Midnight gravitated to her lap. Stroking his head, quieted by the way he purred, she took a deep breath. It was that space in time between twilight and dark when even grasshoppers cast shadows. She heard a truck coming down the gravel road and thought at first that it was Greg, but as the truck came into view, she saw its black lettering, 'Lorain County Game Warden' on the door. The driver slowed down as if he was going to stop. She couldn't see his face, but she could feel his eyes on her. Then he picked up speed and drove away. She could have sworn that all the cats were hiding, including Midnight who was crouched under the swing. Then she heard another truck coming, and a rattling aluminum trailer. It was Greg, coming home with their cow.

The front porch swing squawked with each dip and rise, its varnish flaking at the touch of a hand. Still, it was a peaceful end-of-the-day, when the talking was done, when an early-summer eight o'clock was both the time of day and the time of night. A whiff of wild roses drifted from the creek, a cicada song rose and fell, and a million peepers harmonized into one voice.

Greg sat beside her, the warmth of him against her, playfully crowding her to the edge. She sensed a rambunctious mood. He brushed a strand of her hair away from her face, his knuckle soft on her cheek. She knew it was coming, but wasn't quite sure what 'it' was until he started petting her head. Broad strokes of affection, aggravating at best, down the length of her hair.

"Such a round head," he said, his hand gliding over her scalp.

Anyone else might have smacked him. But this was something his dad had passed down, an induction to the Hamilton family, of sorts. His dad had taken such pride in how round his kid's heads were, or so it seemed. There were so many kids in Greg's family, that maybe any one-on-one attention was better than none.

So Debra sat still. Thinking of that little house and all those kids, she pictured Greg from when he was eighteen and worked in the lumberyard. He was physically stronger than his brothers—a bull, they called him. He never took off his shirt in public, embarrassed by the way people would stare. He was shyer than anything back then, and Debra was anything but shy.

He rested his hand on her knee. He leaned over and breathed a whisper, "It's time to water the livestock. You should give it a try."

23

"It doesn't bite, does it?"

"Not at all. He'll eat oats right out of your hand."

She stood up, reinstating the 'I can do this' mantra all over again. Her charge was just a calf after all, just four months old. How bad could it be?

"Did you think of a name?" Greg asked.

She had thought of a name, something ordinary, something to last the summer and be done with. Nothing cute. Nothing to foster any kind of attachment. "Otto. How about Otto?"

He was saying 'not bad' in a thinking-mode-nod, like when you taste liver and onions for the first time floured and fried in bacon, and you actually like it. Then he said, ". . . Otto ought-to do it." He had a way of making her smile even as she rolled her eyes.

Back by the well she pumped water. This won't be bad, she thought. Otto isn't so different from any other pet; we'll be friends in no time. As she filled the bucket, she caught sight of the three hundred twenty pound toddler—what he was up to. He'd managed to get himself hung up against the tree where Greg had tied him. For whatever reason, the thing had walked in circles until he had only two inches of rope between him and the tree. There he stood, speaking the one-syllable language of moo.

The tenderloin was a Holstein Angus mix with horns so big it was a wonder he could hold his head up. The closer she got to him the worse he stunk, his poop everywhere in plops. She didn't want to touch him. She didn't want him to touch her. Debra got directly behind him, apprehensive, back far enough to reach his hide. She patted his hind quarter to prod him in the opposite direction. "Go on. Go."

He wouldn't budge. She stepped over fresh dung to get closer. "Come on, Otto," she said, giving him a shove with the palms of her hands, impulsively keeping her fingers from touching him.

Otto was immovable, a marble slab with a swishing tail. She smacked his butt; she shoved a little harder. "Come on Otto. Move." Debra leaned in and pushed. Otto urinated a flood, spritzing her feet.

"Great! That's just great!"

Greg came from around the house and stopped at the garage, his arms folded. "That's a L-Otto steer," he yelled out to her, amused with himself.

"Come here," she yelled back.

"Just take his lead and walk him around the tree. He won't hurt you."

Pee-splattered feet, she made her way to the animal's head, saying, "Nice cow." She reached for the leather lead. But, he would not let her take it, his horns targeting her midsection. She hopped off to the side. He gained three feet of rope but he stopped right there. She looked at Greg and back at Otto. "I don't think he likes me."

"Take charge of him," Greg yelled out to her. "You can do it."

She took a step forward. "Good boy. You be a good boy now," she said sweetly. Cautiously stepping in front of him, watching out for his horns, she extended her hand. He aimed for her midsection again. Trying not to be intimidated she trotted backward, him plotting ahead, round and round the tree until Otto had the full length of rope. Quite an accomplishment from her point of view, without having to touch him once. She was glad it was over, glad she'd never have to do it again.

As it was Otto walked in circles around every tree, every day, all day long.

CHAPTER 5

Summer brought temperatures of ninety degrees. Debra unfastened clothespins; towels and sheets stiffening on the line. Out in the daunting sun, the air was still, nothing to flap a single towel, nothing to wave a single sheet. She shied away from looking at Otto. He was tied to a tree near the barn today. A nagging thorn in her side, he was probably tangled already. She heard rustling nearby from a wood pile, and saw the elderberries tussle. It was that groundhog; she knew it; one of the woodland creatures who demolished her garden, one who dug for grubs in the lawn and left big holes where she would trip and twist her ankle. "I ought to get the rifle," she said to Midnight, ". . . for all the good it would do." Midnight rubbed a full-body purr against her leg and curled around her ankle and rolled over her toes. "I know. I'm better off without it. I couldn't kill anything anyway."

Debra had kept her mother's rifle within sight those first few weeks, and carried it with her whenever she heard strange sounds in the house. She hated that rifle, hated what it had done, hated what it could do. Worst of all she hated how easy it took to her hands.

She'd been counting cats for weeks on end, fifteen cats in all. Then two more joined the group, which made her think the cat killer hadn't come back. She'd been dumping cat food in an old hubcap she'd found to keep track of them, calling out, 'kitty, kitty,' to gather them all in one place—rationing cat food she bought on sale.

She'd kept the rifle handy for a few weeks more, and after some time she moved the rifle to the coat closet, trying to rationalize how the wind played tricks on her with the house. A south wind would set a shutter to flapping which she swore was bare feet pit-patting on a bare floor. A west wind would stir up mortar pieces that fell in the chimney, unlike anything she'd ever heard. And a north wind would blow the catalpa tree branches against the windows upstairs which bore the resemblance to someone walking up there. That's how Greg saw it, so it must have been true.

Denying an ever-present uneasiness she put the rifle away, up high in a bedroom closet alongside the Exxon Motor Oil box, and covered it with a blanket, resolved to not see it again. Not for now anyway.

Ninety degrees, it was one of those days when you worked up a sweat by just standing outside, a humid day when the smell of your sweat turned the bugs mean. Carrying laundry back to the house Debra could see Otto—him in his usual spot hung up on a tree. Greg tied him to a different tree every day, further in the field to graze, and every day Otto circled it until he couldn't move—today at the barn. He mooed a never changing pitch, the same no matter what. It was as though he was void of a soul, void of loving or hating or being happy or sad. Seven hundred pounds now and horns to match, he seemed to be growing aggressive. It wasn't one thing in particular, just a change in temperament—as if he hadn't been gelded. The vet had cracked his ball-sacks in a vice-like thing the night they brought him home as a calf. Greg had seen it, heard it, said it sounded like walnuts cracking. It was an awful thing the vet did; Greg had never heard of anything like it.

Debra stood on the deck, laundry basket in hand, looking at Otto. "He has to be downright addle-brained," she said to Midnight. "How can anything be so stupid and live?" She'd tromped down a path for as many times as she'd been there today, and had let him chase her around the tree for the sake of untangling him. She hiked it once more, shielding her eyes from the sun—snapping a red-checkered kitchen towel at whatever was circling her face. There was an awful swarm around Otto's head, worse in the heat of the day. Horseflies. Deerflies. Gnats. All in his face. Crawling. Buzzing. Climbing on sweat, on top of the other, him chewing his cud in gobs of slobber. She'd been waiting for Julie to come over to spray him with some sort of repellant, and was terribly curious as to why she hadn't been there yet, even a little aggravated. She'd made ice tea and finger sandwiches, goose liver and cucumber, which had been sitting in the fridge for what seemed like hours.

Debra swished the towel at Otto's face, trying to lessen the bugs, and snapped it accidentally in his eye. Otto jerked, suddenly spooked. Debra hadn't meant to spook him but she had spooked him and she couldn't take it back. He kicked up his hoofs, bucking like a wild horse, his tree-trunk-neck jerking the rope nonstop.

"Easy Boy. Easy," she said, trying to calm him down. "Easy now . . . ."

He flailed his head. He reared up, fighting the little bit of rope, a wild fire in his eyes. Amid flicks of sweat and slobber something told her to run, an inner voice, like when something tells you to hold your breath under water or you'll drown. She backed away. Then she heard it—a snap. And then she saw it—the rope dangling from his tether. He was so enthralled in senseless ire that his good fortune hadn't occurred to him yet. She walked backward mindful of any quick movements, trying to think of a safe place to run. The house was too far. The barn was boarded up.

He stood still for a moment, suddenly aware he was free—free to chase Debra—and that's what he did. She was already running, knowing full and well that she'd been training him for this all summer. She ran on uneven ground, her flip-flops slapping her heels, weeds waist-high, blackberry barbs stinging her bare arms and legs. She looped around a tree and ran behind the barn, dodging Otto, not like a matador would, but more like the clown sent in afterwards. A clumsy silly no one clown.

On this side of the barn, she saw something odd set way back in the field, an old swing set. The image shifted through heat waves like a mirage, abandoned here for who knows how long. Debra widened her strides, but suddenly stumbled, her foot caught in a tangle of vines. She felt her knees buckle. She felt his horn graze her calf. But somehow she didn't fall, somehow she was able to keep her balance and run. Otto was breathing heavily, she could hear him over her own sinking breaths. It was so hot, so damn hot. This is how she would die, she thought as she ran. He would gore her to death, and they would find her body there. He chased her to the swing set where she climbed up on a rusty teeter-totter seat, and boosted herself up to the center bar that connected the two A-frame poles.

"Julie!" she screamed as if Julie could hear her. "Julie!"

Rusted paint flaked off in her hands, red and yellow. The teeter-totter swung on its own, Otto's new target of destruction.

The rusted bar suddenly broke from under her feet, her hands clenching the bars above. She slid her foot over the bolt that remained, trying to get a foothold. Hand over fist, glazed in sweat, she maneuvered herself to the main overhead bar. She was sweating badly, her wet palms sliding. Otto rammed the swing set. She tried to pull her body up to help her hold on, but lacked the kind of strength it took. The rusty bars seemed to be melting in her hands. Bugs swarmed around her sweat. Horseflies. Deerflies. Gnats. All in her face. Crawling. Buzzing. She felt a sting just under her eye and shook her hair, screaming for screaming's sake. Now she was mad, fighting mad.

"You stupid-ass fudging cow!" She kicked at him and immediately lost her grip. Her feet swung out and she fell, her head hitting the hard parched ground. Blurred images closed her eyes and the sound of waves flooded her head, as she slipped into unconsciousness.

You stupid-ass fudging cow . . . "You stupid-ass fucking brat!" She saw Aida, her mother screaming at her nine-year-old self. Underweight as a child, her clothes hung on her delicate body. She saw three-story houses, lining the street, from inside an attic window, overlooking a steep gabled roof. The houses outside were so close that you could hardly walk between them.

"I told you to never leave this yard! Where were you? I looked everywhere!" Aida screamed, pinching the fleshy part of Debra's arm.

"Ruth went to the circus. She was showing me . . ."

Aida slapped her face. "I've told you and told you. Never leave this yard. There's men out there who experiment on girls like you."

"I didn't mean to . . ."

Aida stopped, her eyes in a glaze, looking up at the ceiling. "They're here. Hide." Aida opened the attic window. "Hurry. On the roof." She motioned to the steep gabled roof. "They're coming. You've got to hide. They'll never look on the roof."

"No. Mom. I can't."

Aida grabbed Debra and dragged her to the window. "You've got to. No one will find you there."

The view spanned the whole neighborhood. She could see the wind stir the treetops. Debra knew not to speak. She knew not to cry. Anything more than a silent observer would throw her mom further into the crazies. She stepped over the low windowsill, and eased herself to the other side. Aida closed the window, locked it, and then stood with her back to it, guarding it, yelling to no one there. Fierce words that Debra couldn't make out. Aida's back against the window, she slid down and curled up in a ball. "No one no one no one no one . . . ."

A thin layer of moss covered the slate roof. Debra hung on to the old wooden window frame, the chipped paint on her fingertips. The wind whistled in her ears and whipped her hair. She angled her foothold, trying her best to be perfectly still. A chunk of old wood came off in her hands, her foot slipped. She felt herself sliding, falling.

Debra's body jerked. She suddenly opened her eyes, lying beneath the swing set, everything blurry. She could smell Otto three feet away. His horns were mangled in a rusty chain. She rolled slowly to slip away. She heard someone coming. Julie.

Julie threw down her bottle of bug spray. "Damn it! Get out of there!" She stormed over to Otto and whacked his behind. Otto turned and snorted. He reared up. Without a word, she grabbed his collar. Julie held him firm with one hand, and she punched him square in the face with the other. "Stop it!' She jerked him down. "I don't need this!" She clipped the tether to his collar. "I've been up since five this morning!" Julie jerked one quick jerk, and led him to a nearby tree. Otto moseyed behind her, subdued, as if nothing had happened at all.

Debra sat up. "I can't believe you did that."

"An old farming trick. Punch him right in the snout next time. You've got to show him who's boss." Julie tied a heavy knot on Otto's rope and went back for the bottle of bug spray. "Sorry I couldn't get here sooner. Are you okay?"

"I think so. Do you lift weights or something?" Debra stood up and wiped her face in her shirt.

"I don't have to lift weights, not with the workout I get on days like these. My boys are supposed to be taking care of those steers, and I'm stuck doing all the work." Julie jerked Otto steady. "Although I like to go jogging," and doused him with fly spray. "Are you sure you're okay? It looks like you're bleeding."

"I'm okay," Debra said. But she really wasn't. She was trembling so. Her face was spotted where she had been bitten. Dried blood crested on her bruised leg, and her head hurt. She tucked all of it inside; whining was not endearing. Whining wouldn't win any friends. "Got time to come inside while I clean up?"

"Are you sure? I'm all sweaty. I've been messing with cattle all day." Julie brushed dried mud off of her sweat-stained shirt. "I can't stay long." They walked back to the house, Debra limping. Julie sat on the porch step, pulled off her boots and then she got a good look at Debra. "You poor kid. You look awful."

"I'm just a little shaken, that's all. Nothing's broken. I can handle pretty much anything else."

Julie rubbed her feet. "I've got to tell you. My balls are killing me," she said matter of fact.

Debra perked up. "Your balls?" she asked surprisingly.

"My balls. You know . . . the balls of my feet?"

It was a dumb joke but that was alright. It brought a welcomed laughter between them. The kind of laughter that makes you look forward to laughing some more.

At a quarter to eight Debra could hear the rattle of ladders, the unmistakable sound of Greg's work truck coming down the road. The pounded gravel spun a dry fog you could taste in your mouth. He got out of the truck, bent like an old man, soot sweat-pasted to the fine lines of his face. She knew he'd had a big job today on a steep roof, tearing off three layers of shingles, and in this heat.

She would tell him what happened, just to get it said. Then he could go inside and she would wait on him. She would give him dinner and sooth his sunburn with apple cider vinegar.

"I had some trouble with Otto today."

"Is he okay?" Greg asked, his eyes on Otto, looking past her.

"He's fine. But he broke loose . . ." she started, figuring she would just get it all out. She told him about the briar bushes, and her flip flop making her fall. She told him about Otto cutting her leg with his horn. It was more of a deep scratch than a cut, but she showed him anyway. The more she told him the faster she talked, until she was rambling on about bugs and bites and how she could have really been hurt.

"I've got to do something about that. I can't have him running loose, chasing you all over the place," he said, fidgeting with his baseball cap, never once looking at her.

"I don't know what I would have done if it weren't for that swing set."

She could tell he'd had enough. He walked past her, toward the garage in what she took as his disappointment. Her gaze settled on the cracked ground beneath a sparse patch of grass.

He took a step back. "A swing set? Where? I haven't seen any swing sets."

"You can't see it from here."

He went inside, looking terribly concerned, leaving her there by herself. It wasn't like him to dismiss her, as such. She knew he was tired and hungry. She knew he'd had a rough day. But it hurt just the same. What was he thinking? All these weeks trying to cope with this house and all of its problems, her driving him crazy over every sound. That it had finally happened? That she was seeing things, hearing things, just like her mother had? She heard the screen door snap shut and saw him coming around the corner. He had a Cherry Nehi, and headed toward the barn in the direction of Otto. She could see him talking to the beast as he tightened its rope, the stupid thing licking his boots.

Staring out at the open landscape, at the horizon, she yelled to him. "I'll show you where the swing set is." She walked out in the field where he already was. "It's on the other side of the barn. It'll just take a minute." She went ahead. She would see it soon and she would show him and everything would be alright.

Rounding the corner, she looked for it. But it was gone, the teeter-totter, the rusty chains, all gone. It seemed as though a vortex tugged her hairs straight up. But there was no updraft, no wind at all, just her and the bugs and the sun. She walked the tall grasses, asking herself, what happened to it? And stood forlorn, her arms folded, trying hard to see it, trying hard to bring it back, when Greg sauntered over.

"So you got to see Julie today. That must have been nice. You've been wanting to see her again," he said, taking her hand. He squeezed her fingers as though that alone would keep her from crossing the path her mother had.

"Don't." She slipped her hand out of his. She walked on. He followed a bit and then he fell back.

A few steps through the thistle; a few steps through the blackberry briars, she saw something strange—a fallen-down pile of rusty swing set bars that had been here so long the soil embedded them. She saw the same faded red and yellow colors that she had washed off her hands. And then she saw blood on one of the bars— her blood.

Greg came up beside her. "Deb? Are you all right?"

CHAPTER 6

Debra mixed Epsom Salt and cool water in the tub. Naked she could see all the bruises.

'Are you all right?' Greg had asked her that just after they'd met. 'Are you all right?' The words repeated in her head. She sank down into the bathtub and laid back in the cool water. Her mind wandered to that place in her mind she'd do anything to erase, the memory of her mother that night. Debra was sixteen at the time, living with her mother and stepfather in Cincinnati.

* * *

Debra never understood why her mom married Bill, the man her mother had met in the nut-house. He'd been a patient there although Debra didn't know why.

Debra was outside with Greg, a boy she'd just met. At eighteen he was a couple years older than her. The two of them sat on a picnic table in a small fenced-in yard which was like all the yards on West 17th. The house was in the inner-city, and rundown, where she lived with her mother Aida and her stepfather Bill.

She could see inside the kitchen window from the yard, and she could see Bill downing a shot of whisky, plain as day. 'Bill seemed nice at first,' she thought to herself—before the drinking started. Then her step-dad would sneak into her bedroom at night. He'd slip under her covers, and try to lay on top of her, and say be quiet, his whisky breath dampening her ear. But she would tell him right off, "You're forgetting that I have a case worker. Lay one hand on me and she'll throw you in jail so fast you won't know what happened." That would stop him cold. Just to make things easy though, she would sleep in a closet cube under the stairs where she'd made a soft bed for herself out of old coats. He'd never look there.

"Would you like something to drink?" she asked Greg. He was fun and sweet and made her feel good.

"What have you got?"

"Root beer, milk." She paused. "I've been drinking water. It's very good for the skin."

He ran his fingertip down her cheek, "I can see that," and pulled her close. He nuzzled a kiss on her neck. She loved it when he did that. But she saw that Bill was watching them from the kitchen window which made her pull away.

"I'll get us some water. Don't go away," she said.

"I'll go with you." Greg held onto her arm.

"No. I'll be right back." She went inside through the back door and walked into the kitchen where Bill was pouring a second shot of whiskey.

"What are you doing out there? He's got his hands all over you," he said, spittle on his unshaven chin.

She wanted to say none of your business, but held her tongue. "Nothing. I just came in for a couple glasses of water."

"Don't lie to me. You need water to swallow drugs. Don't you? That's why you want water. Isn't it? You're one of those hippies." Bill slammed down his emptied glass. "I won't have it. Do you hear me?"

"You know I'm not a hippie. I'm not taking drugs." She said, anxiety, frustration burning.

Bill pushed the screen door open. "Get out of here before I kill you. You hippie son of a bitch."

Greg hopped to his feet, red-faced. "Sir?"

"Don't sir me. Get out."

Greg left through what used to be a garden gate. Debra ran to her bedroom and locked the unreliable door, sick inside. Two hours later, Debra was still in her room when she heard her mother come home from work. Her mother seemed almost normal on this new medication. Debra could tell that even Aida was afraid of Bill. Aida walked softly; she closed the door silently, and kept the metal hangers from clanging when she hung up her coat. Debra stayed in her room, fretting about Greg, worried she would never see him again.

Debra heard the phone ring, and she heard her mother answering it.

"It's 9:00 at night. Don't you have any good sense? Call at a decent hour and you can talk to her." Aida hung up the phone. Debra knew it was Greg.

It was 10:00 at night when Debra slipped out of her room as quietly as her mother had come into the house. Stepping heel to toe, softly, not wanting to make a sound, she snuck down the hallway to the darkened kitchen. Bill's face reflected the glow of the television where he stretched out on the couch. Her mother was ironing clothes that she had dampened the day before, the sour smell hot in the air. Not wanting anyone to hear her, Debra opened the cupboard door without turning on the light and reached for a glass, but it slipped out of her hand. She froze to the sound of breaking glass and closed her eyes, and thought for a minute that if she closed them tight enough, if she could hold her breath long enough, that she could take it all back. She heard the fake leather couch crunch. Footsteps.

"What the hell are you doing up?" Bill staggered around the

corner, pulling off his belt, and turned on the light.

"It was an accident." Debra went for the broom.

"I'm sick and tired of your attitude. You think I don't know what you're doing?" He doubled his belt. The belt slapped her legs.

"Please . . ."

"You're on drugs! Say it!" He threw the belt down and drew back his fist. Debra felt the blunt force. Once. Twice. Three times. The pain so bad her mind went numb, a disconnect. It was as though he was hitting somebody else. Maybe she died just then. Or maybe she surrendered to a kind of escape that comes to those who can't stand the pain.

Then it happened. Her mom. The rifle. The shot.

Bill was slow to die. So Aida shot him again. His body folded on the linoleum squares. The smell of spent whisky. Sour clothes. A cheery commercial played in the other room, "plop plop, fizz fizz, oh what a relief it is . . ." Debra and her mother waited, watching for Bill to move. A minute. A minute more. Watching. Waiting. Each of them holding their breath.

The doorbell rang.

"Look what you made me do." Aida said. "Go live with your father. See if you can ruin his life, too."

Police flooded through the door. "Drop your weapon," an officer yelled. Aida complied, her face grave, hard. Handcuffs clanked. A voice of authority recited a speech of sorts, talking about rights and such.

Debra was guided outside, the cement cold on her feet. She clutched a blanket one-handed, and tasted the blood on her split lips. The neighbors stood, gaping in the front yard, summoned by the sound of gunfire. Greg was there, too, and tried to get through, but the police wouldn't let him. Two policemen guided Aida out of the house in handcuffs to a waiting police car.

Greg saw his chance and his way to Debra. "What happened? Are you all right?" He wrapped her shoulders in the blanket she was holding. Her face was green and bloody and swollen where Bill had punched her. Under a streetlight, Debra stared without blinking at the space behind her eyes.

"I just wanted some water." Her eyes finally focused on Greg. "I just wanted some water." Tears hung on wet eyelashes. ". . . I can't live with my father. How could she say that? My father is dead."

Greg pulled her into his own full warmth. Debra's breath soft on his neck, she cried silently, the only way she knew how.

CHAPTER 7

Wanting to tell someone, anyone, Julie paced on her front porch with a troublesome letter addressed to her from a man who said he fell in love with her. It was an invasion of privacy a nameless man watching her jog, being so close, telling her his sexual fantasies. Whoever he was. Julie had been a waitress at a fancy restaurant, afternoons, where she'd served businessmen lunch which must have been where he'd met her.

It was 9:30 in the morning. Kyle was on a job. Nate and Jeff, her teenage boys, were in the barn. No one would miss her now. Burning to talk to someone she walked to the end of her driveway and gazed at Debra's house. It was strange seeing the house now. The towering lightning rods, the scary old place that simple-minded people whispered about. Who would have thought that someone like Debra would live there? Someone who didn't fawn over tea and cupcakes, the pretense for idle talk among PTA and 4-H women around here. Debra was different. Julie was sure of it.

She crossed the road and jumped the ditch, sparrows chattering on wires above which flocked to Debra's catalpa tree when Julie walked under it. It was funny how she noticed the birds just now, like they were following her just for the sake of little-bird gossiping. Debra was sprinkling roses that seemed to flourish since she'd been there.

"Hi Deb," Julie called out as she neared.

"Hi." Debra pulled the hose for the length across the lawn. "I've been meaning to call you this morning. You won't believe what happened. You know that swing set?"

41

"That old thing?" Julie had no interest in this and it showed in her face. But that was alright with Debra. Julie's remark was an acknowledgment. Julie had seen it, touched it, washed it off her hands, too.

"The strangest thing—it collapsed out of the blue, and when . . . ."

"I'm surprised it was still standing."

Debra stopped short. Julie had said what she needed to know, that she'd seen it upright. That's all she needed. So instead of going on about it Debra said, "It's a wonder it didn't fall in sooner."

"I'm going to have one of my boys chain Otto to an anchor. I've got one that screws in the ground about two feet down. That ought to stop him from being a nuisance. I don't know why I didn't think of it sooner." Julie fidgeted with her hand in her pocket, crimping the edges of the letter. "I want to show you something. Just between you and me, I got this in the mail today." Her back to the sun Julie handed the letter to Debra. "I don't know who sent it."

The sun in her eyes Debra asked Julie to come inside, and unfolded the page as she walked. It felt good to be the one who Julie trusted with something so private. Whatever this letter was Debra was glad for it. Glad that Julie picked her above anyone else. They came in the kitchen by way of the garage and utility room and sat down at the kitchen table, Julie watching Debra's face as she read.

Julie,

You don't know me, and I really don't belong to the church. I put this letter in a church envelope, so your husband wouldn't open it (if he's like most men). I feel as if I have known you for years and finally got the nerve to write. I used to see you at lunch every chance I could. What a disappointment I had when they told me that you quit. I secretly asked questions about you in hopes to talk to you someday. Well that day never came. As with most things I do in life, I gave up. I still want to see you. If I don't, I will hate myself for not trying. I just moved to a new development two months ago, and to my surprise, I saw you jog right passed my house Thursday night. Well, that did it. Almost blew my mind! You are so pretty! I love the way you look. I have never felt this way for anyone before. I must be crazy to write this, and you must think I'm a nut! But I have to tell you that I love you. From the second I saw you I knew I loved you! Well, don't panic, I too am married and won't make any moves toward you, but I had to let you know anyways. I won't tell you my name because of feedback, but I will tell you I'm married, got three kids, and am 40 years old. You have been in my dreams every night since I first saw you. Even when I make love to my wife I see your face. As I said before, I won't approach you, but I may write again, or if you're brave enough, jog past my house again on Thursday about 7:00. I will be outside. I do trust you; please don't get me in trouble. You will always be my lover in my mind and heart! Smitten

Debra looked up from the letter. "This is serious. What are you going to do?"

"There's nothing I can do. Even if I knew who wrote this he isn't breaking any laws. I don't plan on meeting him; although I'd like to know who sent this."

"I don't know what I would do if I got something like this."

"The worst part is he knows where I live. He might be looking in my windows. He could even be stalking me."

"Julie, think. Are you certain you can't think of anyone who might have written this?"

"Not an inkling. I can't tell you how many men I waited on in that restaurant. Mostly businessmen, and for the most part they seemed normal. I'm a waitress. Being nice to customers is just part of the job."

"Has Kyle seen it?"

"He was the one who got the mail this morning. He read it before I got the chance and then he asked me 'what the hell is going on' as if I knew who wrote this. Do you mind if I grab some water?" Julie helped herself to Debra's kitchen cupboards. "Where are your drinking glasses?"

Before Debra had a chance to stop her, Julie stumbled on her mismatched collection of cups and glasses. It would have been embarrassing for anyone else to see how little she had, but Julie didn't draw attention to it. Debra read one line that was particularly disturbing, 'When I make love to my wife I see your face.' Makes me wonder what he was doing when he wrote this. Makes me want to wash my hands."

Julie exaggerated a wide-eyed stare. "Next time he sees my face I hope he sees me slap him."

CHAPTER 8

On the days when the house was quiet, it wasn't all bad living here. Debra knew all her neighbors by now, the ones beside Julie and Kyle. Sam and Marie lived down the road; and even though Debra had been there several times, she kept forgetting to give back Marie's cookie plate from when she and Julie first met.

Debra was frosting homemade brownies with that purpose in mind. The frosting melting, she cut them into squares; and trying to make them look pretty she arranged several on Marie's plate. Mrs. O'Shell always said that you should never return an empty plate. Mrs. O'Shell had been her foster mother for a time, a church-going woman who Debra held in the highest regard.

Because the frosting was sticky Debra didn't wrap them in foil or plastic; and left the house without covering them. The minute she stepped outside a deerfly wouldn't leave her alone, bouncing off her face repeatedly. It seemed as though they were always waiting for her to come outside. She swatted as she walked, the insect biting her in jabs. "Go away!" She stopped halfway across the road, her swatting, it coming back in a maddening cycle. Of all places to land, it landed in the frosting which sucked it down like quicksand.

"I can't believe this," she said out loud. Trying to edge the bug out she shoved it in deeper. Still hearing it buzz she moved the finger-stamped square to the edge of the plate, to make sure that no one would eat it.

She neared Marie's back yard from the edge of the ditch and saw their bantam rooster running loose. The rooster, a fighting breed,

45

lorded over the borders, its wings flapping wildly when she crossed into the yard. It was the kind of rooster that could peck the eye out of an egg-sucking weasel which was what these neighbors wanted according to Marie. Debra was cautious, seeing it, baffled why anyone would let something so mean run loose.

"Hi, Marie," Debra said, eyeing the black-spotted tail feathers. Marie had been bent over in a tomato patch. The rooster flapped right up to Debra, her heart leapt into her throat, but Sam wedged himself in the rooster's path and shooed it away. She could see where Sam had missed a patch of chin-whiskers he must have thought he shaved. Smelling of pipe tobacco his big belly seemed to smother his belt buckle. This elderly couple had a grandma-grandpa way about them, a cozy kind of pleasant, an unconditional acceptance that Debra had only read about.

"What have you got here?" Sam asked in his second-childhood way, immediately scooping up the segregated brownie that he popped in his mouth.

"Uh . . . brownies," she said, feeling wicked, hearing it crunch in his teeth. How could she let herself be sidetracked? She hadn't come here to feed bugs to old people. She lied, "I thought I would put some walnuts in. There must have been some shells."

"Oh how nice," Marie said. "I've got a fresh pot of coffee." Her enormous bosom ended at her waist which Debra felt up against her when Marie wrapped her arm around her. Holding onto Debra as tightly as she held onto her cane, Marie led her back to the house. Without intending to, Debra ushered her up the porch steps, through the screen door, and on inside.

Amid a collage of pictures that covered the walls, mountains of newspapers were stacked haphazardly in every corner and on the kitchen table. Debra could definitely smell garlic but what was that other smell? Eucalyptus? Ben Gay? Nearly everything inside dated back to the nineteen-fifties—teapot wallpaper, paisley carpeting, and a green boxy refrigerator. Stacks of dishes, pots, and pans, left to dry upside down, were piled next to the sink, and old jelly jars of what looked like dried peas and herbs were jammed together on the counter tops.

"The paper said someone killed a rabid raccoon in Grafton," Marie said, letting go of Debra's arm. "A raccoon's been dumping my garbage and chicken feed all summer. I hope it doesn't have rabies."

"He must live in my chimney. I swear I think something's alive in there." Debra scanned the array of faces within the pictures. "You wouldn't believe all the weird things I hear in that house." Now that she'd said it here, of which she hadn't in all this time, she would give them the chance to say something about her farmhouse, something they might have been keeping from her. Forks clanked on dishes with Marie at the sink. A sticky fly strip overhead buzzed with a fly that hadn't died yet.

Marie's voice broke in. "Would you like some coffee?"

"No thank you." Debra shifted her attention to the many pictures. Sam and Marie were young in some, posing with their children. A graduation picture of a young man was in the mix, and a picture of a young girl who looked like Julie.

"Marie, is that Julie? Are you related?"

"Not legally. We tried to adopt her when she was four but they said we were too old. It didn't seem to matter that we'd raised seven kids. We were her foster parents. Her brother was a baby at the time.

We wanted him, too, but another couple adopted him. It was terrible how they split them apart just because those people didn't want a little girl."

"Does she stay in touch with him?"

"It was a closed adoption. We were never able to find him. Funny thing though, her mother was real sick, and had two pendants made, so they could match them up if they ever found each other. I'm sure Julie still has hers. Used to be, she'd never take if off. Marie sipped her coffee. "I never would have known about Julie if I hadn't been the nurse on duty that day. Julie was so little when her mother died. It just broke my heart."

When Julie was four years old her mother was dying of cancer. Snuggled up to her mother in the hospital bed, the little girl seemed to think, if she lay perfectly still, that she would be invisible to everyone there. That no one would take her away. Atop her mother's bosom, their bodies moved as one with every rise and fall of her breaths. Listening to her mother's heart, Julie's eyes followed the heart monitor behind the saline drip.

"Isn't there anyone Fay?" Marie asked Julie's mother. "A sister, a cousin, an aunt?"

"My husband and I came over from Ireland. My family disowned me because I married a Catholic. His family disowned him because he married a protestant. It's been just me and the children since he died. Someone ran a red light," Julie's mother said, her eyes on the ceiling as if she saw heaven there.

"I wish there was something I could do," Marie said, a salty taste in her throat.

Another nurse came inside. "It's time," she said. "The social worker's here."

Fay rubbed her eyes clean of tears. "Julie. Be a good girl." She smoothed Julie's hair and patted her shoulder. "Come on, Honey. We talked about this. You know I love you."

Julie stiffened, gripping her mother's hospital gown. A portly woman introduced herself as Miss Huntley, and nudged passed Marie. All business.

"I have another appointment at ten. Say good-bye now." The woman took hold of Julie's waist and whisked her up like a five-and-dime doll.

Julie was suddenly hysterical, crazy hysterical, kicking, screaming, and writhing in the woman's fat arms. Marie could still hear her being carried down the hallway, and to the parking lot. Then suddenly remembered the necklace and hurried after them. Marie stopped in her tracks when she saw the kind of care that Julie was in for.

Miss Huntley had set Julie down on the pavement, and taken Julie's face in her vice-like hand. "Listen, you're in my charge now," she said. "Stop it." She shmushed Julie's face in her oversized fingers. "Stop it now."

Julie hiccupped her breaths.

"Wait a minute," Marie yelled from inside the door. "I have something for the little girl."

"I'm already late," Miss Huntley said to Marie. And said to Julie, "Come," like you would say to a dog.

"Just give us a minute," Marie said, and knelt down to Julie's level. "Oh Honey, don't cry. Look, this is from your mother," Marie held a necklace in her open hand. "It's half a heart. There's a rose and a drop of water engraved on the back. Your baby brother has the half that matches yours. When the two of you get separated, you'll be able to find him with this.

"Where is he?" Julie hiccupped her words. "Where is my brother?"

"Please, I'm running late." The strict woman said, squeezing Julie's hand.

Marie clasped the necklace around Julie's neck and cradled her cheek. "It's going to be all right. This nice lady will take care of you." She looked to Miss Huntley. "Won't you?"

"Of course," she said, jerking Julie's hand. "Come now. Pick up your feet," which Julie did kicking the portly woman hard. The woman released her grip just long enough for Julie to get away and run to Marie. She hugged Marie's legs, and through a tear-stained face she pleaded, "Please don't let her take me."

CHAPTER 9

Marie finger-dusted a picture of Julie from when she was ten, the first time Julie milked goats. She still milked them once in a while when Marie's fingers got stiff. And she still collected eggs for her, too.

Marie wandered into the hallway, looking at pictures of her children, of Julie. She stopped at a picture from when Julie was fourteen—the first time she wore lipstick. Julie was so pretty, so happy then. In the next picture Julie was sixteen. It had been taken on her wedding day when she married Kyle, who lived just past the wheat field where they live now. They had ridden the same school bus as children. Marie could never figure out why Julie had such a crush on him. He wasn't particularly good in any sport, he ignored her, and he wasn't any better looking than any other boy. Marie took off her glasses and wiped her eyes. "Sam, you've had enough of those brownies."

Marie couldn't look at the picture anymore. After what Kyle had done to Julie, it had taken a long time to forgive him. Deep down Marie wasn't sure that she had. She could still see Julie watch the school bus drive away without her. She could still see that sorrow in her eyes. Bad girls were not allowed at school. It had taken a long time for Marie to blur what she pictured when Julie confessed.

Julie was so excited when she turned sixteen. She finally had a date with Kyle. In her bedroom she applied lipstick and pressed a tissue between her lips. She twisted the top off a bottle of liquid eyeliner, the one she'd been practicing with, and drew a delicate line in her lashes.

Her stomach felt funny, imagining what it would be like to kiss him. The doorbell rang and she started sweating in all the wrong places.

"Julie! Kyle's here!" Sam yelled down the hall.

"I'm coming!" Julie yelled back, licking her fingers, trying to tame a tiny curl with spit.

Kyle stood just inside the doorway with his hands in his pockets, rattling his car keys, examining the wood-grain in the door. There was no expression on his face, happy or sad, pleased or displeased. It was always hard to read him.

"How is your mother, Kyle?" Marie asked, arms folded. The three of them stood by the door—Marie, Sam, and Kyle.

"She's well, thank you," Kyle replied, nodding his head, still rattling the keys in one pocket and rattling change in the other.

"And how's your dad?" Sam asked.

"He's well, thank you," Kyle answered, glancing at Marie once and back at the door.

Then Julie came around the corner. Kyle opened the door and motioned for her to go first, smiling politely.

"I'll be back by eleven. Is that alright?" She asked halfway through the door.

"You'll be back by ten, or you'll have no pie." Sam always loved to tease her.

"That never made any sense to me. Who eats pie with mittens?" She said good-bye in a finger-wave. "I'll see you at ten."

The two teenagers jumped inside his father's old Cadillac.

"Come on and sit next to me." Kyle motioned. Julie scooted closer. It seemed story-book magical, the scent of him, Brute aftershave and leather.

52

"Where are we going?"

"Royal Castle." He slid his hand over her knee. "Or maybe you want to go somewhere else first." He didn't smile or turn his head which made what he'd done even more uncomfortable.

"No. Royal Castle's fine." She stopped his hand before it went too far and sat back. Kyle slipped his arm over her shoulders and kept it there the entire way, trying every once in a while to feel more than she would allow. He pulled into the parking lot still struggling to reach the C-cup prize.

"How many hamburgers do you want?" He asked as he got out of the car.

"Uh . . . two?" This wasn't what she expected, none of it. She thought they would go to a restaurant, nothing extreme, just a place where people would wait on them. She thought he would at least open her car door, but he didn't. He went inside without even waiting for her. She wasn't sure if she should follow him or not. And she got out anyway and went inside and she stood next to him.

"You're a hard one to figure out," she said.

"Oh. I guess I was thinking about something else." He rubbed the back of her neck.

"Like what?"

Kyle eased his hand inside the back of her collar and studied her eyes. "Like what color your panties are."

Julie stiffened, planting her wide opened eyes on the wall directly ahead, thinking maybe he said that to test her sense of humor, maybe to see if she was a prude. Trying to look unfazed, she blinked once and giggled half-heartedly. "Silly. Fridays are blue. If you must know Saturdays are pink, and Sundays are always white."

An approving look, he whisked their bag of hamburgers to the car and they ate them there in the parking lot, listening to Herman's Hermits on the radio. Julie sat quietly by the window and sipped her Pepsi. She hoped she'd said the right thing without giving him the wrong idea. Kyle bunched up the wrappers and crammed them in the bag and then he leaned over and nuzzled a kiss behind her ear. She could hardly breathe.

"Let's go somewhere," he whispered.

". . . sure," Julie barely squeaked out the word, in love, scared, happy, anxious. Two people sneaking off in the night. To cuddle. To kiss. This was everything she always thought it would be.

"Why are you sitting over there?" He tugged her close and started the car. It felt sublime sitting so close, him wanting her, her wanting him. Driving, songs playing on the radio, *The Doors* singing, "Come on baby light my fire," then *Frankie Valli* singing, "Can't take my eyes off of you." A mood of romance, the warmth of him beside her, they drove for almost an hour and came to a farm in Medina. He pulled off the road into a cornfield, the tires jostling on the uneven ground. Someone else was parked in the field, their car windows steamed up, panties hanging from their rear view mirror. This isn't right, she thought to herself. He moved in, his arms around her, and slow-kissed the nape of her neck.

"No. Not this way." She pushed at him.

"I shouldn't have come here," Kyle said. "It's late."

Feeling a bit of relief, Julie flashed her watch in the moonlight. "It's almost nine. I think you'd better take me home."

"I was thinking that, too. We'll go back home. You sneak out after everyone's asleep and I'll meet you behind your house. We can spend the whole night together." He ran his hand up her inner thigh. She stopped him.

"Kyle . . . no." She was taken aback. They hadn't even kissed.

"I thought you liked me. I thought you liked me a lot."

"I do. But . . . ." She hesitated. This kind of being in love was all wrong. Being in love was supposed to feel better than anything you would ever feel in your whole life, not like this. He quietly withdrew from her and turned the car down a country road. Julie moved back to her own window in silence. What had she done? It was a long drive home, the radio low, she wouldn't let herself cry.

At home again, Kyle stopped the car on the driveway's edge. He shifted to park and turned the engine off. "Julie," he said, a tenderness in his voice. "Can't you tell how I feel about you? Don't you know?" He pulled her close and kissed her, his tongue wetting her lips. "Midnight. We'll go out to the wheat field and just kiss. That's all."

"That's all?" Julie asked.

"I promise."

". . . okay," she said, the aftertaste like whisky burning your throat, warm in your belly, a kind of drunkenness that stifles good sense. They met at midnight. He brought a blanket and a condom. The wheat swaying in the wind, he told her not to scream. He told her not to tell anyone. Her telling him no, he took her in the open air. He pinned her down and he took her against her will.

Julie snuck back inside the house, bleeding and raw. How could she tell anyone what he'd done? It was all her fault, he told her so. The sex part was over. The crying lasted all night.

The next day, Kyle told her to meet him again. She would do what he said. He would love her, she thought, and they would be happy. He brought a blanket again, and another condom. She brought Vaseline, which melted the condom. Julie got pregnant that night. Believing abortion was an act against God, she had two choices, put the baby up for adoption or keep it. Then the doctor told her she was pregnant with twins. Kyle called her a whore. Julie called him things she'd never repeat. But she married him anyway, him resenting her, her knowing it. When twins Nate and Jeff were born, Kyle quit high school and worked for his father's small masonry company, paving cement and laying brick. By the time his father retired to a warmer climate, Kyle had taken over the masonry business. By then he knew what an Irish temper was. Julie made sure of that.

Julie told Marie everything, and never spoke of it again, because Julie loved her and couldn't bare to see her cry. Julie hadn't come out and said that. But Marie knew.

CHAPTER 10

Bruce slipped off his game warden hat and pulled his hair back in a pony-tail where a cobra tattoo seemed to crawl out of his shirt onto his neck. He'd driven for an hour to get there, away from the city, and parked his car where he thought no one would look twice—in the empty parking lot of Brentwood Pines Development. It seemed oddly strange, these new houses in the middle of nothing, a deserted-looking place this time of day. You'd go half-a-mile before you'd see another house, probably three of them on the whole road. But it was a barn he was looking for, set way back in a field, half a mile away, a dilapidated barn where the cats were.

He hacked from the back of his throat and spit. He opened the trunk and flipped through a mess of torn maps and oil-stained rags, uncovering a hunting knife in a leather case that he snapped to his belt. He shoved aside an empty gasoline can where a tin of Fancy Feast rolled out of the variety pack. He unpinned a sturdy pole equipped with a retractable leash. In his mind he was doing his job. It was justified. These cats were neglected. They would die anyway.

He crossed the street, jumped the ditch, and trudged in mud through a barrage of trees. It had been some time since he'd been here. The briars, the path through the thistles, had grown. Underfoot the ground was uneven by means of deadwood and corroding junk. It was as though every passer-by had thrown their garbage out into the field, years and years' worth, half buried now. He could see the barn. He told himself no one would know. What was it anyone's business anyway? At the barn he looked inside through a crack in the wood.

57

The cat was mostly rotted from the last time he'd been here. He would cut it down, pitch it in the field. He would feed the cats Fancy Feast and pick out a pretty one. But when he came around front he saw that someone had boarded up the barn. He could see the old farmhouse from here. No one had lived there for years. Heading toward it he smelled something fowl, the stench of a cow. He remembered now. He'd seen a girl on the porch, in the spring, some time ago. "Must be some desperate sack," he said to himself, drawn to the farmhouse. In a quiet approach he came to a window where he saw the young girl, long hair, a pecan kind of brown.

She was wearing denim shorts and a white tank top, her hair swept up in a single clip; wisps falling on her cheek as she folded clothes. She was a pretty girl, prettier than any cat. The basket on the floor, she bent over and stood and folded, bent over and stood again. Her shorts hung loosely and they rode up her thighs each time, revealing a little more skin. Hidden, watching, seeing the soft parts of her body; he took the hunting knife from its case. His reflection in the cold steel, he held the smooth flat side to his face. No one was around but her. No one would ever know. Treading quietly as not to alarm her he went inside the garage and up to the door which opened easily. In this room there was a sliding glass door to the deck on one side, and a café door to the house on the other side. He heard a car come up the driveway. He flattened himself against the wall as if that alone would hide him. He heard a car door slam. He heard someone say, "Debra," and he went back to his own car the same way he had come.

CHAPTER 11

Debra leafed through a variety pack of legal forms, quarterly statements to the State of Ohio and the IRS, unemployment, worker's comp, city and school. All this to keep a business going. They couldn't afford to hire a hand, much less a crew. So Greg worked on his own from the first thing in the morning to just before dark. And that was fine because they were trying to get ahead. At least he was home at night.

Debra had the radio on, not that she could hear it. The water pump kicked on loud, straining to bleed water from the shallow well. Greg had diverted all the gutters to it, but it hadn't rained for such a long time. A forty-dollar check in hand, she was waiting for a truckload of city water, something she'd taken for granted before she'd come here. The pump straining loud in the background, would burn up if it didn't stop soon and it was getting on her nerves. Debra fed an unemployment form into the typewriter and lined it up just right, trying to ignore the noise. Aggravated, Debra stood straight up. "Fine!" she said to no one. She would shut down the straining pump by pulling the fuse, which would be a trial because she didn't know which one it was.

On her way to the basement, the pump kicked off. She unclenched her hands, loosened her shoulders, and stretched her back. There was water for now, at least enough to wet her flowerpot garden. Then the truck would come and she could wash clothes and give all her plants a proper drink.

When she stepped outside she saw two groundhogs on the deck

59

who were chewing up the yellow beans and lettuce. She'd given up on a sprawling garden for this very reason. All those weeks of digging the dirt on her hands and knees, pulling weeds, fertilizing, hoeing, plucking slugs and inch worms, and spraying for white flies—just to feed wild rabbits and groundhogs.

"Get out of there!" she yelled. The small one took off. The big one stayed. It was surprising how it seemed to be sizing her up. Prompted to look for something, a broom, a stick, she took hold of an old shovel just within reach which was odd because she didn't know where it had come from. Its aged varnish sloughed off in her hands in a déjà vu moment of when the swing set flaked yellows and reds. "Go on, get out!" She poked it with the rusty shovel, its teeth clanking the metal blade. It stood up on its hind legs completely out of character in some declaration of dominance. She took a step back thinking to just leave it alone; and she would have, if it hadn't dropped on all fours, bared its teeth, arched its back, and growled.

"No you're not," she said, fed up. "You're not going to chase me inside. I won't have it." She jabbed at it with the shovel. "Get out of here . . ."

The groundhog went wild in a violent fit, biting the shovel between her and itself. The shovel smacking it—the groundhog biting, snarling, foaming. The shovel fended it off as though her hands were a conduit for some other force. Blocking. Hitting. Blocking. Hitting. The groundhog bit her shoe, her waiting to feel the pain. She smacked it full force. The animal backed off. He stood up just like he had. She could see blood. Was it her blood or its? Was her foot numbing the pain where it had bitten her? It dropped on all fours and arched its back in what she saw as round two. Then it came at her. She hit him and hit him and hit him, blood splattering all the while until he didn't move anymore. Her insides shaking she flipped her tennis shoe off to see where he had bitten her. Rabies, she thought, what if he has rabies? Feeling like she would be sick, she saw where he had bitten the tip of her toenail, no blood, no broken skin. That's why it didn't hurt.

The groundhog gurgled amid its pooling blood. Time rewound to her stepfather's own pool of blood. When would murder be justified? Surely if a creature was suffering. She would get the rifle and would do what had to be done. The groundhog lifted his head and dragged its broken body down a deck stair. Now that she knew it could move, she knew it would be gone by the time she got back with the rifle. It would hide and suffer terribly before it would die. Debra raised the shovel, getting strength behind it; feeling justified somehow, and sliced its head half-off with the sharp edge. This was too much.

She gagged over the edge of the porch. Already a turkey buzzard was circling overhead. A hot gamey scent would be an unbearable stench by noon. She had to bury it. She brushed her hair away from her face, her hands shaking, and dragged him to the field in the bloodstained shovel. Here she looked for a spot to dig a grave.

Two dragonflies spun overhead. Turkey buzzards dipped uncomfortably close as they circled. In the distance that dumb cow was grazing this whole time, swishing flies with his tail.

That night, Greg came home just before dark like he'd done all summer. Debra had been waiting for him to come home and as soon as he did, she told him, "You won't believe what happened. One of those groundhogs threw a fit today and went after me. Right on the deck." She told him about it biting her shoe, about her killing it. "I just hope it didn't have rabies."

"It didn't hurt you. Did it?"

"I don't think so. It didn't draw any blood." She stopped herself from saying too much. His face and arms were dirt crusted in dried sweat. He'd worn a hole in his jeans at his knee in the course of the day. She'd taken care of the problem. Now it was time to take care of him. That's what a good wife would do.

"What did you kill it with? The rifle?" He started walking to the house, her next to him.

"I didn't get the chance. All I could find was that old shovel. Where did you get that?"

"Do you mean the hoe? We don't have a shovel."

"Yes we do. It's on the deck." She guided him through the garage, through the utility room, to the deck where groundhogs had chomped lettuce and yellow beans.

No shovel. No blood stains. Only the tennis shoes she'd washed and left to dry.

"It's here somewhere," she said. "I left it right there. I hosed it off when I cleaned the deck, and put it back where I found it. Right there."

She'd seen that look before. It was the look she'd seen on a mental-ward-aid where her mother was. Debra concentrated on the empty space. "Maybe I . . . ." She walked slowly toward the field, "It's here somewhere. I'll find it."

Greg walked with her. "Are you sure you're alright?"

"I'm fine." Her words floated out in a hush. She was the right age for Schizophrenia to manifest, early twenties, the same age her mother was. That's what the doctor had said. Greg knew it. She knew it. What would life be like if she couldn't find that shovel, if she couldn't find that grave? She walked deeper into the field, trying to retrace her steps, thinking about which direction she'd gone earlier. It seemed so long ago, and now there wasn't any trace of it in the overgrown weeds. The neon glow of lightning bugs dotted the darkness. They tromped in circles, slapping mosquitoes, looking for anything to prove it happened. "I believe you. Let's go back," Greg said.

"Wait. I know where it is."

He followed her to the broken mound of soil, proof of the burial. Yet there was no trace of a usable shovel, just an antiqued bug-riddled shovel handle, unfit to wield the weight of the rusty metal tool lying next to it—milkweed and thistle sprouting through its holes. The same aged varnish had sloughed off in her hands.

A cold chill mocked the humid summer night.

". . . I made some brownies today."

CHAPTER 12

Julie was here to end what had started with a jog by his house, without even knowing who he was or where to look. Kyle asked to come, asked her nice, the day that 'Smitten' told Julie to jog here. They watched from inside their car, Julie and Kyle, cruising through Brentwood Pines. She wondered what Smitten would do, and thought probably nothing, not right there in public. She knew what she would do, absolutely nothing, not with the temper Kyle had.

Brentwood Pines used to be a soybean field, these boxy houses jammed together in river-stone landscaping, lined in starter bushes and maple trees, a Victorian lamppost at the end of every driveway. People around here didn't like it; they called it a plague on the rolling farmland. But Kyle was in favor of it. He picked up the contract to lay the cement. And Julie, too. She jogged on the new cement instead of gravel roads. No one would stop her from jogging here, not if she knew which road to avoid.

"Anyone look familiar?" Kyle asked, a soft tone in his voice, a side of him she mistrusted right now. He would start off this way, irritated but suppressing it. He would be nice, smiling and all. But the veins in his neck would give him away.

"I can't believe how the men here seem to look alike," Julie said.

Each of them quiet for the time being, his composure came and went from one minute to the next, his jaw line taunt then soft, his lips pressed then not. Tension mounting, they rode past white-washed houses, brick front houses, stained houses, a blue house, past compact cars, sedans, a white cargo van, a minivan.

"Look at you," Kyle said flatly. "You must really think you're something. Men tripping all over themselves."

There was no way to respond, not with his moods changing like this.

"You had to give this guy a reason to send a letter like that." He staggered his words as to let them sink in one at a time. Then picked up the volume, "For crying out loud. Don't tell me you don't know who he is."

She chose her words carefully as not to start a screaming match. "Why would I be here if I knew who he was?" Her chest tightening, she measured her breaths just to get them all in.

"How do I know what you do all day," He turned another corner. "How do I know you're not whoring behind my back?" he said it like he meant it. She suddenly went back to her teenage self in that Medina cornfield so long ago when she hadn't met his 'sexpectations.' She glared at him, stunned, hurt. This was all backward. He was supposed to be on her side.

"You know me better than that. You know that half those men were trying to impress other businessmen where I worked. And the other half were trying to get their secretaries drunk. Why would I want any part of that?" She stared straight ahead, out the window, reliving the gut-wrenching first date in his father's car. Each posed at far windows, where they were now. "You know why I jog?" She grabbed hold of herself. She would out-mean him. "I like to imagine the further I run, the further I'm running away from you," which was partly true. When Kyle came home in a manic mood, jogging was like duct tape to keep her sanity from oozing out. "I have to say though, sometimes I think you and I are friends. I won't make that mistake again." She could tell she upset him by the redness of his ears, and worried that she'd gone too far. His breaths in and out were heavy.

"You tell your secret admirer, if I catch him I'll kill him."

Julie shut up. She would be back. Not tonight but tomorrow. Not by herself. Tomorrow she would ask Debra to come.

Debra heard the farming tractor before she saw it, the ping-ping-ping of the motor. A diesel smell rose above the freshly-tarred gravel. She stopped pumping water for Otto and came to the front of the house, motioning for Julie to bring the straw in back to the lean-to. It was time to corral Otto, time to limit the greens in his diet and treat him to nothing but corn-mash. It seemed strange, Debra thought, tenderizing meat while it was still alive. The tractor was loaded down with more than enough straw to bed him down.

Julie jumped off the tractor. "How's Otto behaving?"

"I honestly don't see how he can poop so much." Debra climbed in the tractor bed and rolled a bale of straw off the edge. The calico cat unexpectedly scrambled up to her and purred against her ankle. "Kitty Callie," Debra said sweetly, rubbing its head. "Julie. Look. I can't believe she came to me. She's always been so skittish." Debra sat down on the edge of the trailer, petting the mother cat for as long as it would let her. Julie hopped up on the trailer and sat next to her. Dangling her legs over the edge, her hands inside her knees, Julie shrugged innocently.

"I've got something to ask you. It never came up before because I wasn't sure if you would be interested. How would you feel about jogging with me?"

"I'd like that, if you don't mind me starting out small." Debra stopped right there. How could she tell Julie that her lungs had been compromised in a fire? How could she tell her that her legs had been broken and ached something awful sometimes. Julie would want to know how and why and where. Debra wasn't ready to say that much.

"You'd be surprised how fast your body adapts."

"You think so?"

"Only one way to find out."

Garnering a wait-and-see attitude Debra agreed. If she could be company in any sense of the word, Julie wouldn't be dragged off and murdered, not without a witness anyway. Waist-high in bales of straw, Debra told Julie what she'd been waiting to tell her, about the groundhog. She told her about the blood and the killing, how she got sick to her stomach. Julie nodded in all the right places, shook her head just the same, yelling out once, "Holy cheese Louise."

Debra flipped a straw bale off the trailer, chaff clinging to her clothes. "That shovel really got to me. I probably left it in the field and just forgot. I was so upset. I guess I didn't realize how bad a shape it was in." Now that she had said it out loud it seemed to make sense. "I probably dropped it at just the right angle, so it appeared to have weeds growing through it, like it had been there a long time."

"It's amazing how our minds can play tricks on us. Did you find the missing shoes?"

"It's the strangest thing. I can't find either one. But you know . . . I've been so forgetful lately. I lost a jar of mayonnaise a week ago and I still can't find it. It's so weird. One minute I was spreading it on a sandwich and the next minute it was completely gone. And I can't understand how my flip-flops ended up in the freezer. Julie hadn't nodded this time nor had she shook her head. She was splitting bales with a pitch fork, spreading straw in the lean-to; she hadn't even looked up. Debra had taken a chance in saying all this, maybe saying things she should have kept to herself. "Here I've been going on. You never got to tell me what happened when you and Kyle went looking for that man last night. Was he there?"

"I'll never know. Kyle got all pissy with me. He thinks he can make me feel bad. I let him have it." Now it was Julie's turn. She told Debra about her and Kyle, about their fight, how she was afraid of him sometimes because of his temper. "He'll just start screaming and yelling and breaking things. He was so mad once he broke everything in the kitchen, the blender, the toaster, smashed a whole dish-drainer-full of dishes at the wall behind me. I left him for three days over that."

"What made you go back?"

"He said things would change. And they did for a while."

"Please tell me he doesn't hit you."

"He wouldn't dare. He knows I'd leave him for good. The things he says, though, sometimes he won't stop till he sees me cry . . . . I've never told that to anyone."

Debra was here to run interference, going with Julie. It was before sunset. Julie had said it was the best time to jog because it was cooler then. But it was still hot, eighty degrees or so.

Debra jogged a slow to moderate clip as far as the first stop sign, a quarter-mile-run. Julie beside her, she made herself push on, breathing heavily. This was hard. But nothing hurt so far, not her legs, not her chest, which meant her childhood injuries must have healed like doctors hoped they would. Julie did all the talking; telling a story about her car, her voice wavering in time to her steps.

". . . I took Marie to lunch on our way to the hearing aid center, and I couldn't figure out why my key wouldn't unlock my car . . ." Julie was talking with such energy, breathing with such ease.

Debra said, "uh huh . . ." barely able to speak, trying to regulate her breaths. Keep going, she told herself, breathe in, breathe out, one foot in front of the other, she'd been asked to come and was glad of it, glad to be here with Julie. Keep going, she told herself.

". . . so I went back inside the restaurant and called triple-A. It took a whole hour for them to get there. You should have seen Marie. She set herself down in one of the rocking chairs in the shade, and greeted everyone coming in and out of the restaurant. It's funny how people take to her. She has a way . . ."

Debra focused on the next stop sign way up ahead, a stitch in her side getting worse. What was hard at first was brutal now. Where was that second wind she'd heard about? Where was that runner's high?

And here Julie was, talking like she was serving tea, ". . . by the time the mechanic got there, Marie seemed to have gathered a crowd. The mechanic wedged a coat-hanger-thing in the door hinge. He messed up the rubber piping around the car door, but I was so relieved when he finally got it open, I didn't care. You're not going to believe what happened when I got inside."

Debra offered a breathy, "What?"

"I realized. It wasn't my car. I didn't say a word. So here I am sitting in someone else's car with Marie, thanking the triple-A guy like crazy, just wanting to get rid of him." Julie was laughing and breathing and talking—no trouble at all. Debra couldn't help but laugh, slowed down to do it, holding a painful stitch in her side. Breathing heavily she barely got the words out, "give-me-a-minute." Julie was still jogging and talking like Debra was right beside her. Twenty feet or so Julie looked back.

"Come on Deb. Walk it out. It's not good to completely stop."

Debra walked slowly, still holding her side, tickled by Julie's tale ". . . someone else's car," she said between breaths. "I can't believe it."

The next day Debra went jogging with Julie again. Keeping the same moderate pace, she pushed on until the stitch in her side became unbearable, and walked the rest of the way. She came back the next day and the day after that. Julie would run ahead and circle back, the entire time chit-chatting up close, then far off. There was an energy between the two, Julie's inexhaustible, Debra's relentless, an energy that bonds two people, as different as they were.

Debra pushed on farther and farther every day, until she could keep up with Julie. In all this time, not a single man stood out among the rest, at least it seemed that way.

There were trails and circles and lanes and drives and courts and roads packed into one development. Julie had always jogged a different route to be adventurous. But she didn't know which way led to the house of Smitten; that would be the route to avoid. He could have been watching them from anywhere. Maybe one of the sidewalk people, the few there were, who smiled sometimes and offered polite hellos with mechanical nods.

Being the middle of summer there was no shortage of men. He could have been riding a bike, or walking a dog. He could have been mowing a lawn or watering plants or washing his car or one of the men outside listening to the ball game on the radio. Without a letter in all this time Julie figured the home wrecker had moved on and that was that. She would learn later that Kyle was hiding the letters, lots of them. It was by chance that Julie was vacuuming, moving tables and chairs and the like. Kyle always tossed the mail on a small table next to the phone at the base of the stairway, always as though he hadn't gone through it. She dusted the table first and then moved it to vacuum, and saw an envelope that had slipped behind. It was dated three days ago, and addressed to her, a letter from Anonymous.

Julie,

> *Have you guessed who I am? Thank you for not getting me into trouble. I go crazy whenever I see you jogging past my house. Your friend is cute, but she's not beautiful like you. I found out some things about you to see how much we have in common. My favorite dish is Lobster Newburg, the same as yours. My next favorite dish is you. I'll bet you taste good. I love the way your hair curls around your temples and the way you smile. I love you so much that it is getting harder every day to keep my distance. I want to feel your body against mine. I want to make love to you. Don't worry, I would never force myself on you or even try to approach you. I will wait until you come to me. Meet me. Please meet me Friday night at 8:00 P.M. in the restaurant where we first met. Not on the main floor, but in the lower floor lounge where it is dark and crowded, no one will know.*

> *Every time I close my eyes, I see you. You are all I think about. Please meet me. I have to know if I have a chance with you or if you are going to break my heart. I will love you as long as I live. I am Smitten.*

CHAPTER 13

Debra hurried to the basement; Julie would be here any minute. The dryer door was still open, a freshly dried load in the laundry basket on the floor. She'd left it there when she'd heard the phone ring and had run upstairs. That's what you did before answering machines, you ran from wherever you were. The answering machine was a great invention, if only she could stop the impulse to race to the phone.

It still irked her that the laundry room was downstairs, a place where spiders beget generations of spiders. No matter how much she'd pleaded to have it anywhere else, that's where all the wiring was. She tried to make do, broom-scrubbing the quarry-stone walls with a bleach solution, vacuuming the unfinished ceiling. But spiders came back in full force—hanging from the ceiling, spinning spider sacks between water pipes overhead. She started out by spraying them one at a time with ant killer spray. One spun down its web and landed on her. She figured it must have died somewhere in the middle of her tribal dance, a dance that she'd perfected. She'd set off a bug bomb, the basement sealed shut; but it didn't take long for a new batch of spiders to migrate back to their old breeding ground.

Because the well had been low for at least a month, she'd been taking clothes to the Laundromat, and had been hanging them on the clothesline. Unchecked in all that time, the spider webs in the basement had multiplied to outrageous proportions. So much so that she wound webs like cotton candy in a broom so they wouldn't cling to her hair.

Anxious to be ready when Julie got here, she hurriedly whisked up the left-behind basket while on the lookout for crawly things. And carrying it, she could have sworn the clothes in the basket were moving. She looked closer, thinking the sparse lighting had shifted shadows somehow. That's when a snake slithered out through the weave of the basket, over her arm, and dropped to the floor. Screaming all the while, Debra pitched the basket straight up, reinventing the tribal dance to a secondhand chair. Still screaming, she swiped her arms in a fury, as she teetered on the chair.

A voice yelled to her from the top of the stairs, "Deb? Is that you?"

"There's a snake down here. It fell out of the clothes all over me. Now it's under the chair . . ." Debra said, her words high-pitched rolling together, ". . . I can't move. It's right under me. I can see it. It's huge . . ."

Julie came downstairs and stopped at the bottom step. "How'd it get down here?"

"I don't know."

Julie scanned the dungeon-like setting. "You've got some juicy spiders down here," and let a shudder take hold. "I think I can move it away from you." Julie tiptoed off the bottom step and took the broom from the corner. "If you leave it alone, it might just eat all these spiders," she said, big-eyed, a sideways grin.

"How about I move out and let the thing keep the place?" Debra stuck to the wooden chair, its broad seat gummed in old varnish.

"I'll sweep him over to the corner, you get the clothes. You can decide what to do with him later." Just then a snake coiled in the broom bristles slid off, onto Julie's shoe. She screamed the way Debra had, flinging the broom, joining Debra on the chair. Huddled together they saw a third snake crawl out from under the dryer, both of them pointing it out in a duet of screams. Then Julie said, "I hate to say this, snakes can climb you know."

They bounced off the chair, and ran up the stairs two steps at a time. Breathing hard, they slammed the basement door shut behind them, and leaned into it with their backs. On this side of the door, the two of them started to laugh. It didn't make sense but here they were, laughing anyway, holding their stomachs, their eyes tearing in senseless laughter. Happy senseless laughter.

"Greg's heard me scream so often, he regards it as part of the ambiance," Debra said in a gleeful laugh.

"And you're so good at it. You could put yours in a scary movie. This whole house would make a good scary movie. I love the kind that make you jump out of your skin. And boy did I ever."

"You can have it. The house and all. I'll box up those snakes and wrap them up in a big red bow."

"You'll have to catch them first."

"I'd shoot them if I had to. If my mom taught me anything, she taught me how to shoot."

"Your mom? Your mom taught you how to shoot? Does she live around here?"

Debra felt her face getting red. The laughing was done, the smile gone. The last she heard, her mother was having shock treatment therapy in the psychiatric ward of the Hamilton County Prison. "She's in Cincinnati. I don't see her much."

"You're so lucky to have a mom. I'd love to meet her."

"Look what time it is. We better get going. I wanted to be back before Greg gets home."

CHAPTER 14

"Did you bring the letter?" Debra retied her tennis shoes, a long stretch of sidewalk ahead.

"It's gone. Kyle ripped it up and threw it away." Julie was pulling her spiral curls into a ponytail, talking through a clip in her teeth. "I should have hidden it."

"Did he read it?"

"Yeah. Then he went crazy. He got so mad I swear I think something's wrong with him."

"You should tell him you might need those letters. What if that man breaks in your house or something? Is there any way of taping it back together?"

"He dumped coffee grounds on it. I should have known better than to let him see it."

"What did it say?" Debra asked, keeping pace, jogging next to Julie.

"He thinks you're cute."

"Me? I can't believe it. He's seen me?"

"Evidently. And somehow, he's learning more about me, personal things."

"I think it's time to call the police."

"I did. We don't have a police department out here; I had to call the sheriff. They won't do anything, not unless he threatens me. To them, he's nothing more than a secret admirer." Julie started jogging faster. She always did that when she was anxious. "I have an idea . . . ."

"Yeah . . ." Debra quickened her pace to match Julie's.

75

"I'm going to be at the fair all next week . . . . I've got just enough time before I leave. How would you like to go out for an evening?"

Debra struggled to pace her breathing. "Sure." She wished that Julie would slow down. This pace was too fast. She could feel her legs starting to hurt, a growing stitch in her side.

"Let's go out Friday night."

"Where to?"

"You don't think Greg will mind, do you?"

"Why would he? It's not like we're going to a bar." Debra's words were spaced between breaths.

"What about a lounge?"

Debra didn't answer. She hated bars or whatever they were called. She hated men like her stepfather; their drunken liquor smell, their suggestive leers, their clumsy-feeling touch. She remembered how she cowered in a corner booth while her mother Aida pointed out the evil men at the bar, her mother saying these men will hurt you, they'll strip you naked and they will hurt you. But then left her there so she could drink with them.

"Why do you want to go there?"

"His letter said to meet him in the lounge at the restaurant where I used to work. If I could actually meet him, I'd tell him to knock it off. I'd tell him it's not flattering; he's just upsetting my husband, and he needs to stop," Julie answered. "Besides, I want to connect a face to the letters. It really bothers me that I don't know who he is."

"Do you think it's safe? I mean . . . look what his letters suggest."

"I've thought about it and thought about it and you know what? I think he's just a businessman who got wrapped up in his own fantasies. I don't think he's dangerous. Probably just the opposite."

76

"Aren't you worried about Kyle?"

"Kyle doesn't have to know."

"I think he'll figure it out if you just happen to disappear on the same night that man wants to meet you."

"I'll figure something out. I have to go, but I don't want to give him the wrong idea. Go with me . . . please."

". . . I'll talk to Greg." Debra focused ahead on a big oak tree, watching it get closer as she jogged, visualizing the different bars that Aida had taken her to. Debra would go for Julie's sake. If that's what she had to do.

Later on that night Debra talked about it to Greg.

". . . because Julie's my friend."

"But you hate those places. You've said it a hundred times." Greg was sympathetic to a degree. "I don't care if you go, but I can't understand why you would."

Debra cooled her hands around a glass of ice tea. "You know I don't want to. I get the impression that women in those kind of places line up like chattel, and let themselves be auctioned off to the highest bidder. People say they're meeting places, but they're more like meat markets to me."

"You wouldn't be in this spot if you had just said no. If she really was your friend, she would have understood," he said, studying her eyes.

"It's a non-issue. Kyle won't let her go."

"Your eye looks funny. What did you do to your eye?"

"I must have been rubbing it." She took a compact mirror out of her purse and saw a small bald spot in her lashes where she'd mindlessly pulled them out. "I need a bigger mirror." Debra went right to the bathroom, closed and locked the door. She'd never told Greg about pulling her eyelashes, too ashamed to tell anybody. She quickly filled in the spot with an eyeliner pencil. Something she did very well. Then she went back to the living room where Greg was. "I must have been rubbing it. It's just a little red."

"How well do you know Julie? I think she's already made up her mind. You were the deciding factor, not Kyle."

"Then I guess I'll just have to go," Debra said.

"Then I'm going too. You never know what a man like that'll do."

"Julie says she thinks he's just a businessman who's got a warped sense of love. He's probably harmless. If he sees you, we'll never get this over with. It's in a ritzy restaurant. You don't have to go."

Greg took her hand and kissed her palm. He loved her so. She knew this much. She rested her head in the nape of his shoulder. "I hate those places."

"I know . . . .You've got to learn how to say no."

"By the way, we have snakes in the basement. I don't know how they got there, but we've got to get rid of them."

"You can use your mother's rifle."

Up until then it was just a rifle, not her 'mother's rifle'—the extension of her mother's insanity. Her grandfather had given the rifle to her mother when she had convinced him that someone was following her. He'd said he'd shot a Smokey Mountain black bear with that rifle. He'd said it had saved his life. After Aida's murder trial, her grandfather took possession again, which was legal at the time, and insisted that Debra keep it.

Having good aim wasn't the same thing as killing something, someone. "You wouldn't mind if I said no right now, would you?"

At Julie's house.

". . . I'm going out with Debra on Friday." Julie stood behind a dining room chair, clenching the back of it, slowly tipping it back and forth, nervous about what Kyle would say.

Kyle looked tired, his newspaper spread out on the mahogany dining table to the same page since he'd sat down. "Why can't you just be honest with me? I know what you're doing. And with everything else that's been going on . . . ."

She saw a strange sadness in his eyes. Of all the reactions she expected, she hadn't expected that. She softened her voice. "I just wanted to tell him to stop sending letters. That's all." She sat next to Kyle, her hand on his knee. "He's probably just some businessman with romantic attempts that got out of hand. He needs to know what he's doing to us. I've never seen you so upset, not even when Matt wrecked the car. Please understand. I have to do this."

"I do. I understand." He looked away, like he couldn't feel her there.

An air of anxiousness, Julie asked, "What did you mean when you said, 'with everything else that's going on'?"

"I don't know what's wrong with people. I've been losing work all summer. These punks are stealing my jobs because they're cheap. They don't pay taxes. They don't pay insurance or workers comp. They only know enough about cement to steal my jobs. Then they party all weekend. I work like a dog, and I'm handing out dollar bills like I'm dealing a deck of cards. And then I've got some guy having sex fantasies about my wife . . . . But you go on. Go with Debra." He stood up without looking at her. "At least one of us will have some fun," he said, walking away.

Friday night, Debra rode as a passenger in Julie's Pontiac Bonneville, which seemed like an expensive car. Julie was dressed in clothes that looked expensive, a flowing black skirt, silk red blouse, and black heels. She had never seen Julie in lipstick and mascara and couldn't get over how beautiful she was. Debra had clipped her long hair to one side. Greg told her that he liked it that way, how it accented the soft features of her face. She wanted to look conservative, unassuming, so she wore a white tailored shirt and black bell-bottoms, loose fitting, no heels to speak of. They pulled into the ritzy parking lot, and drove past the parking valet. The parking lot glistened like a high priced show room. A Jaguar, a Regal, a Porsche in one row of cars. A BMW, a Mercedes-Benz, and a Mustang were in another near a white windowless cargo van that seemed out of place.

Inside the lounge, candlelight glowed through a fog of cigarette smoke in the dimly lit room. 'Shake it Up' by 'The Cars' pounded so loudly it seemed to vibrate the fillings in her teeth.

All of the barstools were taken. Every table and every booth was packed. Chattering people everywhere, talking loudly over the music, laughing in every pitch. People danced on their little bit of space here and there, which made it even harder to navigate the floor. Julie and Debra shifted into a space near the wall, and stood together, getting bumped by everyone that moved. Debra hated it. Hated the smoke and perfume and liquor smell. People bumping into her, bodies touching. A hand suddenly groped her butt. She jerked around angry to face the group. It could have been any one of them.

"Someone grabbed my butt!" She said to Julie.

"What? I can't hear you." Julie yelled like everyone else over the music and noise. This was the loudest part of the room where life-size speakers were.

"Someone grabbed me."

Debra could see Julie's lips moving but couldn't hear what she said. Her first reaction was to say, "What?" and draw in closer, but she saw a table open up. "I see a table. Over there."

There in the center of the crowded room, two empty chairs beckoned every butt in the place. Julie and Debra squirmed through the crowd toward them, but a couple of women plopped down as if they were playing musical chairs. To make matters worse, now they were in the way of people who were trying to talk to each other; they pushed themselves back into the crowd and then somehow they got separated. Debra saw two people stand up right next to her and promptly sat down in a warm seat. She threw her purse on the other seat and motioned to Julie. A hand reached through the crowd and grabbed the empty chair, but Debra hung on until Julie sat down. Within minutes a waitress came by with two glasses of wine, "From the gentlemen at the bar," she said, and tossed a couple of coasters on the table. "I need to see a driver's license."

Debra raised her hand in a gesture, about to say, "No thanks, we're not sluts," but Julie slipped the waitress a ten. The waitress set the drinks down and left, Debra's face an obvious red; she wanted to leave so badly. Julie pulled a cigarette out of her purse and lit it. When did she take up smoking? How well *did* Debra know Julie? Julie smiled a sexy smile and waved to the two men at the bar, which was

81

their cue to join them.

"Oh no," Debra uttered. She hadn't sipped the wine; she would simply hand it back.

The men were closely shaven, clean and pressed. Average looking—more or less a clone to every other man here, They made their way through the crowd with smirking grins. At the table one of them introduced himself specifically to her.

"I'm sorry, but I'm married. We're both married." Debra showed them her wedding ring.

"That doesn't matter, so are we," the man admitted, bent over so close to Debra's ear that she could have sworn his breath had singed it. The smell of his Aqua Velva and liquor over-powered the smoke of two hundred cigarettes. Her eyes were bright, her chin was lifted indignantly. How could anyone be so crass?

"Are you two together?" Julie asked.

"We work together. It's loud in here. Let's go someplace where we can talk," one of them said.

"I'm sorry, I'm waiting for someone else; thank you for the wine," Julie shouted over the music. Debra pushed hers toward the edge of the table.

One dejected man straightened his tie with his sweaty hands, looking around for fresh game. The other man smoothed back his hair with the bulk of both hands. "Do you live around here?" he asked.

"We're meeting someone else. Really, thank you for the wine." Julie answered.

"You think you're too good for me?"

Julie drew a puff of smoke and blew it in his face.

"Just remember what you passed up when some drunk pisses on

you."

"Just leave." Julie said. Debra stared blankly, hating every minute of it, on the brink of leaving.

The men stepped back into a crowd that seemed to absorb them.

"I think he would have showed up by now. Let's go." Debra said.

"Wait. Just a little longer; I promise," Julie answered. "A man over there's been looking this way."

The man, maybe forty something, was sitting in a booth, intently watching Julie. His hair was almost black like his thin mustache. He looked very business-like, yet tough as though he could be featured in a Mafia movie. For most of the evening Julie had been glancing at him intermittently to see if he was still glancing at her. This time he came over, bringing a chair.

"I was trying to work up the courage to come over after I saw what you did to those guys." He sat down close to Julie, their bodies touching. Debra focused on the glass of wine she hadn't sipped, running her finger over the rim, grasping the seat of her chair. She began to doubt their friendship. This was worse than awkward.

Julie leaned in. "Are you the one?"

"I'm the one if you want me to be." He said in her ear, lingering there.

"Are you the one who's been sending me letters?" she asked.

"I could be. What kind of letters do you want?"

"Oh . . . I thought you were someone else. You kept looking at me," Julie said.

"I thought we made eye contact," he said, gliding his fingers down her shoulder.

Debra rolled her eyes. "That's it." She stood up. "I'll be outside," she said, glaring at Julie. She stepped away from the table, bluffing of course, hoping that she knew Julie at least this much. "Are you coming?"

"I can't stay," Julie said to the man. She stood up and grabbed Debra by the elbow. "Give me a minute, Deb."

"Someone's been sending me perverted love letters." Julie said to the man. "That's the only reason I came here tonight. I thought I could tell him to leave me alone, but he didn't show up. Being a creep is bad enough, tonight he proved he's a coward. You wouldn't believe how much trouble he caused. I have to go. It was nice meeting you."

Debra guided the way out as they struggled through the crowd, each of them saying excuse me again and again. Even as they fumbled to the door, the 'eye contact' guy didn't seem to get it. He followed them all the way to the car, and just as Julie touched the car door, he wrapped his arms around her waist from behind.

"Where're you going? You're leaving before the fun starts," the man crooned.

"Go have your fun somewhere else; we have to go," Julie said, peeling him off.

With that, the man patted her butt. Not once, but twice.

Julie's butt was definitely the wrong body part to show disrespect. Round and protruding, out of proportion to her slender frame, her butt was off limits. No one patted it, not even Kyle, not without generating the ire of a thousand women. Julie whirled around; she balled up her fist and punched him square in the face. With as many drinks as the man must have had, Julie knocked him out with a single punch. Now he was lying face down in the asphalt.

"Get in!" Julie yelled flinging the door open, startling Debra who was still standing with her mouth gaped open.

Julie's car left the parking lot as politely as it came. Debra could see the man in the passenger mirror.

Lying there, drunk and rubbing his jaw, the man looked up from the asphalt. He was memorizing the license plate number. Debra was sure of it.

CHAPTER 15

Debra unlocked the door and came inside. It felt so good to be home. She couldn't stand the smell of stale cigarettes and booze another minute. It was in her clothes, her skin and her hair. It was 11:30 at night. All she wanted to do was take a shower and go to bed. "Greg, I'm back. Greg," she called, walking into the kitchen. All the lights were off except for one. She wondered why he hadn't waited up for her; and went upstairs, gingerly stepping on each stair step, trying in vain to prevent the floorboards from creaking. "Greg?" She opened the creaky door to their bedroom. "I'm home," she whispered. "Are you awake?" She walked softly in the dark and sat down on the bed. "That place was packed . . . ."

She stopped. Something wasn't right—the way the mattress reacted to the weight of her body. Flashes of distant lightning freckled the darkened room. She slid her fingers over the flattened blankets, over the vacant pillows.

Where was he? She turned on the bedroom light, went to the hallway, and stood at the top of the stairs. "Greg?" The tree branches scraped against the house, against the four-paned windows. Distant thunder rippled. She didn't remember seeing his truck, but he never mentioned going anywhere either. Wherever he was, Debra was sure he'd be right back.

Unable to stand that bar smell for another second, she decided to go ahead and take a shower—trying to minimize the feeling of dread, all alone in a presumably haunted house. She went downstairs and into the bathroom. 'Grow up all ready,' she thought to herself, slowly undressing. She turned on the shower. The lights flickered, but they didn't go out. She hung a clean towel next to the tub, still waiting to hear Greg come home at any minute. Completely naked, she locked the bathroom door. The lights flickered again. She stepped underneath the warm shower and closed her eyes, letting it run over her face and hair, down her soft shoulders. Soaping up, she started thinking about scary movies she'd seen. Why did they always depict women stupid enough to look back whenever they were running from a fiend? If she'd learned anything from watching those movies, it was to never look back when you're running. 'Of course,' she considered, 'Greg would probably not run at all. He'd be looking for a logical explanation right up until whatever it was ate him.'

She lathered up with the clean fresh scent of soap, feeling relieved to finally smell good, and for some reason the movie popped in her head about an invisible ghost who was raping a woman in her own home. The movie's only dialogue was screaming. Just then, the shower curtain moved. Her heart pounding, Debra peeked out from inside the curtain "Greg?" then rinsed the soap off as fast as she could, telling herself to stop thinking about murder scenes; and practically fell, getting out of the shower. Through the steam, she could see the door was cracked open, the lock was undone. She slammed the door shut and locked it again, ran the towel down her back and over her wet skin and quickly got dressed, listening carefully for whoever was inside the house. She slowly opened the bathroom door and peeked out at the clock. "It's almost midnight."

She told herself to stop it. No one was in the house. There were no such things as ghosts. Maybe she hadn't latched the lock all the way. Why did she let the horror movie mindset suck her in? From that point on, she had the full intention to go to bed, and wait there for Greg, and put ridiculous movies out of her mind. At least that was her intention.

Debra lay down in bed, listening to raindrops from the open window as fragments of lightning lit the room. Faraway thunder echoed seconds apart. She crawled under the sheets, snuggled up to the pillow, and closed her eyes. 'He probably planned to be back before this or he would have left a note. He'll be home any second now.'

Just then, the stairs began creaking one by one. Someone was coming up the steps. "Greg?" Debra sat up in bed. She waited. "Greg?" She crawled out of bed and opened the bedroom door. No one was there. The hallway light flickered and all the lights went out. She flipped the light switch on but nothing happened. She tried another light switch and then another. The electricity was out. She heard something that sounded like fingernails scratching from inside the wall.

Bam! Bam! Bam! Doors slammed shut. Her body wrenched with every one. The curtains suddenly billowed as gusts of wind sailed through the open windows and down the corridors. A bolt of lightning struck and thunder shook the house. A deep breath sunk in her chest.

"I'll never watch another scary movie as long as I live," she said out loud. Standing at the top of the stairs, she clutched the banister in the dark. Lightning flashed—thunder crashed—rain pounded.

Seeing only when the lightning let her, she fumbled in the dark from room to room, closing windows, wanting to be anywhere but here. She groped her way downstairs and lit a candle. Downstairs, in the living room, she curled up on the couch in the dark, clutching a blanket, waiting, waiting, for Greg to come home.

Thump . . . swish . . . thump . . . . A hushed whisper followed the wind-swept sound.

Her heart pulsing through the tips of her fingers Debra called out, "Hello?" She slipped on her shoes in a panic, and just as she snatched her car keys, she saw someone pull up the driveway. She heard a car door slam, and Greg came through the door without seeing her, and started toward the stairway.

"Where were you?" she asked quietly, sternly. Thunder rumbled and lightning reflected Greg's face.

"Deb? Are you still up? Did you have a good time?"

"Why didn't you leave me a note? I was worried sick."

"I didn't even think about it. My brother called me at the last minute to meet a few of the guys. He just got in town. I didn't think you'd mind," Greg said. "What's up with the lights?"

"I was hoping you could tell me. You should have left me a note."

A golf ball size 'thud-roll' sound came from the ceiling.

". . . did you hear that?" Debra whispered as not to disturb the sound, sidling up to Greg.

"It's just the storm; did you shut the windows?" Greg asked. He flipped an unresponsive light switch.

"I've heard plenty of storms—never a sound like that. I'm telling you something's going on in here that can't be explained. Something unlocked the door when I was in the shower. Someone was coming upstairs when I was in bed. You should have heard it."

"The house is settling; that's all. Old houses make strange sounds settling in; believe me. How come the lights aren't working?"

She gave him a look of frustration, as if to say 'we've been over this.'

"It's probably the circuit breaker." Greg fished a flashlight out of the kitchen cupboard and went to the basement. Debra followed, but just to the stairs. She wasn't going down there with all those spiders and just a flashlight. Greg flipped the circuit breaker; she could hear it; and the lights came on.

"Someday you're going to come home and my hair will be white. This place scares me to death sometimes."

"Let's go to bed; it's late."

They quietly went up the stairs to their bedroom. She would say no more, he would dismiss it as nerves. Lying in bed, she heard scratching sounds come from the wall again. "Greg . . . Greg . . . did you hear that?"

"Hear what?"

"Listen . . . scratching . . . don't you hear that?"

"It's probably mice; buy some poison at the farmer's market tomorrow, and put it around. Let me sleep, I've got a long day tomorrow." He put his arm around her, snuggled close and patted her shoulder. "Don't worry so much."

CHAPTER 16

At home Julie set her keys and purse on the dining room table. She could hear the television from the living room where Kyle was. Not sure what to expect she went into the living room, a little bit scared, a little bit guilty; telling herself she shouldn't be. The brown leather couch in the dimly lit room was disarray with rumpled newspapers and McDonald's wrappers. An empty beer bottle sat on the coffee table next to a half-eaten hamburger. Kyle was in a reclining chair with the remote control as if he barely noticed her. "Well?" he asked, without losing focus of the nightly news. "Did he show up?"

"I don't know. He could have been. But I'll never know it. Maybe he got scared because Debra was there." Julie hesitantly sat down, still not sure how he was taking this.

Kyle voiced a heavy breath and mumbled. "Maybe he just likes watching you. I'll bet you put on quite a show tonight. Since when did you start wearing makeup?"

"What are you talking about? You know why I went." Julie felt the blood rushing to her face. This had the feeling of a Mr. Jekyll night.

His face hardened. Out of nowhere, he threw the remote control, nearly hitting her. "You encouraged him! Following along with whatever he wants you to do! What's next? Meet me at Motel Six?"

Julie didn't answer, she couldn't. She left the room, not wanting him to see her cry.

"That's it! Just walk away! I can't even talk to you! Fine, just leave!" he yelled at her back.

Upstairs in her bedroom she closed the door and kicked off her shoes. Clothes and all she flopped face down on the bed and buried her face in the pillow and let herself cry. It hurt so badly.

Gusting wind blew the window curtains and cooled the room. She heard a loud crack of thunder and then she heard rain. Sheets and sheets of rain which soaked the carpet, but she didn't care. Right then, she didn't care about anything.

In that moment a lifetime of sorrow hit her all at once. This kind of crying, the kind that grips your stomach all the way to your throat, brought back heartaches that had festered for years. She felt the anguish of that pregnant teenager all over again—the birth of twins. How she loved those little boys—she would be losing them. They would leave for college soon. They had their own friends now, their own lives. This week at the fair would be their last fair. The steers would leave the barn empty. Her boys would leave her heart empty. She couldn't imagine the next four years without them. And worst of all, she'd be completely alone with Kyle.

She remembered being four years old and how it felt when her mother would hold her. Miracle of all miracles she wanted her mother to hold her again, to hear those words, it'll be all right. She could barely remember her mother's face. She could barely remember her brother. He was a baby so long ago. How would she ever find him? She longed for him to rescue her. She longed to be loved. She muffled a breathless sob in her pillow.

Then she heard footsteps coming down the hallway. Kyle was coming to bed. Maybe he was sorry for the things he said. Julie climbed under the sheets and quickly wiped her nose. She dried her face and pretended that she was asleep. But instead of opening the door to their room, Kyle opened the door across the hall to the guest room. She heard him open the rollaway bed. He hadn't touched her in months. Was it her fault? Maybe if she was thinner or maybe if she was a better wife. Maybe if she didn't argue so much, but how else would she stand up for herself? Why couldn't Kyle feel about her the way the man in the letters did? "What was it? Why can't he stand to touch me?" Crying took her every breath, as though it were a being in itself, thriving within her.

Just then the bedroom door opened. "Are you crying?" Kyle asked from inside the doorway.

"I . . . ." Julie inhaled a quick breath.

He walked over to the bed, sat down, and rubbed her back. "I don't know what's wrong with me. I've just been under so much pressure lately. I don't know why you put up with me."

She sat up, wiping her face. "Because I love you. I don't know why. But I still do."

"Well, you won't get anywhere by crying like a spoiled child."

CHAPTER 17

Another hot day, the temperature was ninety-two, and because of the overnight storm, the humidity was thicker than ever. Debra rattled a bag of cat food which was just as effective as calling them. Heaping a pile in the old hubcap, she called, "Here Kitty, Kitty." Midnight came first, then Kitty Callie. Soon enough, the cat clan streamed from every direction, and she began the morning ritual of counting them.

She was still upset about last night. Something was going on in that house and whatever it was disturbed her terribly . . . four, five, six . . . . Greg had blamed the mysterious thumping sounds on the storm. He blamed what sounded like scratching in the walls on mice, and blamed the electrical outage on an overload . . . seven, eight, nine . . . . All of which could have been true . . . ten, eleven, twelve . . . . But what about the sound of footsteps coming upstairs? Greg had told her, don't worry so much. But what about the lock on the bathroom door when she'd been in the shower? The house was a hundred years old and built with its own funeral parlor. Why would the realtor have said that if it hadn't been true? Someone must have died here within the last hundred years and was probably mourned in this very house. She had been subtly asking for months and months, gone to the church in the square where the graveyard was, asked inside the church—no one could say.

. . . twelve, thirteen, fourteen, fifteen, sixteen, ... She counted again to make sure, hearing dried cat food crunch as they ate, the territorial cats growled. One of the cats was missing. "Here Kitty, Kitty!" She yelled, shaking the bag fierce, looking for the last one to

94

come. "Kitty, Kitty. Here Kitty, Kitty."

Her skin luminous with sweat, she watched the goldenrod as it waved in tides. The seventeenth cat was gone. Only the living remained.

CHAPTER 18

The day was done. Debra would leave tomorrow. She disrobed, watching Greg through the glow of the bedside lamp. His heavy brow, his deep-set eyes, his clean-shaven chin. He was in bed, reading a cycle magazine, and let it fall to the floor when she closed the bedroom door. The scent of lavender and ginger lingered in her hair, the last of a free sample from an expensive boutique. She'd asked Sam to water Otto while she was gone, and feed the cats, too. Julie would be gone for a week at the fair. Debra would leave tomorrow.

Greg sank back in the pillow, elbows back, his hands clasped behind his head. Debra turned off the light and crawled under the blanket where he was. "I'm going to take some time to see my mother tomorrow. They said her memory is coming back," she pillow-whispered, resting her head on the rise and fall of his chest, her body molded to his.

"Let me go with you. I just need a couple days to finish the job on Sprague Road." His soft baritones lulled her.

"That's alright." Her breathing slowed to the rhythm of his. "If I leave by nine, I should be in Cincinnati by two. I'll stay with Mrs. O'Shell for a few days. It'll be nice to see her again."

She had a late start that morning, the traffic was heavy and she got lost when she couldn't find the right exit in Cincinnati. Driving through a blowing rain, the wind whistled through a window that wouldn't completely close. It was four o'clock and the brown-brick building loomed ahead. Debra felt her stomach tighten, her hands already shaking. They'd told her that shock treatment therapy was standard treatment, a cure-all for the most baffling mental cases, severe depression for instance. She'd seen this kind of depression, the kind that took its victim to a faraway place inside their own head. A place where reality boils away, until it becomes a fog.

The facility towered over a barbed wire perimeter where a long stretch of field surrounded it. After parking and going through security screening, she found herself in an elevator. Anxiety growing, she pushed the button for the 23rd floor, the psychiatric ward. The elevator ascended higher and higher in conjunction with Debra's rising pulse. She inhaled—slow, deliberate. She exhaled—easy, purposefully. She had lost count of how many times she'd been taken away as a child, and placed in a foster home. Doctors would play with her mom's medication and her mom would seem okay for a while, and social services would give Debra back. Then her mom would start drinking again and would stop taking the pills because she said she was fine, and it would start all over.

An armed guard frisked Debra like a common criminal, guided her through an iron gate, and left her on her own to find room A312 down the long narrow hall, the heaviness of her heart, thumping, pulsing. She saw a caged nurse's station, and four armed guards.

A big-bellied nurse and an unkempt man were blocking the hallway so Debra tried to nudge past them. He held an unlit cigarette in one hand and a lighter in the other, his hair was uncombed and his vacant eyes beheld dark circles.

"Give me that." The nurse commanded. "You have to wait till I take your temperature."

"No," The man grunted, and shuffled right into Debra, probably without seeing her. She flattened her back against the wall, trying to get past. The nurse grabbed his wrist, and shoved the thermometer in his mouth.

He bit it. Debra heard the glass break as she inched along the wall. His lips tight, he held the broken bits in his mouth.

"What did you do? Spit that out!" the nurse yelled, fighting with his hands. "Call Doctor Strong! Stat!" she yelled to the nurse's station. He wasn't fighting back so much as he was keeping his mouth closed.

"Calling Doctor Strong . . . Calling Doctor Strong, Ward five," echoed over the PA system. "Calling Doctor Strong to ward five." An armed guard rushed in and then another. Debra crept further away, watching them strong-arm the frantic patient, watching the guards pin him down. She turned away from the commotion, hearing the yells and screams all the way to room 312. Standing in the doorway, looking inside, she saw two cot-like beds in the small cramped room that were bolted to the floor. It was an eerie feeling to see her mother sitting there, stringing beads, as if each one were a rare jewel. Hardly recognizable, her hair was up in a pretty French twist, white strands at her temples. When did her mother get old?

"Mom?"

Aida jumped, startled, dropping her box of beads. "My . . . my . . . m . . ." She seemed stuck on one word and then stopped short, her glazed-over eyes fixed on the wall.

"Mom, it's me." Debra said from the doorway, suddenly that daughter again who couldn't do anything right. Aida dropped to her hands and knees, picking up beads that had rolled under the bed. The woman who shared her room scooted inside the doorway behind Debra.

"They messed with her brain you know," the woman said, digging in a used-up Kotex box that was on a shelf. "Do you have a match?" she asked, pulling out a cigarette.

"No, I don't smoke." Debra said, still watching her mother.

"Poop. Everyone else is allowed to have lighters, but they took mine. Isn't that asinine? All I did was mention to that idiot scrub woman that I could set fire to these curtains just as good with a lighter as I could with a match."

"Really . . . ."

"She told me to hand it over. I told her I was allowed to have it. I told her it was mine. She tried to take it away—it was mine. Do you know what they did then?" The woman's straw-like eyebrows straggled to the wrinkle lines in her forehead as she spoke; the fat under her arms jiggled with every move of her hand. "They called Doctor Strong. You know what that means?"

Aida broke in, her words monotone, "Every able bodied man, get to the psych ward." Aida seemed to acknowledge her surroundings now, the people around her. "They jumped her all at once and crucified her to a gurney. They've done it to all of us. It was just your turn," she said to the woman, a haunting laugh lingering. "It'll be your turn someday," she said to Debra. Aida got up from the floor, her eyes on Debra's. Aida got up close. "They'll come after you, you'll see."

Debra stood there without moving, watching her mother close in to an inch away from her face. Nose to nose, staring into her mother's eyes, she dare not blink, she dare not speak. Shock treatment had erased Aida's memory, the white-coats had said, reserved only for extreme cases. Pieces of memory would be reintroduced so the patient could accept their lot in life. Debra was one of those pieces.

"You smell—like me," Aida said as if she was onto to Debra, onto some sort of charade.

"That's wild," came from Debra's lips. Here she was in a crazy place, this crazy person saying crazy things. It didn't seem real.

"Don't get smart with me. I'm still your mother," Aida said, working hard for each word. "This is all your fault."

Debra froze, gripped by a lifetime of guilt. She'd blamed herself. It wasn't her fault but she blamed herself just the same. Aida had killed Bill because of her. Aida pled insanity at the trial which brought her here to live out the rest of her life. Debra said nothing, knowing too well trying to reason with a mentally unstable person was the same as trying to reason with a drunk. They just don't get it, no matter how much you want them to. "Mom," Debra said nicely. She would put a spin on it. She would turn it around. "I love what you've done to your hair."

"Just who do you think you are?"

Debra smiled politely, her insides wrenched. "It was nice to see you again. I have to go now," she said, rounding up a seemingly cordial visit, promptly turning her back, and leaving the room. It hurt so badly, first to see her mother in this awful place, and then be assailed because she'd come.

"Debby I'm sorry. Don't go." Aida wrung her hands nervously, prattling on. "Please. Don't do this. I'm your mother. Please don't leave me here."

Debra focused straight ahead as she walked down the long hall, the click of her shoes echoing within its walls. She would be strong. She would blink back the wet in her eyes, and she would be strong.

"Debby. Please. I love you. You're everything to me."

Debra stopped. She bounced a glance off the gate and at her mother. This was the woman who would knock her to the floor. The woman who would sit on her chest, grab her hair and pound her head on the floor, in one of her psychotic frenzies. Why did she have to think of that? It was done now, over. Things were different. So very different. She told her mother she loved her. She said she'd stay longer next time. "Next time you'll feel better." Looking into Aida's eyes, she could see they were empty now . . . electric-shock empty.

A guard unlocked the chain-link door. Debra kissed her mother's cheek, and squeezed through the door as it opened.

She dove inside the ladies room, and sitting on the toilet, she brought herself back to the present. She took a purposeful breath. Things were different now. Her mother's insanity was not meant to be shared, that's what a caseworker had said, 'Aida's insanity belongs with Aida. Your sanity belongs with you.' She took another breath. 'Disconnect. Disconnect.'

The case worker had said, 'A mentally ill person is like someone who's drowning. They'll drag you under. You've got to let go.' Debra washed her hands, splashed cold water on her face, and dried with a paper towel—telling herself to settle down. She mindlessly tugged at her lashes, displacing a few at the root. A tight bunch came out in her hand. It hurt. Eyelashes fell down her cheek. She rubbed her fist in her eye, stopping herself from pulling out any more.

She would go to Mrs. O'Shell's house, a woman who fostered her once. She would go to the quaint little house where clusters of roses and baby's breath grew. Where a baby grand piano held a hymnal, a red and gray afghan on the seat. She would smell stuffed cabbages cooking. Mrs. O'Shell's house—this was where God dwelled—not in any pew in any church, but here where this faithful servant lived.

Debra rang the doorbell, and rubbed her face in both hands as she waited. 'My sanity belongs with me. My sanity belongs with me. I am not my mother . . . .' The door opened.

"What a wonderful surprise," Mrs. O'Shell said, hugging her like a long lost child. "It's so nice to see you. How have you been?"

"I'm good. How are you? It's been so long."

Mrs. O'Shell looked right at the bald spot in her lashes, Debra could tell. She hid her face in her hands. "I haven't done that in years and all of a sudden . . . ."

"Oh, Honey. It'll be all right." Mrs. O'Shell took Debra's hands in her gnarly fingers, examining the delicate torn strips of skin. "Look at your cuticles." She held Debra's hands as if in a prayer, her hands small like Debra's. "I don't know anyone else who could have handled all this as well as you. I admire you so."

Debra found solace here. She would lay down all of her burdens and Mrs. O'Shell would help sort them all out. "I saw my mother today . . ." Debra stopped mid-sentence when she came inside to something she wasn't prepared for. The house was terribly unkempt. There were clumps of dirt and dust and shoe-crud. Piles of junk-mail littered the couch and a broken toaster for some reason. Dusty old knick-knacks were strewn on a stained carpet that hadn't been vacuumed since who knows when. This wasn't what she had pictured.

"How is your mother?" Mrs. O'Shell asked, limping along with a cane. Debra suddenly put the bits and pieces together, conversations they'd had, letter she'd read. Mrs. O'Shell was seventy-nine, diabetic, and three of her toes had been amputated one at a time.

"She's . . ." seeing this happy face, Debra wouldn't spoil the old woman's joy. "She's well," Debra said. They would go to the kitchen and have cookies and tea, she thought. They would sit and laugh and reconnect, and then she would help the old woman clean. The kitchen was just as bad. The flowered linoleum floor was sticky where something must have been spilt. From the way it looked, it must have been a while ago. There was a sink-full of rancid dishes, a box of adult diapers against a wall. And here was Mrs. O'Shell smiling for all she was worth. Debra guided the old woman to a kitchen chair, and prepared the sink to wash dishes.

"I would say you don't have to do that, but I'm afraid you'd stop," Mrs. O'Shell said, covering a laugh like a Geisha girl—a very old Geisha girl. Debra knew she always hid her laughter because she was afraid her false teeth would fall out. Not that they ever had.

"We bought a house," Debra said, dipping into sudsy water.

"A new house . . . how exciting."

CHAPTER 19

It had been a week since Debra had seen her mother. She looked forward to jogging with Julie more than ever—even in the heat. Julie's letters had seemed to stop, but this time when Julie swung by, she showed up with another letter.

Julie

I hope you received my letters. I don't think I had your whole address quite right. I hope you did because I could never rewrite them. Well, if you did, you probably know who I am, right? I wonder if you came Friday. If you did, I'm sorry I missed you. I couldn't make it because I got called away again (NY). Work is getting to be a problem. I was looking forward to meeting you at our restaurant. We would have had such a good time together! My, how romantic it will be to sit next to you, holding hands. We'll order the best meal and my favorite wine (you remember?). You are so gorgeous, so pleasant to be near. I bet you look terrific in a beautiful evening gown, so fragile, loving, and sensitive. It will be the most memorable time of my life! You sitting with me would make me so proud! I will always remember your warm smile. It will be so nice to talk to you! On the other hand, I'm afraid you're going to tell me that you're happily married. I don't know yet. I didn't know how else to make you love me. I am so in love with you, Julie! Give me one more chance! Meet me again next Friday, same time & place. Please give me that one experience of a lifetime! If I don't see you, I will let go and try to stop loving you. This will be extremely hard because I know you would like me and, perhaps in time, love me like I love you. I have to say, this has been real exciting writing to you. Remember, there will always be someone loving you for the rest of your life. ME

Debra stood motionless. "Julie, I don't know what to say. What are you going to do?"

"Nothing. He said if I didn't show up that he'd stop. Besides, Kyle would go nuts if I tried to meet him again. Most likely this guy just wants to watch me and pretend he isn't there."

"Can you be sure that will end it?"

Julie's hand trembled as she took back the letter. "What if this guy's lurking around my house and looking in my windows? What if he's following me? I can't call the sheriff unless he threatens me or actually does something, and he hasn't. Yet. And how can I avoid contact when I don't even know what he looks like."

"What does Kyle say?"

"He says he's going to find out who he is and kill him. I've never seen him like this," Julie said as they crossed the road. She looked worn out, like she hadn't slept for days.

"What do you say we jog in the morning, tomorrow?" Debra asked. "We can get a breakfast first and split it like we did last time."

"I don't know. Call me in the morning."

CHAPTER 20

A fire breathing dragon coiled the body of a naked woman down the length of his arm, a heart of blood, the tail a pitchfork. A string of skulls encircled his wrist—part of a whole tattoo. His arms and back, his chest and stomach, were a canvas of hearts and snakes, skulls and naked women, and flames. Bruce pulled a black muscle-man shirt on over his head, and wadded up the game warden shirt he'd just taken off. He reached under the car seat and retrieved the hunting knife that he'd wrapped in a kitchen towel—its bloody case still in his trunk where he fetched a crowbar. His car was parked where it had been the last time—the deserted-looking parking lot in Brentwood Pines Development—the place down the street from Debra's house.

It took an hour to get here. Always an hour, always while his wife was sleeping. She worked nights at a bar on Brook Park Road and slept until well after noon. A can of Fancy Feast cat food in hand, he crossed the street, jumped the ditch, and forged a path over new fallen deadwood, and into the field, the brush so thick you couldn't see your feet. Shoulder-high trees camouflaged blackberry barbs that had grown and spread. The willowy briars piercing his skin brought a new vibrant color in the mix of tattoos. How it should be, his blood to her blood.

The barn had lost its dead animal smell where the small skeleton had fallen through the noose. He wedged the crowbar into a board and pried it off, enough room for him to squeeze inside. The cats scattered to the thistles and woodpiles. He punched an overhead rafter, solid enough to hold a naked human. He tied a heavy rope around it and tested its strength—swinging from it like the Hunchback of Notre Dame. He'd pictured this in his mind for so long.

He made his way toward the house, knowing the only car there was hers. She was always alone this time of the day. He'd been watching her.

His footsteps light, underbrush snapping as he stepped, he made his way past the cow, the moo-thing lying in his own excrement, chewing a cud. Suddenly a black cat came from nowhere, hissing, and clawed its way up a tree trunk.

"You're next," Bruce said, pointing his knife at the cat. Once in the open yard he quietly sprinted to the deck in the back of the house. Through the screen he could see the window open about six inches— the window where he'd been watching her. He cut a hole in the screen and tried to open the window enough to get inside, but something was jamming it. Glancing up, he thought he saw a moving shadow inside the house, and ducked down. On his hands and knees he made it to the sliding glass door, and easily unlocked it with a nail file. The door slid open, but stopped at an inch. A wooden bar was wedged in the track, keeping it closed.

He duck-walked to another back door and cautiously looked in the small window. The door was peeling paint badly. He could see an old piano inside and a rickety staircase. It didn't look like anyone lived in this part of the house. Glancing over his left shoulder Bruce wedged the file inside the doorframe, and slid it down. It caught right away. He pushed on the door but something was holding it closed. He looked in the four-paned window again and couldn't see why the door wouldn't open and shook the doorknob, trying to be quiet. "Shit," he whispered, sniffing, choking back and swallowing the phlegm that was building in his throat. He couldn't go to the front door, someone might see him from the road. Maybe she would come outside. She'd have to feed the cattle sometime today. He peeped in the window where he'd seen her before. Where was she?

"I'll see you tomorrow." He heard a woman's voice, someone walking down the driveway from the end of the road. Bruce backed into a covey and crouched behind a patio chair. He heard the jangle of keys and heard the side garage door opening. A few more minutes and he'd make his move. The black cat suddenly jumped on the deck and started purring as it butted its head against Bruce's leg. Bruce nudged it away with his foot. The cat shot back and rubbed its back on Bruce's leg, purring loudly. Bruce shoved it this time, trying not to make a sound. Then he heard the door open and close again, and he heard the sound of gravel as Debra's car backed out of the driveway.

He glared straight ahead. "Shit! And jerked the cat up by its neck and held it in his fist. "You dumb ass cat!" The black cat hissed. Bruce stabbed him, gutted him right there. He retraced his steps to the barn and suspended the lifeless cat from the rafter. The sun beamed in narrow stripes between the wood-slat walls. Alabaster rabbit bones sank in the rubble, and poison ivy hung down through holes in the roof.

Bruce unzipped his pants. He looked down at himself and up at the cat. This wasn't what he wanted . . . not now, not anymore.

CHAPTER 21

A black plume soared above a pile of burning branches—Kyle's growing bonfire of deadwood and old papers he didn't want anyone to pilfer through. Julie hurried up their driveway, coming back from her jog, in time to see Kyle throw in his version of useless mailers. He picked out a stack from a cardboard box.

"Wait a minute. I wanted to go through those. You burned some of my recipes last time."

"Is this what you're looking for?" Kyle held up a handful of letters.

"What is that?"

"The rest of his letters. The ones I never showed you." Kyle tossed a letter into the fire. "He stays home from work sometimes just to watch you. But you probably know that. Don't you?"

"You're making that up. Let me see those."

"I know why you leave the shades open, why you dress up to go to the bank. You like to be watched."

"You're starting to scare me. Where did you get those? How many are there?" she asked, barely seeing the handwriting.

He singled out a letter. "He talks about your black lace bra in this one," then he tossed it in the fire, "you must have given it to him. He says he likes to sniff it." He singled out another one, waved it in her face, and jerked it away before she could grab it. "Did you find the panties he bought for you? Red-zippered, he says. He left them for you in the barn. I burned those, too."

"Let me see that." Julie grabbed his arm, trying to get the letter, but he flipped it in the fire with all the rest. "Kyle. Don't!" He grabbed her arms forcefully, enough to leave bruises, holding her back, her yelling, "You're hurting me. Let go."

He loosened his grip. "Didn't want you to get burned, that's all," he said, dusting ashes out of her hair.

She smacked his hand away and took a step backward, her face aglow with orange and red hues of the fire pit. "He was stalking me this whole time, and you let me think he was some stupid businessman. Don't you care about what happens to me? Do you think I would have gone to that bar if I'd known about those letters?"

"You know as well as I do, these were sent *after* your night at the bar. I don't know what you did that night, but he wants more." He turned his back to her and jabbed at the fire with a pitchfork. "Go away. I can't look at you."

That night Kyle slept in the guest room again. The next morning, he was gone before Julie woke up. She'd barely slept, visions of a faceless man watching her through her windows. She let the boys sleep in and was making coffee when the phone rang.

"Hi Julie. I can be ready by nine o'clock. Is that okay?" Debra asked.

She'd forgotten all about Debra, all about a morning jog. "I've got a lot of errands this morning. How about later?" Julie lifted a section in the closed blinds and briefly looked out the kitchen window. She wouldn't open the blinds in the kitchen or anywhere in the house. Something had snapped inside, something during the night when her eyes wouldn't shut. A stalker had been here, had seen her in every light. It was as though Kyle had welcomed it as a means to torment her.

"I thought you had a 4-H meeting later."

"That ended when the fair did. The boys are leaving next week for college." Julie nervously twisted the telephone cord around her finger as she talked.

"I can't believe it. I barely got to know them and they're already leaving." Debra's cheery voice was a welcomed reprieve, if only for a moment.

"I can't believe that Kyle had them working across town all summer. The only time I got to spend with them was at the fair and then for orientation for Bowling Green." An awful thought crept in, "For all I know that pervert was there, too."

"Well at least that's over, "Debra said.

"I'm not so sure."

"What makes you say that? Did something happen?"

I didn't know it, but he kept on writing to me. Kyle hid all the letters, and was burning them when I came home last night. I'll talk to you later. Okay?"

Julie chose her clothes carefully that morning, making sure that whatever she did, she would not look nice. Wearing jeans and a Bowling Green t-shirt, she poured coffee in a travel mug and left the house. The target of unwanted affection, she could still hear Kyle say, 'he's watching you,' something that had troubled her all summer. Now she knew for sure.

Julie parked her car in the bank's parking lot. As she walked to the door, a man was waiting there, holding it open, "Morning," he said, smiling sweetly, nodding his head, giving her little room to get by him.

"Morning," Julie said quietly, squeezing through the door,

unavoidably brushing against him. A cloud of aftershave and hair gel swirled her in. Standing in line, she brushed off his essence the best she could. Now he was standing behind her, so close that he was almost touching her. She moved up a little. So did he, closer than before. She moved up again—so did he. Without the slightest touch, she felt the warmth of his body, and suddenly saw herself naked. The stalker, her stalker, had one of her bras. He'd been buying her panties. He'd been watching her undress.

Fumbling in her purse to find her transaction, she rushed up to the cashier. Then quickly left. As she drove away, she realized that she hadn't actually looked at the face of the man behind her at the bank. She'd never be able to describe him, if he was the stalker. She'd never be able to recognize him, if it came to it, in a line up.

She drove to the grocery store where she impatiently rattled the cage of grocery carts, struggling to pry one out.

"Let me help you with that." A pinstriped arm reached from behind her and pulled out the cart. This man was wearing a paisley tie and had a dimpled chin. He was so tall that he towered over her, and he was the right age. "There you go." He gestured for her to take the cart, almost bowing.

"Thank you," she mumbled, taking the cart, suspecting even him. Sailing down the first aisle, she pulled a shopping list out of her purse. The paisley tie guy seemed to be following her. He was subtle about it, yet there he was. She would study the face of this man just in case he was the stalker, and looked right at him.

"Well, hello," he said, smiling like he'd won a prize.

She said, "Hello" like a gavel dropping, and walked abruptly out of the store. She was so flustered in the parking lot; she couldn't find her car keys.

Pure happenstance, a man got out of a car parked next to hers. "Excuse me," he said. "Do you know where the wine shop is?" A nothing man, he wasn't unfriendly or friendly, just a man asking a question. But wasn't that the guise?

"You'll have to ask someone else." She ransacked the bottom of her purse and suddenly found her keys, opened the door, and quickly got inside her car. Coffee on an empty stomach was churning acid.

Who was the man in the letters, the man who shared their favorite wine? What wine? She never drank with anyone where she worked—she simply opened the bottle and poured.

On the long drive home from Southland, a nobody man in the next lane was driving a black Mustang, keeping the same speed as Julie on the four-lane road. Every time the light turned red, their cars were neck and neck. She could feel his eyes on her. The road ahead seemed to narrow into a long concrete tunnel.

Miles away, Debra stared out her kitchen window, her arms folded. She watched a calico cat lick her kitten and then itself. A faint wind hummed through the cracked window. Then a disquieting racket, a 'whoosh-scrape-rattle-rattle-rattle' intruded. She harnessed a rogue shiver, suddenly thinking about what her mother had said, 'It'll be your turn someday.' The house was quiet—uncommonly quiet. Debra went outside in spite of no shoes, lugging a bag of cat food, then dumped a pile right on the ground. Overhead a formation of geese announced their southward journey in conjunction with a premature autumn breeze. One by one the cats came, but only after she'd stepped away from the food. Midnight was always here first, but not today, not anywhere. "Here Kitty, Kitty," she called. She counted fifteen cats. Midnight was not one of them.

On the other side of the driveway, in the thicket as tall as her, she heard something, someone, rustling and crackling the dead underbrush. Sam had been watering Otto while she'd been gone and she called out, "Sam? Is that you?" hoping he'd answer back. A phantom footstep crackled the underbrush. That did it. Two cats missing. Someone was out there, she knew it, someone who'd taken them and killed them for some sort of sick pleasure. Debra marched inside and retrieved the rifle from the bedroom closet. No bullets though. She came back, and aimed it at the edge of the field. "Whoever you are, you better leave now!" she yelled in her childlike voice. The wind rippled her long hair over her arms and down her back, the rifle butt in her shoulder, her eye on the sight down the long barrel.

Just then Julie pulled in the driveway and got out of car, ashen; angst etched in her face.

"Julie, what's wrong?" Debra asked, taken out of her own uneasiness.

Julie suddenly found herself smiling. "Look at you, barefoot, surrounded by cats, and toting a rifle. Are you shooting some supper or shooting at some government agent man?"

Debra let herself laugh. "I heard something out there. Come on in before it figures out I don't have any bullets." She would tell Julie about everything.

"I think I might have seen him Deb, the guy who wrote the letters." Julie meandered through the garage with Debra and into the house.

"Where? Did he try something?"

"No . . . no, they . . . he didn't try anything. There was a man at the bank, a man at the store, and another one in the parking lot, and then I think someone else on the way home . . . . I don't know which one was him." Listening to herself, Julie hesitated; her story fell under the headlines of terribly vain and highly unlikely. "I mean, four different men acted funny in four different places. You know, like they all . . . . It's so confusing." She sat down at the kitchen table and covered her face with her hands. "I must sound like an idiot."

"Don't say that. Some men act as if they've never seen a pretty face before. You should ignore them. Tell me about the letters?"

"There were maybe five or six. He's been watching me through my windows. He's got one of my bras and he bought me red panties. And Kyle waited all this time to tell me. I don't know what to do."

"Call the sheriff again?" Debra said.

"I did. They won't do anything—not unless he threatens me—not unless he commits a crime . . . when it'll be too late."

"I don't know what to say. I wish I could help." Debra bit her cuticle, fixing her gaze on the rifle she'd set in a corner. Julie leaned on the table and rested her chin in her hand, watching Debra's face. A quiet hushed over them. Debra's gaze turned to a blank stare.

"I shouldn't be dumping all this on you," Julie said.

"No. Really . . . I don't mind."

"Then something else is upsetting you. I can see it in your face."

"Two cats are missing. Midnight's gone. I'm afraid to look for him. I have a feeling he's dead."

"Tomcats roam for days sometimes. I bet he's on the scent of a female. He'll be back. Don't worry about it."

Debra got quiet, her face worried.

115

"Is there something you're not telling me?"

"I don't know. It's . . . It's nothing. It's dumb."

"Are you still unnerved about that swing set?"

"The swing set isn't the only thing . . . . Do you remember me telling you about that groundhog?" Her eyes shifted to Julie.

"It had rabies. You had to kill it."

"The shovel I used disappeared and then it, I mean another one, showed up where I buried the groundhog. I know I said it was in worse shape than I thought. What I didn't say was, we don't even have a shovel . . . . I feel like someone's watching me, maybe playing tricks on me. I almost thought that Sam took the swing set down or switched shovels, but now I don't think it was him."

"Alzheimer's affects Sam more some days than others. He can't concentrate on anything long enough to finish what he starts. Sometimes he wanders over to my house. By the time he gets to the door, he usually can't remember why he came. And other times he seems so lucid. It's not Sam."

"I know. I have to ask you though. What do you think about ghosts?"

"You know there's no such thing."

"Just for argument's sake, let's say there were. I like to imagine something greater than me erected this old swing set and planted that shovel when I needed them. I hear things in this house, too, like footsteps when no one's there. You should have been here that night in the thunderstorm. I could have sworn someone was in the house."

"It's funny how the mind can play tricks on you. I think that anyone with even a staggering belief in ghosts can make themselves believe they've seen one. If you stare at something long enough, it can actually appear to move. Maybe listening for something long enough works the same way."

"You're probably right," Debra said, her voice soft. She would say no more. Julie would think she was crazy, the kind of crazy people tolerate because they liked you once.

Julie knew how to read her face, or so it seemed when she said, "I'm not saying you should ignore it. My advice—buy some bullets."

CHAPTER 22

It was September now. Julie's hollyhocks had gone to seed, and the coral bell had curled up inside itself. The letters had stopped, and Julie wasn't sure if they'd stopped because Kyle was hiding them or because Smitten had stopped writing them. Neither she nor Kyle spoke of it, and even though the hoopla died down it was never far from her mind.

Jeff and Nate had left for college, and Julie found herself in their bedroom, missing them terribly. A poster of Bruce Springsteen hung over Jeff's bed. A poster of The Cleveland Browns hung over Nate's dresser, and their high school graduation tassels were tacked on the corkboard inside the door alongside wallet size pictures of their closest friends. She ran her fingers along Nate's pillow, still fragrant with his scent, she inhaled it, and inside the silent room, she cried.

A door slammed and she heard Kyle yell, "Did you take care of the stock trailer? Julie! Where the hell are you?"

She wiped her eyes. "I'm coming."

"Where were you? I left my truck here because you were supposed to hitch the trailer. Is it ready?" His faded jeans were smudged with bits of dried cement and flecks of blood where he'd cut his hand. "I only have an hour before I have to get back to work." Dried blood encircled a big Band-Aid that he'd slapped on his knuckles. "And Greg's probably got less time than that," he said, opening a jar of peanuts for a quick lunch.

"It's ready," Julie said as she brushed by him, her dark ringlets of curls pulled back, her tissue clutched in her fist. "It's ready." There was no use in telling him how much she missed the boys. There was no use in telling him anything, especially not today. He was already in a bad mood because a new hire hadn't showed up for work, and on top of that he'd taken all of Kyle's tools. A temper tantrum was on the horizon, she could feel it. One word from her would set him off. At this point, she wasn't sure why she was still living here. Maybe it was because there was nowhere else to go. Julie got in the truck with him and stared straight ahead. As they left, the aluminum trailer clanged over a rut at the end of the driveway—she hated that rut, the rut she endured every day.

Kyle backed up the trailer. Greg was holding Otto's leather lead, looking amused as he watched the fourteen-hundred pound steer lick his worn out leather work boots. Greg's tar-ridden jeans were frayed at the knees, and soot highlighted his collar and his baseball cap. Debra waved from the porch when Julie hopped out of the truck.

"It's a good thing he likes my boots," Greg said. "Wherever Otto wants to go, Otto goes." Julie's face softened when she smiled at Greg. She waved to Debra and pulled down the ramp, and then meandered to where Debra was. Her job was done. This was Kyle's gig.

"You've been crying," Debra said.

"You can tell?" Julie opened her eyes wide and finger-swiped any telltale signs of tears. "I don't know why I'm so emotional. The university is only a two-hour drive."

"We should take a day and drive up there. I heard it's beautiful." Debra tucked her long hair behind her ears.

The fourteen-hundred pound steer pranced backward, throwing cow-kicks. Kyle circled back and smacked the animal's hide. Otto's nostrils flared, he snorted and barreled up the ramp and into the trailer.

119

Then Kyle maneuvered around him, secured the tether, and Greg pulled up the ramp.

"You girls want to go for a ride?" Greg yelled. "We can stop for a quick hamburger on the way back."

"No, you go ahead," Julie yelled back. "I'm holding out for a McOtto burger." Julie waited for Debra to laugh or giggle or something. Nothing.

Debra, standing with Julie, watched the trailer drive away and out of sight. "I can't believe he's gone," she said.

"Oh, he'll be back." Julie leaned into her a little bit with her shoulder and smiled, anticipating a cheerfulness here. But Debra wouldn't be cheered which seemed strange because no one should have been happier to get rid of that bull than her.

"How long do you think it will take? I'm mean . . . until he's freezer meat?" Debra said in all seriousness.

"You don't have a tender spot for that steer, do you?"

"Yeah . . . I do." Debra's face, the arch of her brows, were poised in regret. "It's reserved for the end of my fork."

Julie gave her a sideways glance. "How long have you been waiting to say that?"

"It sounded better in my head."

They shared a grin, two women and one silly grin. Here was Debra, Julie thought, at least ten years younger than herself, practically a girl, someone too young to have ever known real sorrow. She loved that about Debra, her innocence. "You're not going to eat any of it. Are you?"

"I'd have to be starving."

CHAPTER 23

The accountant had shown Debra, tax-wise, what to do when they incorporated Greg's carpentry business into a Sub-chapter S corporation. She had separated each form on the dining room table for Hamilton Carpentry Inc. and now she had to fill them out—Ohio Unemployment, Ohio Worker's Comp, 941, IT 501. The quarterly federal tax and the State of Ohio quarterly tax were two more slips of paper bundled with their own instructions and mailing envelopes. But there were bills, too. Banner Supply, Builders Loft, Decker Steel, Landmark Fuel, and Bradley Dump-yard were in a neat pile of unopened mail, shoved in the corner. Every last one of them wanted money—money they had scrimped together.

Debra sat down and picked up a thick worker's comp instruction booklet, holding her forehead in her hand. Twenty-six percent of payroll per construction worker—down to 10% through the Twinsburg Chamber of Commerce—down to 6% if she followed recommendations mandated for 'Safety in the Workplace' that required eleven typed pages of rules integrated with their own. This was a job in itself. She'd worked in a legal office in Cincinnati, and had wanted to do the same here, but Greg had told her to wait a year so she could organize his business.

"This is nuts. It's just the two of us. Why wouldn't he be careful? He is the company." Debra heard a car pull in. Mr. Brubom was early. She grabbed his contract and a clipboard, and hurried to the front porch where she saw a new white 1984 Cadillac Seville stop halfway up the driveway. The car door opened and a portly man in his sixties set his feet, one at a time, on the gravel driveway. Mr. Brubom wore a leather cowboy hat and held an unlit cigar. He flicked unseen ashes and hoisted himself up, holding onto the car door; his watermelon belly hung over his belt.

Seeing the century home, he stopped and gazed at the one-of-a-kind mansion, as most people did, either in admiration or in sympathy. On his way to the porch where Debra was waiting, he stopped to gaze again, taking his time as he lumbered to the porch.

"I always loved this old house," he said, feeling the gingerbread trim overhead that framed the porch. "You should have Greg take those lightning rods down . . . . Did you know Ed Cummings?"

"No, I don't believe I've ever heard the name."

"Oh you probably wouldn't have. No telling how many renters this house has had over the years. Ed lived here 'bout seven years ago. He was a cop in Brook Park. Loved cats, couldn't turn 'em away. Too bad about his accident though," Mr. Brubom said. "He was so young, such a nice fellow. He'd only been on the force a year."

"Accident? What happened to him?"

"Well . . ." Brubom began. "Him and his two buddies were renting here . . ."

"I'm so sorry, please sit down." Debra gestured towards one of two rocking chairs. Men were never invited inside, even clients. The garage was an option in case of rain or snow, but then she'd have to stand at the edge of it and flag them down. Everyone that came to the house seemed to be drawn to the front door, "Would you like something to drink?"

"No . . . no, I'm fine." He stood, leaning on the pillar. Debra could see the old chalky paint coming off on his nice jacket. But she would keep it to herself.

"You were saying?"

"Oh yes, Ed Cummings; he had an accident right here in this house. Killed him, you know. It was such a shame. He was only twenty-three."

"Really?" Her eyes opened wide. "Here?"

"Right here, in the basement, knee-deep in water . . . it used to flood, you know. You don't go down there, do you?" Brubom used the white pillar as his personal scratching post, unaware that he was smudging chalky paint all over his back.

"Greg fixed it so it won't flood anymore. What were you saying about the policeman . . . Ed?"

Oh yeah . . . Ed was standing knee-deep in water and he plugged in the sump pump. Electrocuted him right there on the spot," Brubom said. "How did Greg fix it from flooding?"

Debra didn't answer at first. The way he kept switching subjects was making her dizzy. She collected her thoughts. "Someone cemented over the original drainage, but Greg didn't know that until he pick-axed a hole in the cement . . . . This man died? Here?"

"Yeah, electrocuted to death, it was a shock." He cleared his throat to signal that he hadn't meant to make a pun. "What made Greg take a pick-ax to the floor?"

The abrupt subject change got her again. "Greg? Oh. He was looking for the lowest spot to set the sump pump. Greg tells this better than I do. When he broke the cement, water came bubbling up from underneath, and the more it rose up, the more he thought, 'what the hell did I do?'"

"What the hell did he do?"

"At the time, nothing. The water drained back out through the hole he'd made, and the basement's been dry ever since. He says he'd kept wondering what they did a hundred years ago when this house didn't have electricity.

"I'll be darned. Where does it drain to?"

"The original underground tiles were over here." She stepped off the porch, pointed to a line of new grass. "Believe it or not, the lowest part of the basement is just above creek level. He rented a backhoe and replaced the clay tiles with a corrugated pipe. It drains to the creek over there," Debra said, showing him the row of cherry trees and wild raspberries that hid the creek.

"You know, when I was young I used to have that kind of energy. My wife sucked out every last bit. We're getting a divorce, you know. She's got a high-priced lawyer whose going to drain me of every last dollar."

"Oh." Debra sighed, wondering how he'd landed on this subject, knowing she'd never get rid of him now that he was on a roll. "I'm sorry to hear that."

"I retired last year and then right before Christmas, she tells me I get on her nerves. She tells me I've been getting on her nerves for thirty years and she can't take it anymore."

Debra stood there, listening to him ramble on with her arms folded, shaking her head to say too bad, nodding her head to say good thing, thinking about the man killed in her house. How would she ever sleep here again? She started biting her cuticle, muting Brubom's words, looking past his moving lips. Anticipating Midnight's purr at her ankles, she looked for him. She knew somehow he was dead.

124

CHAPTER 24

Debra and Julie were jogging close to town in Edgewood Park this morning, the perfect place for endurance running—up steep hills and down again. There was a quiet between them, the kind of acceptable quiet between two friends. At least that's what Debra liked to think.

The weeks had drudged by so slowly. It was November now, 1984, which was a long time coming. It was thirty degrees, too cold too early for this time of year. The trees were almost bare and scatterings of leaves floated down on a whim.

Debra would visit the Laundromat after this. Her laundry had piled up long enough and she'd stuffed it in the trunk of her car. She wouldn't go in the basement. Even with the basement door closed, she envisioned vapors of death wafting up through the cracks in the floorboards. Greg had tried to console her and she had tried to be consoled, but it was no use. The Laundromat was a half hour drive— coupled with a few other errands, it was worth the drive.

"I think it's going to snow today. It's so cloudy," Julie said in frosty breaths.

"It smells like fall. I've always loved that smell." Debra would trick herself into being happy. Sometimes she was good at it.

The length of sidewalk was piled with fallen leaves that crunched with each footstep. "When I was little, we used to rake up leaves and burn them. I don't know why but I always loved the smell of burning leaves."

Jogging next to Julie, Debra listened to the rhythm of their feet. She was grateful to be away from the house where creaks and rattles seemed to speak their own language. Strange things were happening in that house; shoes somehow ended up in the bathtub, scissors ended up in the freezer. She could just hear what Julie would say; that there were no such things as ghosts, there was no such thing as Ed. Greg was growing impatient.

The conversation today was pleasantries, timed to the rhythm of their feet—a superficial camaraderie for the duration of their jog and back to their cars.

After they'd said 'good-bye' to each other, Debra sat behind the wheel of her car, counting her change, thinking about what to make for dinner. Greg would have steak. He could have steak every night, no vegetables, no bread, just a hunk of meat. Not her. Not Otto—even if she was short on cash. And she was always short on cash. Six dollars and twenty cents was all she had, barely enough to buy eggs, and milk, and enough gasoline for the next couple days, let alone store-bought meat. She had the choice of starving or washing clothes in the basement. How could she eat freezer meat when she could still see Otto chewing its cud?

Debra drove past the Laundromat, pining to stop there, watching it grow smaller in her rearview mirror. Instead, she drove to a brand new Kroger's grocery store, where she parked amidst an immeasurable number of cars. The wind bustled flags strung all the way to the road. It was much windier than before, so much so, she fought with the car door to open it.

Inside the new store, aisles seemed to go on forever. She guessed which way the canned tuna fish was, bypassing the fruits and vegetables, skipping aisle after aisle and barreling past Greg's nemesis—store-bought chocolate chip cookies which would have cost half of everything she had. Reading the aisle markers, she caught a glimpse of Julie who was speed walking down an aisle toward the exit. "Julie," she shouted, trying to get her attention. "Julie!" Debra raced to catch up with her. "Wait up!"

Julie stopped dead in her tracks, "Deb?" Her face was void of color.

"What's wrong?"

"He's here. The stalker. I know it's him. He's following me in the store," Julie said between short breaths, searching with her eyes.

"Where is he?" Debra asked, looking beyond a bread rack and then around a corner. "Are you sure?"

A breath sunk in Julie's chest. "Believe me. He followed me through every aisle. Just to be sure I skipped one, and so did he. No cart. Nothing in his hands. He's not buying a single thing here."

"Maybe it was an awkward coincidence. Maybe this man couldn't find what he was looking for."

"That's what I thought at first. So I went to the other end of the store." Julie's eyes flashed. "He followed me again. I walked off on my grocery cart somewhere in the soup section."

"What does he look like?"

"He's got on some sort of a mechanic's overall and a black baseball cap. His eyes are dark like he's wearing eyeliner or something. I think his black mustache is fake. He could be Greek or Italian, maybe Lebanese."

"I would report him to the store security."

"What am I going to say, that I'm paranoid? He's not standing right here. They'd never take me seriously."

"Come on. Let's find your cart; I'm ready to check out anyway."

She tossed a can of tuna fish in her cart. They found Julie's cart and went to the checkout line. Standing in line at the checkout, Debra saw the man just as Julie described. He was right behind Julie as though he were browsing through a magazine.

"That's him!" Debra pointed right at him. "That's the man!" She yelled confronting him.

Julie closed her eyes as though she'd made peace with dying, her back to him all the while. The man locked eyes with Debra, penetrating into hers, giving her a horrible feeling that he could fry up her brain, pull it out through her tear duct, and eat it. Motionless, wordless, he held her spellbound for what seemed like an eternity— all within a fraction of a second. He backed away still holding her prisoner in his eyes. Then he released her. Then he was gone—quietly, swiftly. Julie hadn't moved, hadn't made a sound, her face etched in dread. It was odd how no one around them had any idea.

"He left. I saw him leave. We need to report him to security."

"What good would that do? They'll ask if he threatened me. He didn't. Now he's gone."

"Where are you parked?"

"Not far." Julie answered.

"Let's stay together till we get to your car." They were leaving the store when Debra asked if he looked familiar.

"Kind of. Remember the man from that night in the lounge? The one who wouldn't leave us alone?" Julie asked, pushing her cart.

"It was dark in there. And he had one of those faces . . . . Do you think it was him?"

"If it was . . . ." Julie stopped halfway to her car. "It could be the answer to both our questions." The wind swept up Julie's spiral curls

128

and whipped Debra's long hair. "I feel like my brain is plugged into a high-tension wire . . . . Where are you parked?" Julie asked.

Debra pointed five double rows away. "Over there. On the other side."

"Go ahead; I'm fine. He's gone now," Julie said. Go ahead. You've got things to do."

"Are you sure?"

"Yeah, my car's just up ahead. I'll see you later. Okay?"

Feeling uneasy about it, Debra left Julie there and headed in the opposite direction. She kept looking back, still watching Julie who was now fumbling in her purse for her keys. Once Debra got to her own car, she scanned the sea of cars. She saw Julie open her trunk. Then she saw him, the man in the black cap, standing next to a white windowless cargo van. He was half-hidden watching Julie load her trunk. Debra stood on her toes, trying to see him better. She stood on the bumpers of the opposite car and hers. He slid open the side panel door where it would have been impossible for Julie to see. But Debra could see clearly; there were no seats in the back which was perfectly suited for kidnapping someone, for doing all sorts of unimaginable things. This very thing had been on the news with a warning not to park near them when a woman's body had been found in one.

"Hey!" Debra yelled as loud as she could, frantically running between cars. "Julie!" The wind blew the words back in her mouth. Debra yelled out again, practically screaming Julie's name, desperately trying to get her attention, but Julie didn't look up. It was more than strange, of all the cars in the parking lot, not one single person was there, not one single person to call for help.

Julie closed her trunk and scooted inside the driver's seat. Debra stopped cold. The man closed the door panel and eased into his driver's seat. Debra jaunted to her Chevy Cavalier and jumped inside. Snowflakes danced across her windshield, a gust of wind rocked her car. She watched Julie's Pontiac Bonneville pull away. The white van was right behind Julie.

Debra backed out and slipped the gear in drive, but as she accelerated, an elderly driver pulled out right in front of her. A handicap tag hung from the old woman's rearview mirror, a short woman who could barely see over the dash, who turned the steering wheel painfully slow. Debra watched the van follow Julie out of the parking lot and onto the road, with herself still blocked by the old woman. By the time Debra got to the end of the parking lot, the light turned red. She waited for a brief minute, and gunned the engine. Flying around the car in front, swerving into the oncoming traffic. She drew in a never-ending breath to the sound of burning rubber, screeching brakes, and blaring horns. From here she could see them at a red light by the Laundromat. With only Julie in mind she carelessly weaved around another car to get behind them. Another red light. They were all stopped. Only one car between her and the white van. Traffic started up again. The one car turned. The cars were lined up, Julie's, the crazy man's, and Debra's, driving over Fulton Bridge. Julie's car went through a green light, the van went through a yellow light, and Debra sped up to go through the red.

"What am I doing? What am I doing?" she repeated, cringing, barreling through the red light.

The traffic was stop and go until the speed limit hit fifty-five. Julie suddenly turned into a speed demon and flew through a pre-red traffic light. He flew through the red light, too. Debra floored it, screaming through it. She could hear the squeal of brakes. Her body stiffening, she braced for a car wreck. The oncoming car swerved into a mailbox instead of hitting her.

She could see up ahead, the railroad tracks, the crossing bars come down. She could see the train coming full on. Debra slowed down and thought Julie would, too. The train whistled. But Julie sped up, careening around the crossing bars just as the train barreled by. She must have known, Debra thought. The man slammed on his brakes—his tires locking, smoking, screeching. Debra was right behind him at a dead stop now. The train rumbled on and on. Debra's shoulders seemed locked in place, her hands tight-fisted ten and twenty, clenching the steering wheel. She could see him as he mouthed profanities, his eyes darting off in the rear view mirror. As far as she knew he hadn't regarded her as anything more than the car behind him. Not yet anyway. She franticly shook her purse upside down to find a pen, glancing at his license plate. The first letter was A. She popped opened the glove compartment. The second letter was Q. All she could find was handful of napkins. She saw him take off his baseball cap. He was suddenly staring at her from his rearview mirror—a thinking stare, she hoped, like his mind was somewhere else. She slumped down in the seat. There was nowhere to go. She couldn't drive forward. She couldn't drive backward. There was a gulley on one side and a line of cars on the other. He had to have seen her. Slumped into the seat, she locked the doors, waiting for him to trek over and smash her car window. She wrote down the first two letters AQ, and peeked over the dash, but something looked funny about the rest of the license. There were bits of masking tape covering little sections of the numbers. She couldn't make out the rest.

The train went by and the crossing bars slowly lifted; cars rolled over the tracks again. Debra put her car in gear. Her car was behind his as she drove her way home for another seventeen minutes of speeding up and slowing down, of stopping at the occasional red light until she finally came upon the road that led to her house. Nudging her left blinker to turn, she thought she'd finally be rid of him.

His turn signal mimicked hers.

The light turned green, and they both turned down the gravel road, her gravel road—five miles from where she lived. She was suddenly itching, and in shallow breaths, she glanced in the rearview mirror and saw red blotches on her face. So this is what it means to be tough, she thought, you break out in hives.

Distancing her car from his, she followed him down the gravel road. She would follow him right into Julie's driveway, and then what? They drove past the first stop sign, past the second stop sign, closer and closer to her house, and to Julie's house. They stopped for one more stop sign, but instead of driving straight ahead, the man turned into Brentwood Pines. This was where they jogged. Could he live there? Could he know she's following him? Debra hesitated when the man turned, watching his van get smaller and smaller as he drove away. What if she kept following him? What if she got his address? She wanted to go home and be glad it was over. But she could lose him if she didn't turn now. She turned the wheel, a surge in her stomach, a distance between them. It felt so terribly wrong. She watched him go around a bend and followed. She watched him turn down Jaycox Avenue. This had gone too far. The way he had looked at her was how her stepfather had when he'd thrown that first punch. She let her car inch closer.

And then it happened. He turned into a driveway. Debra watched the garage door open from a distance. He drove his van inside and the garage door closed. She crept closer and wrote the address on a napkin, the address for the only blue house on Jaycox.

CHAPTER 25

Jumbled coats hung haphazardly from hooks inside Julie's small foyer. Shoes and boots were piled in a corner by the door. The mahogany dining room could be seen just past the refrigerator, just past Kyle who kept shifting his weight from one foot to the other.

"Why didn't you report him to the store security?" Kyle shouted at Julie just inside the entryway. Marie was there, too, in her coat and hat carrying a dozen eggs, smelling like she'd been in the goat-barn.

"What's wrong with you?" Kyle smashed his fist in the wall.

Marie jumped, undoubtedly caught by surprise. "Kyle," Marie started, "Haven't you been listening? Can't you see she's already upset?"

"Marie, I'm sorry you had to see this, but this is none of your business. This has nothing to do with you." Kyle stuck his hands in his pocket and rattled his change. Just then someone knocked, almost pounded, on the door. "See who it is," he instructed. Julie opened the storm door an inch.

"Deb . . . it's you. What's up?" Julie said, holding the storm door open.

"What's up? What do you mean; 'What's up?' Didn't you see that guy following you?"

"And he followed you home?" Kyle shouted from inside.

"Oh . . . Kyle's home," Debra said, glancing back at his truck like she hadn't seen it the first time. She glanced back at Kyle, the veins bulging in his neck. "I'll call you later." Debra hopped off the step and started walking quickly toward her car, obviously trying to get the hell out of there.

"No, wait. I want to hear about this. Come here, Deb." Kyle ordered.

Debra came back and reluctantly stepped inside the foyer. The storm door closed behind her. Stepping over shoes, she backed up to the coat-laden wall. Her face and neck were a mass of little red blotches that she was rubbing with the back of her hand.

"Hi, Kyle. Short work day?"

"What were you saying about some guy following Julie home?" Kyle asked.

"I was trailing both of them, and then Julie lost him at a railroad crossing," she started to explain.

"You were behind him that whole time?" Julie asked with a 'you've got to be kidding' look on her face.

"Yeah, the whole time. When I saw him follow you out of the parking lot, I almost killed myself trying to catch up." Debra looked about as stressed as anyone could look.

Kyle seemed to hang on every word, resting his elbow on the wall, cradling his ear with his hand. Marie, galoshes and all, seemed glued to the spot where she stood.

"Even after you lost him, I could have sworn that he was going to follow you home. But at the last minute, he turned off into Brentwood Pines down the road. I don't think he saw me."

"Where did he go after that?" Julie asked.

"He went home. I've got his address."

Everyone's mouth fell open to some degree. Everyone eyed the napkin that Debra was holding.

"He lives in the only blue house on Jaycox Avenue."

Both Kyle and Julie reached for the paper. Debra shoved it into Julie's hand before Kyle could grab it.

"I'll kill the son of a bitch! Give me that!" He snatched the napkin from Julie, almost tearing the flimsy scrap of paper. "He's going to be sorry he ever messed with me!"

Kyle brushed against Debra, who had flattened her back against the wall. He kicked the door until it was hanging by its hinges, until he'd broken a good section of glass. "I'll kill that son of a bitch!" The veins in his neck visibly pulsed to his temples. He kicked it again. This time the door bounced back just as he reached for the handle and a fragment of jagged glass sliced his hand. But he didn't groan in pain or even mutter a sound. He kicked the door fast and hard, violently shattering the rest of the glass, straining the hinge of the door. Then he stomped out, steadfast toward his truck.

Debra, Julie, and Marie stood motionless, listening to his truck peel out of the driveway.

"I think you should call the police." Debra said.

Marie's face lost all expression . . . she looked at Julie and then at Debra. "He threatens to kill someone all the time. Once it was Nate's baseball coach after they got in an argument. I have to admit though; I've never seen him like this."

Julie set down her grocery bag and blankly stared at it, playing back the surreal sequence of events in her head—each one as they unfolded, seeing the man in grocery aisles, again at the checkout—his clothes, his face, fondling her with his eyes. She wanted to scream. She wanted to cry. So this was Kyle's way of defending her, she thought. Not for her protection as much as it was for his ego.

Debra picked up the phone. "I'm calling the police."

"Good luck," Marie said. "We don't have police here. You'll have to call the sheriff's department. That might take half an hour if they're close to the county borderline, a couple hours if they're not." Marie guided Julie to a chair. Debra faced the wall, looking up and dialing the number. Still facing the wall, she spoke in hushed tones. After a while she hung up the phone.

"They won't do anything, not with just the color of a house. I was going to give them the address but I couldn't remember it. I couldn't give them the guy's name, or even the guy's license plate number. You're not going to believe this, but they said the man on Jaycox needs to call them if he thinks he's in danger. That's their protocol."

"Did you tell them that this guy was stalking Julie? What kind of person does that?"

"They said that since the man in the store didn't physically or verbally threaten Julie, and because Julie had no previous incidents with this man, there were no grounds to report him either."

"That's ridiculous. Who did you talk to?" Marie asked.

"An officer, Jennings I think. He said it might be different if Kyle had left with a gun or a knife. But he didn't."

Julie could still see Kyle's fist as it punched the wall. She could still see the force of his boot as it busted the door, the glass. She got up, and with the same blank stare, retrieved the trashcan and squatted as she started to pick up shards of glass with her fingers.

Debra picked up the broom and dustpan, and went over to where Julie was. "Julie, don't. You'll cut yourself. I can do that." She touched Julie's elbow and guided her stance. Julie stood back and watched in silence as Debra swept the broken glass.

"Julie, are you okay?" Marie asked.

Julie wiped the corners of her eyes. "I'll be alright. Thanks for the eggs, Marie." Julie shivered fast and short, and straightened her shoulders. "I'll be alright."

CHAPTER 26

Julie stared out the front window, arms folded, watching for Kyle to come home. She'd turned off all the lights but was too upset to go to bed. She glanced at the clock and out the window again, rotating her earring. She paced to the stairway and back to the living room where she straightened an afghan, her hands jittery, and went back to the window. It was ten after eleven when she saw his truck headlights bounce over the rut at the end of the driveway.

She retreated to her bedroom. He had said that he would kill 'the son of a bitch'. Had he? The moonlight, penetrating through the bedroom blinds, cast inkblot shadows. Her eyes rested on their wedding picture that was framed in heavy crystal as she crawled under the blankets. She thought about when she'd first come to live here, how his mother had cowered at a pin-drop and had hid in her room because of her overbearing husband. She never wanted to be like that. But here she was hiding in her room, cowering just the same. Kyle's father had been downright mean at times, critical and controlling. She was glad when they'd moved to Florida. She heard Kyle downstairs, first as a door closed, then as the sound of his shoes hit the wall, the way he always kicked them off. She waited. What was he doing? What was taking so long? She wanted to rise up out of bed. She wanted to ask him where he'd been, what he'd done. She couldn't. She just couldn't. Julie closed her eyes. Tomorrow she'd pack a bag. Tomorrow she'd leave for good. Why argue about it tonight? Tomorrow she would just do it. She heard him coming. She waited for the door to open across the hall where he had been sleeping, but instead her door opened—their door. She closed her eyes, vowing to keep them closed no matter what. Kyle walked softly to the bed and leaned over her. He brushed her hair from her face and kissed her cheek. Then he left the room.

Maybe she wouldn't leave, not just yet. Tomorrow she'd get even. Tomorrow she'd make his favorite dish with a whole lot of extra something-something grotesque, something she could camouflage. She didn't want to poison him, nothing like that. She would think of something, something good. She punched her pillow. Then she'd bleach his underwear. Just enough to make him itch. He'd never smell it the way his sinuses were—at least he never had. Tomorrow she'd get even. Then she'd leave . . . she'd leave him for good.

* * *

The next morning Julie stayed in bed until she heard Kyle leave. Then she made coffee just like she always had, and sat down in the living room, still in her pajamas, to wake up slowly watching <u>Good Morning America</u>. Kyle was heavy on her mind. He wouldn't kill anyone. What was she thinking? He probably went over there to yell at him. Maybe he punched the guy, too. Maybe the guy punched him back, just maybe. Kyle would have wailed on him then. What if the guy had a knife?

But Kyle came home.

She waited for someone to interrupt the morning show to announce the murder on Jaycox Avenue. And when they didn't, she spent the rest of the day envisioning one scenario and then another.

Kyle killed him.

No he didn't.

Kyle killed him.

That's ridiculous.

She listened to the radio, too; hoping, praying that no one was dead in that damned blue house.

It was five o'clock now. She'd made stew, his favorite dish, just as she'd promised herself. One kiss would never make up for what he'd put her through. Eyeing a dead fly on the window sill, she wished she had the guts to crumble it in and disguise it with cracked pepper and dried basil. Knowing just where to find some, she wished she had the guts to add a cluster of maggots to the boiling caldron and disguise it with rice. But she thought better of herself. "Only a psychopath would go that far," she said out loud. "If anything I'm not a psychopath."

By now it was six o'clock. She had toted a basket of lightly bleached laundry to the living room, Kyle's white underwear, and had started to fold them, watching <u>News Channel 5</u>. But she really wasn't paying attention to the news until she heard: "And now a breaking news story," Wilma Smith, a Cleveland TV news anchor, announced. "LaGrange Township is reeling after a local man was found dead in the garage of his home. The dead man has been identified as Devin Hurley, 34, of Jaycox Avenue. Norman Hurley, his brother discovered Devin's body late this afternoon. Police are investigating." A blue house was in the video behind Wilma Smith.

Julie froze.

Kyle was going to be home any minute.

Her phone rang. "Julie, are you watching the news?" It was Marie.

"He did it. He really did it. I can't believe this is happening. He'll be home any minute. What do I do?" Julie stuttered. "I can't . . . I can't

141

be here."

"Get your things, get over here right now. Do you hear me? Leave now! I'm calling the police."

Julie turned off the oven and hurriedly threw some toiletries and a clean change of clothes in a wadded plastic bag. She could still see Kyle ravage the door and break the glass. In that moment she knew— Kyle was a murderer. Who was next? Her? Debra? Marie? She could still see the look on Marie's face; he shouldn't have put her through that—not Marie, not with all she'd done for them. Marie had rescued Julie from an orphanage. Marie had always been there for her, ever since Julie was four.

She wrestled her coat off the hook and slipped on her shoes. But just as she turned the doorknob, she heard Kyle's truck. She rushed to the back sliding door, slid it open and jerked it closed as she left. Then she ran to the other side of the house where he couldn't see her. Breathing heavily, Julie flattened her back against the wood siding. She heard Kyle slam his truck door. Her body lurched.

'He did it. He really did it.' She waited, frozen in place, repeating the same words in her head. He had to be inside now. She peeked around the edge. She didn't see him . . . not by his truck, not anywhere. The bag she was holding made a crinkling sound so she set it down. Then she made her way to the kitchen window and crouched under it.

'Don't breathe, don't breathe . . . .'

She slowly stood up and for a second, just a second, she glanced inside, and crouched down again. She'd seen a bouquet of roses. She'd seen Kyle look in the oven. She glanced inside again and suddenly stooped down. 'Did he see her this time?' She heard the sliding door edge open, and she rolled under the porch. She heard him call her name. Her mind was racing. How would she get to her car? He'd see her for sure. What if she went to Debra's house? No, she might get held up crossing the road. He'd catch her then. She heard the door close, snatched her bag, and ran behind the barn where she waited. He called her name again. She took off for the only place left to run, to the stubble of a wheat field behind their property. The cornfield up ahead hadn't been harvested yet. She rushed toward it, frantic that he might have seen her. Just outside the cornfield, she heard a sickening sound when her ankle suddenly twisted in a groundhog hole. "Shit!" Sitting in mud, cradling her ankle, she looked to see if Kyle was coming. Thankfully not. It was just her and the sound of wind through the corn stalks. Oddly enough, half-scooting, half-crawling, brought back the memory of how the whole thing started between her and Kyle—in that cursed field. Finally in the tall corn, she clambered to stand; and limped the rest of the way to Marie's house.

"Marie, did you call the police yet?" Julie hobbled inside. "What if it wasn't him?"

"What happened to your foot?"

"I twisted it. What if he didn't do it?"

"Sit down Julie, take some deep breaths. We'll figure this out. We're just going tell them what we saw, that's all. If Kyle didn't do it . . . Julie, be realistic." Marie bagged some ice and handed it to Julie. "Hold this on it so it doesn't swell any worse."

Kyle took the roaster out of the oven, set it on the stovetop and lifted the lid. Steaming meat and vegetables, basil and rosemary instantly drew him in. He started to get a bowl but stopped, and looked out the window again; Julie's car was there. For some reason she hadn't answered when he'd called her name. He sniffed his shirt and peeled it off as he headed toward the bathroom, probably thinking she was in the barn or maybe thinking she'd gone for a run. He stuffed his shirt in the bottom of the clothes hamper. Then he showered, shaved, and bandaged his hand—all while the smell of stew wafted through the house. He went back to the kitchen, sat down, and started to read the sports page. He looked at the clock again. It was well past his feeding time and supper was getting cold. He pulled away from the table and got a bowl, but just as he started to ladle stew, someone pounded on the door.

"Open up, sheriff's department," a voice barked.

Kyle opened the door hesitantly. "Can I help you?"

"Kyle Zourenger?"

"Yes . . . . What's going on?"

"We're investigating a crime that occurred in this area last night around seven on Jaycox. Were you at home last night between five and ten o'clock?"

"I was at work yesterday, and then I had a few beers with the guys."

"Where were you having beers and who were the guys with you?"

"I can save you the trouble right now. I don't know anything about it." Kyle started to close the door but the officer nudged against it, holding it open.

"I would like you to come with me. I suggest voluntarily." The officer stepped inside as he unsnapped his holster.

"Hey! I don't want any trouble. There's no need for that." Kyle flipped his coat off the hook and followed the officer.

A second police cruiser stopped at Marie's house. "I'm Officer Wilson and my partner is Officer Wetzel. We're here to take you ladies down to the station to make a statement."

"Can my husband come, too? I can't leave him alone," Marie asked

"Sure ma'am." The officer nodded.

The ride to the police station took forty minutes. Forty minutes of Pine Sol cleaned vomit smells. Forty minutes of listening to police chatter on the walkie-talkies. Forty minutes of Julie fretting.

At the police station, Officer Wilson herded them into a collect-all room of worn out benches where a menagerie of toothless men, scantily dressed women, and scummy looking vermin all seemed to be vying for attention. "The lieutenant will be right with you. If you'd like something to drink, there's a coffee machine and a Coke machine down the hall."

Marie held tightly onto Sam's hand and tighter onto Julie's, huddled together in seats just behind a terribly smelly person.

A few moments later, Officer Wilson guided them down a hall. Julie kept her eyes ahead, still holding Marie's hand, thankful that Marie was there. Sam followed, looking confused. They sat down on a pew-like bench that felt sticky. Julie wondered if Kyle had taken his shower yet. And wondered what she would tell their sons. She saw a nicely dressed man coming toward them.

"Juliet Zourenger, Marie Wachowski, Mr. Wachowski. I'm Detective Barger."

"Julie . . . you can call me Julie." She watched the detective toss back an ice chip from a paper cup. The man looked miserable like he'd been in a fight. He spoke soft and slow, in an almost raspy voice.

The officer turned to Marie and Sam, standing right next to Sam. "May I call you Marie?"

Marie nodded her head. Then she saw Sam smooth his fingers over Detective Barger's silk suit. She silently nudged him in disapproval. Sam drew back his hand slowly, looking confused. Julie pressed her fingers into her forehead in anguish. She'd been so self-involved that she hadn't stopped to think—Sam's dementia always flared up at night and worsened in unfamiliar surroundings.

Barger stepped out of Sam's reach. "Would anyone like something to drink, some coffee, some pop?"

Marie nodded her head again. As of yet, she hadn't said a word.

"I'll bet you'd like some coffee," he said to Marie. "Sir?" he addressed Sam, "would you like some, too?"

Sam just looked at him with that far off look, like he wanted to say something but couldn't think of the words. Julie patted his shoulder affectionately and answered for him. "Not right now. It's a little late for caffeine."

Barger offered his arm to Marie. "If you wouldn't mind coming with me, we'll get some coffee on the way." She took hold of his arm and he helped her stand.

Sam stood up, too.

"We'll be back in a few minutes. I'll try not to keep you waiting. Okay?" Barger said to Sam, clearing his throat, like talking came hard.

Marie's cheeks looked flushed, a sign of how flustered she was as she handed her suitcase-of-a-purse to Sam.

"Don't worry. They'll be right back," Julie said to Sam. "I'm glad you're here to keep me company." She tugged his sleeve for him to sit back down. But Sam wouldn't have it.

"I'm missing . . . uh . . . uh . . . Magnum P.I. What time is it? Mother has to give me my . . . uh . . . uh . . . my pills." The simplest words baffled him now. Sam took a step toward the direction of where the detective had taken Marie, motioning for Julie to follow, looking panicked and confused.

"Wait. Sam. Mother has a watch in her purse. See what time it is first," Julie said, knowing that once that purse was opened, he'd be caught up in Marie's collection of 'just in case' necessities.

Sam pulled out a tissue first, then he pulled out a coin purse, and after that he pulled out fingernail clippers, then a checkbook that was stuffed with receipts. "Magnum P.I. starts at eight. I take my—my pills—I eat my Oreo cookies at eight o'clock." He was talking to himself now, whispering the words again as he opened the coin purse. He dumped at least three dollars' worth of lose change into a tissue. Everything rolled out on the floor. "What the?" He stood up, letting the purse fall, too. "Where is Mother? It's time to go."

Chasing after the coins, Julie tried to calm him down from a kneeling position. "She's coming right back. I just know it. Let's get this picked up for when she gets here. Come on Sam, help me."

Sam acted like he was going to bend over, but froze in a half-stooped position. A puddle formed at his feet.

Sam had wet himself.

Julie heard someone coming, Detective Barger and Marie.

"Her hearing-aid battery died," Barger said. "She left her glasses at home. Let her know that I'll stop by her house tomorrow. She doesn't have to come back."

"Could you please take them home now? They can't take any more of this," Julie said.

"I understand." Barger lumbered to a phone on the wall and picked up the receiver. Within a minute a uniformed officer escorted Sam and Marie to a car outside.

"Well Julie, it's just you and me." He led her down a long grimy corridor. "You must be exhausted. I'll try to keep this as short as possible." He opened the door to a small interrogation room and held it for her to come inside. The black and white tiles were chipped around the edges. 'Probably from years of scrubbing off blood,' she thought. 'Blood from interrogations that must have gone terribly bad.' The blistered chairs and the worn out table had probably seen just about everything, except for, of course, the other side of a five-foot mirrored wall. A coffee carafe was at the end of the table along with a pitcher of ice water. Barger poured Julie a glass of water and spooned out some ice chips for himself.

"I'm not going to mess around here. What happened yesterday?" Detective Barger paced slowly, holding a wadded handkerchief to his mouth. "By the way, this conversation is being recorded."

"I don't know where to start, with the man who was stalking me in the grocery store, with the anonymous love letters, or with my husband saying he was going to kill 'the son of a bitch'?"

Barger sat down. "Tell me everything."

"It all started a few months ago with an anonymous letter." Julie relayed the entire story as it had unfolded; the visuals within the letters, the anger within Kyle. "Then yesterday, this really strange man followed me through the grocery store and then to my car. It scared the crap out of me."

"How? What did he do?"

"He wasn't just following me. It felt like he was stalking me. I

148

can't tell you how creepy it felt. He wasn't buying anything and he was always in my aisle. I skipped an aisle and he went there, too. So I went to the opposite end of the store. And so did he. I went from being uncomfortable to being afraid. I didn't report him to store security, they would have just thought I was being paranoid."

"You assumed they would think that. I'm not thinking that. I'm thinking, if it had been my wife, I would have been very upset. Then what happened?"

Julie relayed the rest of the story, right up to Kyle kicking open the door.

"And what time was that?"

"Yesterday, a little after noon."

"What time did he return?"

"Just before midnight."

Barger had gone through nearly all of the ice. "So he cut his hand on the door." Barger jotted something down.

"Yes," Julie answered softly, feeling terribly guilty for betraying Kyle.

"What kind of a husband is Kyle? Has he ever hit you?"

"He's a good man. No, he's never hit me" Julie answered quietly. She wanted to say that he gets insanely angry at times. She wanted to say maybe it wasn't his fault, from what she'd read he had all the tendencies of being bipolar. But she couldn't say any of that. The guilt she felt was overwhelming. However twisted, going to Jaycox was Kyle's way of defending her.

"You look tired. Where are you staying tonight?"

"With Marie and Sam."

"Why don't you go now? We'll let you know if we need anything else. I'll have an officer take you wherever you want to go." He opened the door and finger-waved to an officer. "We appreciate your cooperation," he said, seeming stiff all of a sudden, as he gathered his notes.

Carrying another glass of ice chips, Detective Barger came into the room where Kyle was waiting. "Kyle Zourenger? I'm Lieutenant Barger," he said, taking note of Kyle's bandaged right hand.

"My hand's a little banged up." Kyle slipped the hand in his pocket.

"What happened there?"

"It was my own fault."

Barger extended a long-suffering breath. "Look around at where you're at . . . ." He paused. A trace of blood crested in the corner of his mouth. Barger's bruised jaw line gave him a seasoned appearance, lean and tough, like punching a guy in the throat was nothing. "Let's try this again. I'm Lieutenant Barger. This is an interview room. When I ask a specific question, I expect a specific answer. Tell me what happened to your hand."

"I cut it on a storm door at home yesterday. The glass broke when I pushed it open." Kyle scratched at his waistband as he talked. "What has this got to do with some guy that got killed? Can't you just ask me if I know anything and get me out of here?"

"Mr. Zourenger . . . ." Barger sat down at the table across from Kyle and leaned in as if he was sharing a secret. "I feel strongly that you can help us with this, especially since you know the neighborhood so well." Barger was careful to use his words, his voice, to reinforce sincerity to ensure that the suspect would be receptive. "You may have seen something or heard something that no one else would have paid attention to. So let's get the preliminary questions out of the way. Were you coming or going when you cut your hand?"

"I was leaving my house."

"Do you remember what time that was?"

"Somewhere around twelve."

"Noon? Midnight?" Barger brushed his knuckles along his lower lip and swallowed hard. His jaw was swollen, blood in his mouth, and he was trying to shove back the pain. He had taken a thug down earlier, but not before the thug had sucker punched him, a roll of nickels in his mammoth fist.

"I wouldn't say it was noon on the dot, but it was sometime around there."

"Okay. So you pushed the storm door open, the glass broke, you cut your hand. You must have been in a hurry. Where were you going?"

Kyle suddenly became quiet, his eyes resting on Barger's notebook.

"This must be very frustrating. A degenerate, a man stalking your wife gets himself killed, and coincidently . . . let's see . . ." Barger flipped a page in his notebook. "Three witnesses state that you said, 'I'll kill the son of a bitch'. That's pretty strong . . . ."

Kyle slumped in the chair, head down, and fingered a crease in his jeans.

"This is your chance to explain. Tell me what happened after you left your house, after you cut your hand? Tell me where you went, who was there, what time it was."

Kyle scratched his elbow and then his head, changing seating positions. "I drove to a job on Fairfax in Columbia Station where I had a paving job. We finished around six, and then I had some drinks with the guys."

"Good. You have someone who can verify your whereabouts that entire time—from when you left your house to when you came back."

"Not entirely. I drank too much and fell asleep in my car. When I woke up, I drove home, near sober. It must have been ten o'clock or so."

"I'm afraid that doesn't fare well. The lapse in time. The pointing trowel."

Kyle sat straight up, planting his feet on the floor. "What trowel?"

Barger didn't flinch. "It was fairly new, no fingerprints. I understand that someone broke into your truck and stole your tools."

"Do you think whoever robbed me . . . but those tools were practically antiques. Some of them belonged to my father. You said the murder weapon was new."

"I didn't say it was the murder weapon. You had to buy new tools, trowels and such. Didn't you?"

There was a silence, a toxic vapor.

"I can get receipts," Barger added.

The stillness of their bodies, their every breath, enforced the silent struggle for power. "That new pointing trowel is yours isn't it? You used it to stab Devin Hurley through the throat. Isn't that right?" The sound of Barger's voice escalated with every phrase. "Did you tell him how wrong it was for him to stalk pretty women? Did you tell him how wrong it was for him to ruin marriages with raunchy letters? That you weren't going to put up with it anymore?"

"No, I didn't say any of that. I didn't kill anyone!"

"Oh come on. Those might not have been your exact words. But you let that deviant know that he deserved to die, that he deserved to suffer."

"No! I didn't . . . ."Kyle jumped out of the chair, almost knocking it over. "I didn't kill anyone!"

Barger jumped out of his chair, too. "Come on. You were insane with anger. You punched a hole in the wall. You kicked the door halfway off its hinges. You bullied three women into believing that you were going to kill this man. Don't tell me you didn't even go over there."

"Yeah, I was mad," Kyle yelled. "Do you think I wanted to lay cement for the rest of my life? Do you think I chose to be lower than a ditch-digger? I was seventeen when she got pregnant, and I've been paying for it for the last eighteen years. And now this damn company is the only thing that keeps us alive. I was counting on laying a roller skating rink to carry me through the winter, and an out-of-state contractor underbid me, that was on top of a hundred other setbacks. Honestly, I don't know how we're going to survive. And then I come home and find out some guy's following my wife around. I just started yelling. I know I said some stupid things. We all do. I didn't mean them, any of them." Kyle plunked down in the chair and rubbed his butt hard against the wooden seat.

Barger's jaw throbbed. His head hurt. This was the part where the suspect was supposed to confess. Not this guy, this guy kept scooting around and kept jabbing at his 'Johnson' like he had crabs or something. "You said some stupid things, huh. How is it the stupid things you said happened?" Barger shouted, swallowing his own blood. "I'm telling you what I know. I know you killed the man you thought was harassing your wife."

"No. I did not. I can show you every last one of my tools, and I can match them with receipts. You go out and find the real criminal," Kyle yelled. "Get me out of here. You have no grounds to keep me."

Barger stared at him, cold and hard. Like any suspect, the more often Kyle says 'I didn't do it', the more difficult it will be to get a confession. Once guilt is flat-out denied, he would have to stop him from talking to keep him from asking for a lawyer. The suspect had already given his reasons why he couldn't have committed the crime. The next step was to reinforce sincerity to ensure that the suspect is receptive, to start all over again.

To hell with it, Barger wanted to go home. Every inch of his body twinged. His shoes choked his feet. His eyelids felt like sandpaper against his eyes. He could keep Kyle for 48 hours, but he wanted a blood sample now. Without that, forensics couldn't match the unidentified blood they'd found at the scene. He couldn't force Kyle to give one, not unless he arrested him. But there wasn't enough evidence, not even for a misdemeanor—if Kyle had only pushed his wife, even just a little. Barger knew that once he initiated a court order, it would take more time today than he was willing to sacrifice.

"You must have cut your hand pretty bad. Did you get stitches?"

"No." Kyle sat on the edge of his chair, gripping the seat of it as if he was going to throw it across the room, staring at Barger.

Barger returned the stare at first, then he softened his stance. "I'd like our doctor to look at that. It might be infected."

"There's no need for that. I want to go home."

"You know, I could hold you for 48 hours. Tell you what, I want to go home, you want to go home. Let someone check that out and I'll let you go. I don't want to be responsible for you ending up with a stump."

". . . fine. Just get me out of here."

Barger tossed back an ice chip, abruptly got up, and left the room.

"I can't stand to look at him anymore." Barger said to the rookie, Yarnolf, a masculine woman with a disheveled appearance. Barger had told her to watch from the mirrored window this time. "There's no fingerprints, no one saw him there. Have him sign a medical release, look in the bottom drawer of the third file cabinet. Then go up to the fifth floor and tell forensics to doctor up his hand. Doc should be able to use the blood on the bandage. Maybe get a little blood sample in the pretense of cleaning it out, or . . . . I don't know. Figure something out. I'm going home . . . ." Barger's voice trailed off as he walked away.

CHAPTER 27

Staying at Sam and Marie's house, Julie came to the door. "Go away!" she yelled from inside the closed door. She could hear Marie arguing with Sam to mind his own business.

"Julie, answer the door!" Kyle yelled through Marie's front door, from the porch, pounding his fist. "Please, open the door. You don't understand." He'd rung the doorbell a dozen times and had pounded on the door a dozen more.

"Open the door, Julie. Please," he pleaded.

"Stop it. Sam and Marie are upset enough," Julie yelled through the door.

"I can't stop. You have to listen to me," Kyle pleaded again.

Julie swung the door open. Every nerve in her body on edge, she would not be afraid, not outwardly. "You killed him. You actually killed him. Why aren't you in jail?"

Kyle stepped inside. The door closed behind him. "Julie, you can't really believe that." He reached out to her, touching her arm, but she jerked away.

"You can fuck yourself all the way to hell and back," Julie shouted.

"Come on, don't be like that."

"You said you're going to kill 'the son of a bitch' and now he's dead. How could they let you go? Are they idiots? Do you think I'm an idiot?"

"Julie, I . . . ."

"No! We're done. I'm not going home with a murderer."

"I'm not a murderer. You have to believe me." Kyle said, his eyes piercing through hers.

Julie rubbed her face in her hands. "Just go home. I've had enough. Just leave me alone."

"Listen to me. Please. There's a reason I've been upset. The jobs, the foreman I hired, this last developer, it's all been torture. Then I find out I've been buying bad cement." The tone in Kyle's voice turned harsh, the tone she knew so well. "Those last jobs," he said, "the cement crumbled and now the property owners are threatening to sue me. We could lose the house."

Julie quieted down, a realization hitting her. It was always something, his excuses for bad behavior, bombs he would drop whenever his temper flared. She wouldn't fall for it this time, not when he was using it to justify a killing. "I can't believe you're bringing all this up now. Not after you killed that man."

"You know me, Julie. You know I say things I don't mean. How could you even think I could kill anyone?" He looked so believable, standing there, sincerity in his eyes.

Julie felt herself tensing, blindly staring at a tear in the flowered wallpaper. She suppressed the layer of guilt.

Kyle must have seen he was losing her. He softened his voice. "I'm not kidding. I was so upset today I wanted to drive my truck off the interstate bridge."

There was a long silence. Kyle's gaze settled on an umbrella stand. Julie watched her own foot tap in slow motion. She wanted to wake up from this nightmare. She wanted to have her boys back home. She wanted a normal life.

"You have to leave now," Julie said softly, her hand on the doorknob.

"How can you be like this? I thought he was going to hurt you . . . . I brought you roses today."

She hesitated. "What did the police say? Why did they let you go?"

"It was just a coincidence, that's all. I went there but he never came to the door. Nothing happened. You've got to believe me. Come home, Julie. It'll be different this time. I'll do anything."

Julie took an exhausted breath. He had risked everything to protect her. He could have gone to jail. Maybe he really was sorry. He'd kissed her last night. Maybe he really did love her.

"Come on, go get your things," he said softly, touching her face, resting his palm upon her cheek. "You know in your heart it wasn't me. Trust your gut. Come on home."

Julie opened her mouth to speak. She heard the sound of 'O' flooding the sound of 'kay' as the word "Okay" slipped off her tongue—almost like someone else had said it. She searched his eyes, his warm blue eyes.

Kyle retorted, "I can't believe you said fuck."

She paused, picking the last of her wits off the floor. Why couldn't she have been psychotic just once? A couple of maggots wouldn't have killed him.

CHAPTER 28

"Are you Kyle Zourenger?" a police officer asked. Kyle looked up from his trowelling position smack dab in the middle of wet cement. Five more officers rushed in from police cars, guns drawn.

"Yeah . . . ." His face sullen, Kyle stood up. The rest of his crew stopped what they were doing, simultaneously gawking at him, at all the policemen, at all the guns.

"Don't just stand there. That cement's hardening by the minute," Kyle yelled to his men.

"Step over here sir," an officer said, readying his handcuffs.

Kyle obliged.

"Hands behind your back, sir."

"No, wait. You're making a mistake."

"Hands behind your back! Now!" the officer shouted, jerking Kyle's wrist. "Kyle Zourenger, you're under arrest for the murder of . . . ."

Kyle pulled away. "No. Wait, this is a mistake!" Kyle exclaimed. "You've got the wrong guy!"

The officer yanked and twisted Kyle's arm, threw him to the ground and stomped his boot in the center of Kyle's back.

"You have the right to remain silent . . ." He wrenched Kyle's body, standing him up. "Anything you do say may be used against you in a court of law . . . ." The officer continued to read Kyle his rights, dragging him to the police cruiser.

Lieutenant Barger and the rookie woman entered the room where Kyle was handcuffed and shackled, the same room where he'd been questioned a few days before. "Mr. Zourenger, this is Officer Yarnolf. I assume you've been read your rights."

"Please. Help me. I didn't kill anyone. We've been over this, you let me go."

"I can't help you. I can't do anything for you unless you're honest with me."

Kyle looked puzzled, not the innocent kind of puzzled but the look of puzzlement that only liars possess. "I told the truth. I thought we had a deal."

"You're mistaken. I don't make deals." Barger sat down across from Kyle, straight faced, setting down a cardboard box. "There're a few things here that I'd like to show you."

Yarnolf paced slowly, cracking her neck, ear to shoulder . . . ear to shoulder. Then for her next order of business, she sniffed her fingers. Call it a habit, call it a quirk, by any means it was an effective distraction. Her presence was the white noise that Barger was counting on.

"I'd like you to look at these things very carefully. Two new pointing trowels, one of which I believe is newer," Barger said, setting them on the table. "The napkin we found in your truck where you can see the victim's address. There's blood on it. This is a picture of a shoe casting from the crime scene." He placed each item side by side on the worn out table. Yarnolf looked over Barger's shoulder and mouthed, 'you did it'.

Barger took a pair of Kyle's shoes out of the box. "These shoes seem to match the castings. See where the tread is thicker here?" He set down the shoes and pulled out an official-looking paper. "But this is the most damning evidence. We were counting on that cut of yours to leave some blood at the crime scene. So we looked for traces of what might have been wiped up before we arrived, blood that wouldn't be visible to the naked eye. Our guys used luminal spray that detected an enzyme that wasn't the victim's. A blood-pattern analysis narrowed it down with an accuracy of ninety-nine percent. Should I go on?"

Kyle's expression turned into a mask of agony. A silent wave swept in like a tide and rolled out with his answer, "I laid the concrete for almost every garage and driveway in that development. Whenever I cut myself, it soaks right in. I trowel over it. It's barely there at all."

"When blood dissipates, whether it's a day or three hundred days, it leaves traces," the detective said. "It's amazing what they can do in 1984. DNA Fingerprinting for one, or DNA profiling."

"I'm telling you, it would have been invisible. How could they do that?"

"Luminal, it picks up on semen, spit, any bodily fluid, including blood, which all have DNA. Forensics spliced the DNA they found. They typed with an ABO test to see the "splice sites" in that particular part of your DNA." Barger watched Kyle's face. "You asked me to help you. Just say you were there."

"I said I was, before the house was built. I also said I might have cut myself. You couldn't possibly have found year-old blood."

"You cleaned up after yourself. Yes?" Barger nodded.

Kyle nodded, too. "Sure I . . . No! I clean up whenever I cut myself. I can't have a homeowner seeing blood."

"You think you're pretty clever. You thought you were covered because of that. Blood is blood. It doesn't matter how we found it or how old it is, just that it is. In this case it's yours. You were there that night! Just say it!"

"You're not going to find a single person who saw me there."

"That just says you didn't see anyone around. You thought everyone was at work or in school. What if I told you that an eyewitness says he saw your truck there?"

The veins in Kyle's neck surfaced. The redness of his ears colored outside the lines.

Barger took a letter from his suit pocket. "I got this from your wife. It was the only one you didn't burn, the first anonymous love letter. I'd probably want to kill the guy myself." He slid it over to Kyle. "This is motive."

Yarnolf peered over Barger's shoulder as she eyeballed the letter. He could smell garlic and something else musty, mothball like.

"Would you mind leaving us alone, Officer Yarnolf," Barger said sweetly, so sweetly that he almost gagged on the left over sugar. She left. The white noise was gone. Silence took her place. A dull ache was coming back in Barger's jaw. His feet were progressively getting hotter and they itched terribly. He needed to focus. Interrogation is an accusatory process—accusatory only in the sense that the investigator tells the suspect that there is no doubt as to his guilt.

"If I were that mad I would have at least gone there to yell at the guy, and you're saying that you didn't? You didn't even try to talk to him?" The detective spoke with renewed authority. "We know you were there. We know you killed him. Tell me. Tell me what really happened."

Kyle's eyes focused only on the letter.

"I know you were there. You stabbed him in the throat. Look at this picture. Look at this mess of what used to be a man." Barger tossed a grotesque picture of the murdered victim in front of Kyle. "You're in a lot of trouble here, murder one for starters. We have the death penalty in this state." The detective closed his folder. "This man was stalking your wife, on the brink of acting out all these unspeakable things, following her, watching her. The letters kept coming and coming. He fantasized about every inch of her body. You wanted to stop him. You wanted to kill him. Just say it."

"You son of a bitch."

"You wanted to kill him. Didn't you? You finally knew who was writing those letters, and you did just that. You killed him. Isn't that right?"

"You don't get it. You just don't get it."

"Then tell me . . . . Set the record straight."

"Those letters made me mad as hell, but they actually did me a favor . . . I was having an affair. That's why I didn't tell you before. I didn't tell anyone. My wife got so caught up in those letters that she never suspected. I didn't fall asleep in my car that night. I was with another woman."

Barger took an exasperated breath. "Okay, so what is her name?"

"I can't drag her into this."

"Then tell me where you went, a hotel, her place? Did anyone see you?"

"I don't know. The hotel manager, some old man. I paid cash. I gave him extra to let me write a fake name in the log. He asked to see my driver's license at first, but I couldn't have that. I didn't want anyone to know."

"And what kind of angle do you expect me to take from that? If you had a witness that could clear you from a murder conviction, you would tell me her name."

"No, I can't. She's married. This would ruin her." Kyle leaned over the table with his face in his hands. "You can't let my wife know. Please. Isn't there some kind of privacy law?"

"What do you think this is? For one thing this discussion is not confidential. You should have listened to your rights. And for another, what could I possibly have to tell your wife? Another lie?"

"I want a lawyer."

Barger slowly stood up. He could be stoic, sticking to the rules of interrogation. The suspect had asked for a lawyer, the interrogation was officially over. "Some story. Too bad though, if you'd stuck to the truth, we might have had something to work with." Barger knocked on the fake mirror. "Book him."

CHAPTER 29

Gone were the days of cotton ball clouds, of brilliant blue horizons. Stratus clouds had seized the sky in a way that redefined gray as the anti-color.

Debra worried obsessively. Kyle was in jail because she had given up that address. It had been four days and Julie hadn't returned her calls. Julie would probably never speak to her again, Debra surmised.

Debra loaded a .22 caliber bullet. There was no one else. Greg couldn't even kill a snake. Alone on the edge of the cornfield behind Sam and Marie's, she loaded another bullet. Julie couldn't handle a gun, a rifle, or anything of the sort, she'd said so herself. She was probably seeing a lawyer anyway.

Debra loaded another bullet and cocked the long-barrel Marlin rifle. A raccoon huddled in a corner growling—grass and feces clinging to the wire mesh inside a Have-A-Heart trap. The trap itself was a narrow cage where a central lure, when triggered, would close the spring-loaded doors at either end without hurting the animal. Debra had set the trap herself. But Marie wouldn't hear of letting their captive loose in a cornfield, 'he'd strip it clean,' she'd say. 'Farming was hard enough.' And besides that, it might have rabies. Marie had gone inside to downplay the sound of gunfire to Sam. Marie would say that Sam couldn't aim a rifle any more than he could aim his pee.

She could do this. One bullet, that's all it would take. One bullet to the head and it would be over. Debra tuned out the barnyard sounds—chickens, Billy Goats, one protecting the only chick left, the other ramming a fence. This didn't feel like an act of kindness, not killing something. But Marie had looked so helpless. Debra didn't ever want to be that helpless, that dependent. If she didn't do this now, right now, she might as well accept her fate.

"It's your fault you know. If you hadn't gone after her chicks, if you'd left her goat feed alone." She squatted down. She steadied the butt of the rifle in her shoulder. There was a five hundred dollar fine if she were caught releasing him in a park. The Animal Protective League had told her to call the game warden. The game warden had told her to call the sheriff. The sheriff had told her to shoot it, or find someone else who would. She could do this. She had to do this. It wouldn't be as bad as killing a groundhog with a shovel—this was clean, simple, fast. He'd never feel it.

"Just one shot . . ." she said to the animal. Somehow the idea, the words felt eerily familiar. She remembered now, she'd heard it before.

A memory flashed, 'Just one shot to the temple, that's all it takes.' That's what her mother had said that day she'd held the rifle to Debra's head, one of her lesser offences.

She placed the tip of the barrel just inside the cage. "Sorry guy." Debra aimed between his eyes and forced herself to pull the trigger. Blood splattered. He thrashed inside the cage. She didn't think, she cocked the rifle and shot him again behind his ear. Blood bubbled out his nose. He thrashed and jerked. Blood splattered even more. She shot him again. "Please Lord. Please let him die." The raccoon rolled and thrashed. She reloaded, her hands shaking so badly that she could barely hold the bullets. Then she shot three in a row, pausing only to cock the rifle in between shots. The shell casings pinged one at a time on her shoes. Now the raccoon didn't move, there was no more rise and fall in its chest. Debra pulled back, staring. Blood pooled like scarlet syrup, just like her stepfather's had. His blood had splattered her clothes the same way they were splattered now. She was holding the very same rifle.

Marie came outside, holding tightly to the railing and even tighter to her cane, stepping slowly, painfully over the length of her yard. "Sam counted six shots. I made him think it was a tractor backfiring," Marie shouted over the wind, making her way to Debra.

Debra didn't answer. Her eyes were wide, her mouth agape, the rifle lying at her feet. The stench of blood and feces, dirt and gunpowder poisoned the crisp fall air.

"Honey, are you okay? You saved me an awful lot of trouble."

Debra blinked. She took a deep breath. "I'll bury him," she said calmly, softly, her eyes following a colorless cloud. Silently inside her head she repeated, 'you're okay you're okay you're okay . . . .' clutching her fist to her mouth as not to let the words escape. Twenty-two-years-old, she looked like a child.

"You dear sweet girl." Marie stroked Debra's shoulder as tenderly as her gnarled fingers allowed. "I don't know what I would have done without you."

"I know." Debra nodded, finally looking at Marie. She liked Marie. They would often wave from their distant mailboxes and yell something that neither one could understand. Sometimes she envied Julie for having been raised in that house. Marie seemed like the mother that Debra had always dreamed about. And the thing of it was . . . Marie had taken that role even from a distance.

"Where do you want me to bury him?"

"There's a shovel behind the hen house. You can bury him there.

167

Bring the cage to the house when you're done. I'll get some bleach."

Debra dragged the bloody cage behind the hen house where the crabgrass and ragweed swayed in the wind that bustled across the open field that whistled in her ears and swept up her hair. She found the shovel leaning against a weather-beaten fence, and started to dig. Worries plagued her. She'd had lots of friends in Cincinnati, school friends, church friends, office friends where she used to work. Julie had been her only friend here, as mismatched as they were.

She balanced herself to stand on top of the shovel, and rocked it into the hard ground. Digging through clay and roots, the hole grew into a grave one hard-earned scoop at a time. Lifting the trap she let the dead animal fall out of it, and then shoveled dirt on top. A memory flashed of her own father's grave, how she'd tossed in a handful of dirt, how she loved him. Then her memory flashed to her stepfather's grave, how she'd thrown the dirt instead, how she hated him.

She filled in the hole, and mounding it with more dirt, she dug into unbroken ground, and hit something, something metal, just below the surface. She squatted down and dug carefully to unearth a small tin box. On its cover an Egyptian bird, maybe a falcon, guarded the lettering 'RAMSES', and underneath that in very small lettering was, 'Three Genuine Transparent.' Something rattled inside the two-inch tin, it sounded like jewelry. She knocked off dirt with the shovel and could barely make out the rest of the lettering, 'Rubber prophylactics'. Debra glanced from across the yard over at Marie, suddenly amused. Unable to resist, Debra pried the rusty clasp open.

"Marie. Look," Debra yelled, heading toward Marie.

"What have you got there?"

"It was buried behind the hen house."

Marie set down the hose, eyeing the tin. "Of all things."

"What's inside?"

Debra pulled out a piece of delicate jewelry and handed it to Marie.

"That went missing . . . let me see now . . . . Julie must have been eight or nine. I told her to put this some place safe. It wasn't . . . I never thought she'd bury it," Marie said. "Was there anything else in there?"

"You mean one of these?" Debra pulled out a prophylactic that was still in the foil. The two of them suddenly laughed. Laughter for Debra, right now, tasted wonderfully rich like eating candy after chewing on bitter herbs. The kind of laugh where you lean in and hold your stomach. The kind of laugh where you throw your face in your hands and start to cry, the kind of cry that takes laughter's place.

"Oh honey." Marie took Debra in her arms. "This is about Julie. Isn't it?"

"I feel sick about it . . . I didn't know all this was going to happen."

"It's not your fault, Debra. No one blames you."

Debra freshened her face in her shirtsleeve; she so desperately wanted to make everything right. "I . . . I might see her tonight," she stuttered, doubt, angst etched in her face.

Marie took Debra's hand. "Give this to Julie. Talk to her." The sun eased through a crack in the clouds just as the jewelry trickled into Debra's hand.

It was a gold necklace. The engravings of a rose and a droplet graced the pendant, the right half of a broken heart.

Cold and splattered in blood, her windblown hair over her shoulders,

Debra hung Julie's necklace on one of her cupboards. Somehow the house felt different, almost alive. The cupboard's agate-like knob, salvaged from one of the original kitchen cupboards, seemed to sway the necklace. She covered her eyes, dizzy, sickened, visualizing bubbles of blood—the foul odor still in her nose.

Debra stripped right there in the kitchen, piling her clothes on the floor, all the while wondering if she shouldn't just burn them. She scrubbed her hands and her fingernails, and in the bathroom she disinfected with rubbing alcohol. She finally dressed and toted the soiled clothes downstairs. Maybe white vinegar could save them. That was pure acid. That would clean anything—a tip from one of her foster homes.

Down in the basement, setting the washing machine, she heard something, something muffled, somewhat like the bottom of a grocery bag falling out. She turned off the washing machine and stood very still, trying to hear it again. It seemed to have come from upstairs. She eked up the basement steps, paying close attention to the narrow passageway—hundreds of tiny newly hatched spiders inundated the quarry-stone wall. At the top of the stairs she heard it again, and suddenly thought of being alone that night. Greg was going out—the first Friday night in a series of Friday nights for the next two months. He had joined a racquetball team. It was bad enough during the day, but in night's darkest hours . . . she didn't want to think about it.

She got as far as the dining room and peered into the kitchen. The mail she'd left on the counter was all over the floor. She stood there, a numbing void in her head.

She finally stepped into the kitchen. A cupboard door was open. A bag of flour was on the floor. Out of nowhere a booming thump shook the house. Eyes wide, she glared at the ceiling, her breaths came in quick stops and starts. It sounded like a heavy dresser had fallen.

Going upstairs to where the bedrooms were, Debra gripped the handrail tighter and tighter. At the top of the stairs she edged toward the long hallway. Except for her bedroom, these rooms hadn't been touched in the last hundred years. No electricity, no heat. She rested her hand on a clear crystal doorknob. She swallowed hard and creaked open the eighteenth century door. Cracked walls, peeling paint, and old cardboard boxes were strung together in cobwebs. She eased through the door, through the cobwebs. A dusty old dresser, the only one that could have fallen, was still standing. A leftover roll of plastic from when she'd stapled plastic over the doors and windows was on top of it. Sunlight flooded through the long vertical windows, the only light source up there. At night the rooms were shrouded in darkness. She never would have gone there at night. She checked the next room and then the next—all in dire need of 'plaster' surgery—all revealing nothing more than the essence of its tenants from long ago.

She suppressed a shiver and headed back to the stairs, then suddenly stopped. Sounds were coming from the kitchen again. She felt her stomach rise up to her throat, taking one step at a time until she ended up in the arched doorway and peered into the kitchen. The bottom cupboard doors were all open. The bag of flour was shredded, cornmeal too—its contents spread over the floor, and dry coffee grounds from one end of the kitchen to the other. As if that wasn't bad enough, there were fingertip-size trails in the mixture. She stood frozen; goose bumps worked their way down to every last follicle. Staring at the floor, she saw what looked like writing—sloppy at that. It looked like the letter E, followed by the letter D. A cupboard door moved. A scream stuck in her windpipe. She couldn't breathe.

Rumbling came from inside her cupboards. A can of soup rolled across the floor and stopped at her feet. Debra backed away, eyeing the front door. 'Heel, toe, heel, toe,' she said to herself, stepping softly, quietly to the door. She'd been good at sneaking away in the past. She had snuck under barroom booths when her mother had stayed too long at the bar. She had snuck to the back of her closet when she'd heard her drunken stepfather coming toward her bedroom.

She finally reached the front door and grappled with the doorknob. The lock was jammed.

"Open. Please open," her voice shook as she whispered, straining her hands to turn the doorknob. Her eyes searched for another way out. The windows were all painted shut and sealed with a layer of plastic. She turned around, her back against the door, her hand still on the knob. Her chest heaved.

"Fine! You want me? I'm standing right here!" She waited, her chin quivering with anger and fear. A vortex of quiet, of stillness, she could hear her own heartbeat. The knob turned in her hand. The wind heaved the door open. Stunned, she stepped through the doorway onto the porch, down the quarry-stone steps. The further she got, the quicker her steps. Coatless, she stopped beneath the catalpa tree and stared at the house. The wind blasted against her back. Where was she going to go? Her car keys were in her purse. Her purse was inside.

Hugging herself against the frigid wind, she jogged across the road all the way to Marie's house.

"Marie! Marie!" Debra yelled through the door, pounding on the wooden frame. "Marie!"

Sam cracked the door open. "We don't want any," he said, peeking through the door.

"Sam, where's Marie?" she asked. "Sam, it's me, Debra. Where's Marie?"

"Oh, Debra, come on in." Sam turned. "Marie, Debra's here."

Marie came around the corner, drying her hands on her apron. "Debra, come on in. Where's your coat?"

"I've been scared half out of my mind."

"What happened?" Marie asked.

"Something's going on in that house. I heard things. But no one was there, no one but me. I know this sounds crazy, but . . . . The house is haunted. I swear it is." Debra was ranting now, about the flour, about the thump from upstairs, about everything that had just happened.

"Come on, let's go over and take a look. Okay?" Marie said. "Sam, get your shoes; we're going over to Debra's house."

"I'm not sure if I want to go back."

"Sure you do, honey. Let's go and set that old house straight." Marie's words carried a patronizing tone. Debra had to go back now, if only to show Marie.

"If only to get my purse and my coat. Are you sure you want to go to the trouble?"

"I have to go out anyway. I'm out of cod liver oil and I need to go to the bank." Marie used her cane to drag one of Sam's shoes out of the corner. "Will you help Sam get his shoes on? My fingers feel numb. He has trouble."

Sam swept up his shoes, "I can do it myself. Why all the fuss?" Sam said lightheartedly, sitting down with them. Sam's shoes were still tied from when he'd taken them off. He didn't untie them, but struggled, trying to squeeze his foot in one of his shoes with a metal shoehorn, but his body would only let him bend so far. Marie was busy struggling to pull their coats out of the hall closet, as she leaned on her cane.

Debra kneeled at Sam's feet and untied his shoestrings. She could see why he hadn't untied them, because he couldn't bend down enough to reach the shoelaces, much less his feet. She guided his foot into the shoe and as she did, she felt the bottom of the shoe to see if they were wet, to see if he'd been outside. Maybe he'd been to her house to play tricks on her. She'd rather it had been Sam somehow. At least she'd know not to be scared. But the shoe was dry. It wasn't Sam. It had never been.

"Just what I wanted, a beautiful girl at my feet," Sam joked.

Debra looked up, half smiling, trying to think of a witty comeback. She only nodded, realizing she hadn't any wits left.

When they finally got to Debra's house, the front door was wide open. Sam led the party right to the kitchen.

"What's for dessert?" Sam joked. He pulled out a chair and sat at the table.

There inside the kitchen the half-empty, half-shredded bag of flour was on its side, but all by itself on the floor. Only one of the cupboard doors was open, and inside the empty cornmeal box was on its side, too. But there was no writing on the floor, no muss, no trails, not enough of anything to back up Debra's elaborate story.

Marie picked up the flour bag. "Is it possible that you could have spilled the flour, and forgot about it when you got busy doing something else? You were pretty upset this morning."

Debra saw right away that Marie didn't believe her.

"Maybe you're right. I was upset," Debra said, trying to maintain a sane exterior, yet feeling insane inside—feeling, maybe like her mother had. This was the scariest feeling of all.

CHAPTER 30

"I'm so glad you're home," Debra shouted through Greg's truck window, her arms wrapped around herself. "You won't believe what happened." Debra's face was drained of color. Her eyes opened wider than ever.

"What happened? Are you okay?" He had barely shifted the gearshift into park when he opened the truck's door. Hard-earned soot settled in the few wrinkles around his eyes. His unshaved face barely hid his wind-burnt skin.

"I was in the basement this morning, and I heard this weird racket. So I went upstairs, and all the cupboard doors were open. I mean, not all of them, just the ones on the bottom," she said, as Greg stepped out of the truck. She'd seen this face before—the one that says he's thinking, here we go again. "I'm not kidding Greg. You should have seen it." Debra tucked her blowing hair behind her reddened ears. "Then I heard something fall upstairs, but I couldn't find anything that fell." Her words picked up speed, racing off her tongue. "And when I was upstairs, I heard that racket again coming from the kitchen." She walked with him as far as the garage, rambling fast and long, telling him every single detail. ". . . Flour and cornmeal and coffee were all over the floor. And there was writing in it. Greg, you've got to believe me. Ed's name was written right there on the floor." She'd held him prisoner in the garage, carrying on so. ". . . you should have seen the look on Marie's face, like nothing happened, like I made it all up." She finally took a breath.

"Deb, why do you have to exaggerate everything?" His voice was stern, his words precise. "I'm supposed to meet the guys in an hour. I have just enough time to take a shower and eat."

"I'm not exaggerating. You've got to believe me."

"You always exaggerate. Can't you ever just get to the point?"

Her stomach dropped. It was as though she was nothing, not even a tiny particle. She didn't love him right then—if she ever had. Her eyes focused straight ahead.

Greg watched her chin quiver. "I'm sorry. I had a bad day." He tweaked her nose. "Are you sure you didn't . . ."

She smacked his hand away from her face. "I know what you're going to say. Marie said it, too."

"Come on, Deb. I said I was sorry . . . Is there any way you could have been looking for something in the cupboard and just spilled a few things?"

"No. I know what I saw. E . . . D right on the floor. I'm sure of it." Just then, listening to herself say it, a mist of doubt clouded her certainty. Her fantastic tale sounded as such—like a fantastic tale.

Greg took her hand. But instead of pulling away, she locked her fingers in his. She wanted . . . she needed him to believe her, or prove she was wrong. Her grip tightened, going through the doorway, fighting the urge to stop there and not go in at all. Inside the kitchen, she watched him open a cupboard, and saw scattered Quaker Oats and Cheerios. The boxes were torn. He opened cupboard after cupboard and found the empty cornmeal container, the empty coffee bag, among other toppled items. One thing or another in all the cupboards he'd checked had been ripped or disturbed. He opened the last cupboard under the sink. And there, lo and behold, a white baby possum hung upside down from the plumbing with his head in the wastebasket, motionless. Greg eased the door closed.

A phase of speechlessness passed between them. "No wonder you were upset . . . without any backs to these cupboards, that possum went wherever he wanted from against the wall. It must have been foraging for food. My guess is, it licked up the floor and hid back inside. Then it found the garbage. What might have looked like an E and a D were just trails that his tail made. A possum's tail is so thick that all they can do is drag it. He must have carried whatever he could back inside for the last crumbs."

"He could never have cleaned the entire floor with his tongue. And before Marie got here, too," Debra said.

Greg knelt down and picked up the cornmeal lid from the cupboard. "Did you leave the front door open when you ran out?" He asked, studying the floor.

"I might have."

"The wind would have whipped through the house." Greg probed underneath the stove. "Look," he said, showing Debra white and yellow powder speckled with coffee grounds. "The flour and cornmeal blew under the refrigerator and stove." Greg took a can of peaches and laid it on the floor. The can rolled to the farthest wall. "The floor's crooked, but you should have known that."

Debra didn't say anything.

"You must have given him quite a scare when you came downstairs." Greg adjusted his baseball cap. "How the heck did he get in here?"

"From the crawl-space?"

"There has to be a hole in the mortar somewhere between the quarry stones. I thought I got them all," he said. Buy a bag of mortar mix tomorrow and I'll patch whatever I missed."

"That doesn't explain the doorknob or . . . ."

"That doorknob's brand new. There's nothing wrong with it," Greg said, looking at the clock. "Get the trap? I'll set it before I leave."

"You're still going?" she asked quietly, subdued.

"You'll be okay. You'll be perfectly fine. Trust me."

Greg had left. Debra set the trap in the kitchen, and called Julie again. This time Julie answered the phone.

"What's up?" Julie asked.

Debra hated that phrase, understanding it as, 'I don't have time for this. Get to the point.' "Oh. I just wondered if you were going to jog tonight."

Julie didn't answer.

Debra waited. An uncomfortable silence. Debra listened closer. Did Julie hang up? Maybe the phone line cut out. "Julie?" she waited. "Are you there?"

"I'm here. I guess I can jog. Let me get my shoes on, and I'll meet you at the end of your driveway."

"Okay. Give . . . ." Debra started to say, 'give me ten minutes', but Julie hung up. She hadn't even said good-bye. Debra quickly clipped her hair up, stuffed it under a stocking cap, and dug a pair of warm socks out of a laundry basket. Then she opened the closet. Every shoe she had ever owned spilled out with Greg's, and not one of them matched the one next to it. She sank to her knees, crawling, sorting through the shoes, starting to panic . . . she couldn't be late. A tennis shoe, she flipped a boot and tossed a slipper, the other one. She shoved her feet inside them, and rushed to get her coat on. Then she heard

Julie at the kitchen door.

"Is anybody home?" Julie yelled, opening the door. Debra raced to the kitchen.

"Hi. Come on in," Debra said, zipping her coat. "I just need to tie my shoes."

"Why do you have a trap in here?" Julie asked matter-of-factly.

Debra opened the cupboard door under the sink. The possum, still in the same position, hung upside down in the wastebasket. "I think he's sleeping. He's been there for awhile," she said, half chuckling. "You should have seen the mess he made."

Julie glanced at Debra, at the possum, and back again. "Only you, Deb. Only you."

CHAPTER 31

It was unusually dark tonight, a phenomenon for this time of year. Debra jogged with Julie past Marie's house, past the recreation complex, and into the development. The quiet between them this time seemed as dark as the nonexistent stars. The only sounds were their shoes hitting the pavement and Debra's own rhythmic breathing. The stale-leaf smell, like wet dog and spoiled prunes, inundated the night. By now the dead raccoon seemed hardly worth mentioning, and besides being alone that night, Debra couldn't stop worrying about Julie, about Kyle, about the address that had put him in jail. Why didn't Julie say something, anything?

Debra focused on the stretch of sidewalk ahead, the perfectly spaced lampposts. Plodding her narrow running path, a grassy edge on one side and Julie on the other; she felt like she was balancing a tight rope, stretched tight from words unspoken, and even tighter from words yet to come.

They jogged half a mile, then another half a mile without saying a word. All the while Debra wanted to come right out and say that she was sorry she didn't wait until Kyle had left. That she should have seen his car. She was sorry that she caused all this trouble, that she'd do anything to take it all back. There was something else that was bothering her, too. Every once in a while she had this feeling that she had forgotten something, but her thoughts circled back to Kyle.

Julie finally spoke. "I haven't talked to Kyle yet. He doesn't want to see me," she said. "Nothing makes any sense. He tells me one story and an entirely different story to the police." The sound of her voice in what felt like the dead of night sounded surreal.

"I can't believe it," Debra remarked.

Julie paused for a moment. "Did you know . . . when you respond with 'I can't believe it,' it implies that you think I'm a liar? You say that a lot."

"Oh . . . I didn't mean . . . you knew what I meant. Didn't you?" Julie was silent again.

"I didn't realize I was doing that. I didn't mean anything by it." Debra felt her shoulders tighten. "Why won't he see you?"

"I don't know," Julie answered. "Maybe he thinks I was the one who called the police."

"Julie, if you need anything . . . if there's anything I can do . . . ."

"I'm sorry I'm so touchy. I'm just not myself since . . . well, you know." Julie cleared her throat like she was trying not to cry, like she was trying to gain a lucid degree of composure.

"I know. It's just that . . . I can't help but thinking . . ." Debra focused up ahead on a patch of orange mums. "If only I hadn't given that address to Kyle. He never would have killed that man." There it was, out in the open. Julie could yell at her now.

"Debra, the thought never crossed my mind. This isn't your fault. This has nothing to do with you . . . wait a minute. I have a stone in my shoe." Julie stopped and took off her shoe. "It's all Kyle; he doesn't think about anyone but himself. He didn't have to act like that. He's always had a temper, but there's no excuse for what he's done, not a single one."

Debra didn't speak. Not after the way Julie had reacted to her 'I don't believe it' comment.

"I feel like a fool." Julie got to her feet, and they started to jog again. "There I was at the police station, asking to see my husband and some smug woman cop says, 'not today, you don't. I got a note here says he won't be entertaining visitors today.' I didn't know what she was talking about." Julie jogged faster. The rhythm of her words quickened with the rhythm of her feet. "You should have seen her. I've never met anyone who was so frustrating."

Debra picked up the pace.

"So I asked her if she wanted to see my driver's license. I thought that she made a mistake or something. And you know what she said?" Julie jogged even faster, her breaths and words intermitting.

It was all Debra could do to keep up with her.

"She said 'What did you do to the guy? He doesn't want you near him. And you're the only one he's allowed to see.' This woman, this mean man-like woman said it just like that, and then she laughed. She laughed at me! You can't imagine how I felt. I just stood there, taking it."

After running for almost a mile, almost sprinting, Debra held her side, breathing heavily. She couldn't talk now even if she wanted to. It amazed her how Julie could.

"I said," Julie's words came in breaths, "I needed to talk to him. I needed to know if he's got a lawyer.' And then this woman cop says, 'Tough luck lady.'"

Debra finally slowed down and stopped for a minute to rub the stitch in her belly.

"She says, 'Go home. You're not the only person who's got problems.'" Julie didn't seem to notice that Debra wasn't there until a half a block down the sidewalk. She pulled off her stocking cap and mittens, now soaked with sweat. She stuffed them in her coat pocket, and ran back to Debra.

"What happened? Are you okay?

They toned the jog down to a power walk.

"Man, you were doing a pretty good clip." Debra said, puffing frosty breaths. "Go ahead . . . I'll catch up."

"See you 'round the bend," Julie said, her voice trailing off.

Debra was fine with that. Right now the best thing in the world for Julie was to work it off, right down to the soul.

CHAPTER 32

Debra was alone. The darkness outside blackened every window, seeping into every crevice in the dimly lit rooms. Amid creaks and rattles, rumblings from the kitchen, she turned up the television. Barefoot, and wearing pajama bottoms and an oversized t-shirt, she arranged a pillow and blanket on the couch and settled in with a box of chocolate Mallomars. 'Dallas,' was just starting, Bobby Ewing, Pamela Barns, J.R.—all a fitting distraction. And after that, a new show, Miami Vice, would distract her just long enough for Greg to get back. At least she hoped it would.

She inhaled—slow and deliberate. She exhaled—easy and purposefully, distancing herself from all the horrible things that had happened today, mentally erasing those two letters that kept coming back, E D—electrocuted to death. Ed, right there in her basement. She didn't care about the noise in the kitchen, whatever that possum was up to. The trap was set, even though she had blocked the cupboard doors to prevent them from opening—figuring that with her luck, the possum would pass up the bait and join her on the couch for chocolate-coated marshmallow bars.

Finally in the perfect position, feet up, sinking into the couch, Debra saw something out of the corner of her eye, something moved. She set her Mallomar on the coffee table, and muted the television, eyeing the spot where she thought she had seen it. Curling the blanket under her chin, she heard a car coming down the gravel road.

Out of nowhere, a shape materialized on the living room wall. Luminous, its twisted silhouette etched in shadows, it inched its way along the wall. The heaviness of her heart, thumping, pulsing, jarred her every limb. Then it disappeared. She sat straight up . . . . "Ed?"

She heard another car coming and the misshaped figured appeared again, slowly traveled along the wall, then vanished. That's when she realized it was only a car, its headlights obscured by the skeletal catalpa tree. The one-hundred-year old tree's enormous leaves would no longer block the headlights since they had fallen off. She turned the volume on, and slipped back inside her show. Finally relaxed, her eyes grew heavy and she fell asleep.

Misplaced at first, not knowing how long she'd been asleep; she sipped from an empty glass. Something had snapped under the couch or maybe she had dreamt that it had, but her body jerked her awake just the same. Sighing she took a bite of the chocolate treat that she'd left on the coffee table. It seemed to tingle her lips, her tongue, her fingers. Sugar ants dripped off the Mallomar. Debra jumped up spitting them out, slapping them off her face; while underneath the couch, a half-dead mouse caught in a mousetrap flopped out. It touched her toe, and she screamed her way through involuntarily aerobics.

Now she was mad. She hated this house, hated that it wasn't a normal house, one that wasn't infested with mice and ants and any critter that happened along. Debra punched the blanket into a ball and grabbed the pillow, stomped her way to the door, and pitched them outside.

She hated being poor, hated the razor that she'd stretched so many times that it cut her legs, she hated using dish soap to wash her hair because she didn't have shampoo. Her jaw clenched, she stomped back to the couch, to the chocolate crumbs, to the mousetrap. She hauled the trap, mouse and all, outside and threw it fast and furious. Then she wrangled the vacuum cleaner out of the closet; and taking the couch apart, vacuumed every last crumb, every last ant.

Clutching a lumpy couch pillow and a stiff decorative throw, she plopped down on the couch. "Ten, nine, eight . . ." she counted backwards ". . . three, two, one," and took a deep breath. "Okay, it's over, settle down," she told herself, leaning back. Nothing else would distract her now. Not the shadows that headlights made, not the possum, not the noise inside the wall. She concentrated on Miami Vice, trying to figure out what was going on. Her feet were up now. Her arms relaxed.

The lights went out. The television flickered off.

"Crap."

Laying there in the dark, waiting for the electricity to come back on, she heard a distant train whistle, its tune long and lean. The sound of a car coming down the road interrupted the not so silent night. She watched misshapen headlights travel along the walls, strumming her fingers on the remote control. The echo of a dog, a tenor, howled. Another dog harmonized, barking the bass. She wondered where the duet was coming from and how far away they were—one mile, two miles, five? How long was this intermission going to take? She waited, laying very still, the couch like a magnet. The wind outside took one long breath, wheezing through the old windowpanes. "Come on," she huffed. This was taking too long. She sat up. There had to be candles somewhere in the kitchen. She got off the couch and stepped carefully through the dark, feeling her way, trying to remember which cupboard they were in. Another train whistled through the stillness; a floorboard creaked; the sound of metal tapping metal came from somewhere else. The source of every sound, all instruments of an ill-orchestrated sonata.

Groping blindly in the kitchen, she found a candle, and remembered that she'd seen matches in a drawer across the room. She stepped too quickly and tripped over the empty trap, and fell on top of it.

"Shit."

She rubbed her knee. The half-moon, filtering through the curtains, offered only gray specks of light. She finally found the matches and lit the candle; then reset the trap. Carrying the candle, guarding the flame, she made her way back to the living room, and set it down on an end table. There she watched the candle flame, the unsteady reflection in the polished veneer and thought about what to do. Sitting there for who knows how long, the only thing left was to go to bed. Guarding the flame through the black stairwell, wretched sounds came from inside the wall. She told herself it was only mice. She crawled into bed.

A door slammed from somewhere inside the house. Her body lurched. She scooted under the blankets, praying, "Now I lay me down to sleep. I pray the Lord my soul to keep . . ."

She heard footsteps slowly creeping up the stairs. Her throat felt like it was closing, she could hardly speak, "Ed, is that you?" She pulled the tough-cord Sears bedspread over her head.

"No it's Greg. ED who?"

CHAPTER 33

"Hi. I'd like to speak to Jeff or Nate Zourenger. Could you please find them for me?" Julie asked over the phone, thankful that someone had finally answered it.

"Who is this?"

"This is their mother calling. I've been trying . . . ."

"Hey! Anyone seen Nate or Jeff Zorro?" the voice yelled out.

She heard heavy metal playing in the background that blasted 'Bark at the moon', so-called music that she would have never allowed.

"Their mom's on the phone!" the voice yelled again.

Julie heard a clunk. Whoever had answered the phone, more likely a freshman, must have let the phone drop. This was the only phone, a payphone, to service the entire floor in that particular dorm. It sounded like someone turned up the music. Julie balled her hand into a fist. They were supposed to call every second and fourth Sunday. That was the deal. Listening to Ozzy Osborn's damning lyrics, half expecting to hear a dial tone next, Julie wondered just how responsible they really were. How could they study in this?

"Mom?" Jeff answered the phone.

"Where have you been? I have been trying to call you for days."

"I didn't know you were trying to call me. I'm not here that much. I've got this calculus test today and I've been studying at my fraternity." He seemed to be explaining too much.

"Where is Nate?" Julie asked, picturing him—his T-shirt, wrinkled and faded. His jeans, torn at the knees.

188

"He's down the hall. Do you want me to get him?"

"Go find him. I need to talk to both of you," Julie said, rethinking what she was going to say. She heard him yell Nate's name. Why had she started out by scolding him, she had intended to start on a positive note.

"Okay, Mom, Nate's coming. What's going on?"

Suddenly everything she wanted to say stuck in her throat. What she was going to say was suddenly all wrong. She took a breath, stuck in a frozen stare.

"Mom?"

Julie blinked hard. Her voice softened. "You haven't heard? You haven't been watching the news?"

"Heard what?"

She was a little relieved. All this time and they still didn't know. She was on some level glad that they could hear it from her. "Remember those letters that someone was sending me?"

"Yeah. What about him?"

"We tracked the man down who wrote them, in that new development. And the same day we found out who he was . . . someone killed him. They're saying it was your dad," Julie said, her palm to her forehead.

"How could they make such a mistake? I'm sure he told them he didn't do it. Right?" There was a long pause. "Mom?"

She wanted to say how sick with worry she was, how she wanted to jump through the phone line and hold him tight. She wanted . . . but this wasn't about what she wanted. A numbing sensation befell her lips and her tongue—the words fell out, "Your father's in jail."

"What?!" Jeff shouted. "Are you fucking kidding me? How could he be in jail? Dad would never kill anyone. What about his alibi? He has an alibi, doesn't he?"

"The police aren't buying it. I guess there's some sort of evidence." Julie kept a calm demeanor, her way of saying don't panic."

"No way. There's no way. Dad wouldn't kill anybody!" Jeff yelled over the phone.

"What?" Nate jumped in. "What did you say? Dad killed somebody? I want to talk to Mom!" Nate grabbed the phone from Jeff. "Mom, what are you talking about?"

"I know it doesn't make any sense . . . your dad's been arrested for killing the man we think wrote those letters.

"He didn't do it! You've got a lawyer, right? You know Dad would never do that. He gets all mad and stuff, but he would never kill anyone."

"Listen to me . . . I'm going to see the lawyer who's taken your dad's case. I'll let you know how it goes. But I'm telling you, this is going to be rough. Do you understand?"

"I understand. Can you come and get me this weekend? I want to see Dad."

"I want to see Dad, too." Jeff yelled over Nate's voice.

"No, I can't come and get you. But I'll make sure dad calls you two."

"That's total bullshit." Jeff said, grabbing the phone from Nate. "You wouldn't let us bring a car here and now you won't come and get us. We have a right to see our dad, and you made it so you're the only one who can get us there. You made it your job." Jeff said in stern determination. It wasn't like Jeff to cuss, not like most boys, Jeff

190

always presented a good argument instead.

Thrown by the swearing, Julie chose not to challenge him. Not now. Not under the circumstances. "What's the best time for him to call you?"

"Didn't you hear a single word I said? Are you seriously going to ignore this? I want to come home!"

"Listen Jeff, I can't leave. I'm not able to. Believe me, I'd like nothing more." A long pause on the line, Julie could feel her son's anger. "It's okay to be angry. I understand," she said. "I'm glad you know the difference between a controlled burn and a wildfire. It's one of the things I most admire about you."

Jeff spoke up. "Tell him to call me between seven and seven-thirty at night. I get out of my last class right before seven."

"How about Nate?"

"We've got the same schedule."

"I've got to go. Tell Nate I said goodbye and that I love you both very much."

"I love you, too, Mom. I'm sorry I swore," he said, his voice soft, boyish. "Bye."

She hung up the phone, damming the tears that were welling in her eyes.

CHAPTER 34

"Hello?" Julie answered the phone, still sitting on the bottom stair where she had just hung it up. A tissue in hand she had tried to sound like she hadn't been crying.

"Hi, got a minute?" Debra asked from the other end of the phone line.

"I was just getting ready to leave. What's up?"

"I forgot to tell you last night. I have something that belongs to you. Do you have a minute to drop by?"

"Something of mine?"

"I was digging a hole at Marie's yesterday, and I found your pendant."

"Why were you digging a hole at Marie's?"

"Oh. I shot a raccoon over there, and Marie wanted me to bury it. It just so happened that I picked the spot where you must have buried your necklace."

"You shot a raccoon?" Julie wadded up the tissue. "You never cease to 'amuse' me. Give me a couple minutes. I'll be right over."

Outside, the morning rain had drizzled into a damp chill where mere breathing fogged the windows inside her car. Julie turned the key and sat breathing warmth into her cupped hands, random thoughts racing to nowhere. 'Debra killed a raccoon? What the heck?' She glanced at her watch. 'The lawyer said eleven fifteen . . . . He has to know that Kyle lied . . . . Another woman? I would have known . . . Kyle has to call the boys . . . . I have to see him . . .'

Her eyes followed a speck of floating dust. 'I would have known . . . .'

How could he?' She shifted the gear in drive, and eased out of the driveway.

High heels and stockings, a spritz of *Charlie* cologne, Julie stood in Debra's doorway.

"You look nice," Debra said, as Julie stepped inside.

"You like this?" Julie opened her coat and then took it off—a white tailored shirt, a black A-line skirt, and a lavender sweater. "I thought I should look nice when I see the lawyer." There was plenty of time to see Michael Cane, the lawyer who had taken Kyle's case. Julie wasn't very happy that he was charging extra for today because it was Saturday, but he'd left her with no other choice

"Nice. I have just the thing to set it off." Debra said, handing the necklace to Julie. "I believe this is yours."

In her open palm, the gold necklace and pendant caught the light. A look of awe on her face, Julie stared at it, thinking of her mother now. Those damn tears welled in her eyes again. "I have to stop this," she said half-smiling, her fingertip stopping a tear. Glaring at the pendant, reddened nose, she wanted so badly to see her mother again, to smell the Ivory soap that scented her skin, to feel her touch, to hear her voice. No one had ever loved her like that, no one ever would. Frozen in grief, she looked up at Debra. A tear dropped off her chin.

Debra hugged her, right then, and there. "I'm so sorry . . . ."

Suspended in time, Debra's silk-like hair against her cheek, Julie mourned the dead. She mourned what could have been, what should have been. Then she finally pulled away. "I'm okay. I'm okay now."

"Do you have time for some coffee? I've got muffins. I know you like lemon poppy seed," Debra said, warming one in the microwave.

Julie half-nodded, studying the pendant in her hand, wiping her eyes again.

"Have a seat," Debra said.

Julie sat down without saying a word. Her gaze caught the stream of coffee as it filled her cup. "You know, I didn't forget about this. I always meant to dig it up and wear it again."

"Why did you bury it?"

"I lost it once when the chain broke, and when I found it again I buried it for safe keeping. I was nine at the time. The way I felt when I lost it was worse than not wearing it at all." Julie repeated what Marie had told Debra, about someday matching her half of the pendant with her brother's half. "I'd really like to find my brother." Julie tried to clasp the necklace, but her hands were shaking badly. "I'd forgotten that Marie replaced the chain. Can you help me?" Julie asked, brushing her hair to one side.

Debra clasped the two ends together. As the necklace took its natural place, the lights flickered. The overhead light bulbs glowed brighter and brighter, and finally the fragile beakers exploded. Fine shards of glass fell like confetti, all over the counters, the floor, the curtains, all over Julie and Debra. At the same time, the radio in the living room came on all by itself, changing stations—static and blurbs, static and bit-piece songs, tuning nothing, tuning everything in one quick search. The radio played the song, *Eyes Without a Face*.

Both Julie and Debra stood straight up. Billy Idol's song drew them into the living room where the light bulbs had exploded, too. Debra turned the radio off.

"The ghost is awake," Debra said, her grin unique. The two of them flicked glass out of their hair.

"You crack me up. What a power surge. I've never seen anything like it. Too many appliances must have kicked on at the same time."

"A power surge would have thrown the breaker switch, which would have killed the radio."

"This house is so old. I think you need an electrician to take care of that." Julie checked her watch. "I have to leave pretty soon."

"Oh. Come and see before you leave. I found a new batch of kittens under the porch. Do you want to see them? The mother is wild, but I've been taming her kittens so I can give them away."

"Let me see."

They grabbed their coats and Debra led her outside. Under the front steps, Julie picked up a gray kitten. "You are so cute."

"I spayed and neutered the cats I could catch."

"How many was that?"

"Just two. There're so many wild cats here. I don't know where they all came from.

If I could get away with it, I'd pass these kittens out to strangers on the street."

"You are so sweet," Julie cooed—the kitten purring in her hands. "You want to come home with me?"

"Maybe you'd like two of them, so the first one doesn't get lonely."

"Oh, that would be lovely; two cats marking their territory. No thanks," Julie said. "But I'll take this little guy." She held him up to her face. "He likes me," she whispered in the kitten's ear. "What's this little bald spot, Deb?"

"I don't know. They must have been playing too rough; they all seem to have one or two."

Julie agreed to take him later, on her way home. She would stop at the pet store first in preparation for the new tenant.

"What are you doing Friday night? Maybe you can come over and watch a movie with me while Greg's gone? I'll make chocolate cake."

"That's almost a week away; I'll see." She scratched the kitten's ear and put him back with his brothers, thinking about the lawyer now, nerves hitting her stomach.

CHAPTER 35

Debra had gone in the basement to offer the electrician something to drink. He was encased in a jungle of frayed wires, holding one to his eye, the other eye closed, cussing under his breath. He wanted coffee, thank you and go away. He was a piano tuner, this retired electrician who had bartered with Greg. There was talk of paying him cash. There was talk of Greg building him a pole barn. He would decide on just how much after he had taken a gander at their electrical box. This seventy-nine-year-old man with the thick eyeglasses and hair growing out of his ears was in the basement for most of the morning, talking to himself. She could hear him from upstairs, his baritone old man voice. She couldn't make out all of the words. But he seemed to favor the expressions, 'aw horseshit' and 'aw hell'.

There was a lull coming from the basement now "I'm going outside for a while. Do you need anything?" Debra yelled down the stairs, buttoning her coat. The old man didn't answer. She walked halfway down the basement stairs. She could hear him now, his back turned to her.

"Well I'll be a son of a . . . son of a bitch! Aw horseshit!"

"I hope you're not charging by the cussword," Debra said, adding her signature smile.

That seemed to make him laugh.

"I just wanted you to know that I'm going outside for a little while. Do you need anything?"

"You're going outside? It's cold out there," he said, whittling the rubber off an end wire.

"I've been wanting to cut down some wild grape vines behind the field. This might be my only chance. It's supposed to get colder later on."

"Wild grape vines, huh." He stuck the end wire in his mouth, gnawed a bit and spit out a piece of rubber. "What on earth do you want with those?"

"I've seen these grapevine wreaths in specialty stores. They're nice, but expensive. They don't look that hard to make. I shouldn't be long."

"Take your time. I'm leaving, too. It's almost lunchtime." He closed his pocketknife, and pulled a white rumpled handkerchief out of his pants pocket and blew his nose. "I'll be back after my nap." His old man nose seemed double-jointed. Every hanky swipe seemed to displace it.

Debra searched for just the right words. What did he mean, 'after his nap'? She didn't have any electricity. How long was he planning to take? "Oh . . . when will you be back?"

"Don't worry. Your furnace is on. I should have your kitchen on by tonight."

It was just after six o'clock. Gus had come and gone for the day. The only working outlet was in the kitchen where Debra had plugged in the microwave. She scratched feverishly at her wrist and up her arm. The dinner table was set. Candlelight showcased a tuna casserole that she'd made in the microwave, and individual servings of sliced cucumbers in apple cider vinegar.

Sitting at the kitchen table Greg eyed the crumbled potato chips on top of the casserole, and scooped a spoonful, looking a little wary.

Debra had tried to stop scratching but now she was rubbing her wrist hard against the edge of the table, "I think something bit me." She edged up her sleeve. "Are these spider bites? Or ant bites? Nothing works, not calamine, not even antibiotic cream. It's just getting worse."

Greg guided her arm to the candlelight. The welts were perfectly round, raised on the outer edge. "How long have you had these?"

"Maybe a week. Do you think they're infected?"

"I don't know, but I've got one, too, on my stomach. I don't think these are spider or ant bites either. You're going to have to see a doctor for the both of us. Tell him I've got it, too." He tasted a fork full of tuna, noodles, and potato chips. "How's Gus doing? Can we watch TV tonight?"

"Sure, as long as it's not more than a hundred feet away from that outlet. He left us an extension cord. That's the only outlet that works. Are you sure he knows what he's doing?"

"Give him some time. He used to be an electrician for the Allison Tank Plant. He knows what he's doing."

The doctor's assistant guided Debra to an examination room, and handed her a paper gown. "Take everything off from the waist up. Put this on, opening in the front. The doctor will see you soon," she said as she left the room. Debra had called for an appointment on Monday, four days ago, now she had two more welts on her hands, and splotches of blistery rash on her upper chest and neck.

She scratched her neck through her paper gown, trying not to break open the blisters. Dangling her feet, sitting on an examination table, she heard the door shut in the next room, hoping that she was next. Muffled voices came from the hallway. Then the door opened.

"Hello. How are you today?" Dr. Banion entered the room.

Smelling of cigarettes, his hair pure white, he shook her hand.

"Good. Except for this rash."

"Lay back. Please."

Debra complied, wondering why she had to lay back.

"When was the last time you had a breast exam?" He opened her paper gown and proceeded to manhandle her breast.

Her face fevered, itching more than anyone could ever itch, she complied. That's what you do in a doctor's office. You comply. Doctor's always know what they're doing. Don't they? There had to be a reason for this.

"Everything looks fine. You can sit up now," the doctor said, "What's this on your neck?"

"I don't know. That's why I'm here."

He opened her chart, sat down, and crossed his legs, reading.

Debra sat quietly, holding her gown close. It was cold in here. She wanted to put her clothes on.

"It says here that you came in because of 'lumps on your breast'." He looked up at her.

"I came in because of 'bumps on my chest.' Right here, now it's mostly my neck. And here." she showed him her arms. "This looks different."

"Well." The doctor studied her arms through a magnifying lens in a bright light, turning them over and back again before completing his sentence. "This over here and here is ringworm." He turned the light on her neck. And this is poison ivy."

"What? Are you sure they're not spider bites. My husband has them, too. And I haven't been near poison ivy." She paused in thought. "Can you get poison ivy after the leaves are gone? I cut down some grapevines last week. Poison ivy doesn't climb trees, does it?"

"Of course it does. Even after the leaves are gone, you can get poison ivy just by touching the stem or the vine. I had a guy who tried to burn it and got poison ivy just from the smoke." The doctor scribbled something down. "Have you been in contact with any stray dogs, cats?"

"You wouldn't believe how many cats there are in that old barn behind my house. They're even under my steps. I don't know where they all came from. I don't let them in the house."

"Do they have any bare patches where there's no fur? Perfectly round spots?"

"Yes," Debra said softly. The word 'ringworm' sounded so unclean, like she lived in filth or something. "Did I get this from them?"

"It's highly contagious." He washed his hands in the room's tiny sink. "You have to spray them with an over the counter fungicide twice a day for two weeks, every last cat, or they'll keep passing it to each other and probably the rest of the neighborhood, if they haven't done that all ready. Then you have to scrub down their bedding and treat it with fungicide, or just throw it out." The doctor took out his prescription pad and scrawled something down. "Here's a prescription for you. Clean your ringworm real good with Betadine soap twice a day and apply this . . ." he wrote another prescription, "this is for cortisone." The doctor stood up and walked to the door. "Take two at bedtime. You can put calamine lotion on the poison ivy to help with the itching." His hand was on the doorknob.

"My husband has it, too. And I know this sounds strange, but those cats were there before we were. They're not used to people. Out of seventeen cats, I can only catch two. The rest are wild."

"You have to call the game warden. If they are truly wild, and they can't find homes for them, they have to be euthanized. Do you have any more questions?" He opened the door.

She'd been in that waiting room for an hour and a half. And he had been there all of six minutes. Her face, still feverish—her neck still itching—she froze, staring blankly. There were questions. There had to be questions. Why couldn't she think of any?

He left the room.

Debra felt sick, and boy did she itch. She drove straight to the pharmacy, trying to think of everyone who had touched the cats. Greg had ringworm and Julie would get it next. Then there was Sam and Marie. She'd given them a kitten. Gus had held a kitten, too, but couldn't take one home.

She leaned into the steering wheel. "It's an epidemic."

Waiting at the pharmacy, she thought of all the questions that she should have asked the doctor. How long would it take for ringworm to clear up? How long was the incubation period? She pictured an angry mob of neighbors, boils and blisters, and scabs, marching to her door with torches and a hangman's noose.

The pharmacist pulled out a reference book. His rounded belly rubbed against the counter as he read. "It takes four weeks to clear up ringworm if one maintains the course of treatment, and the incubation period is ten to fourteen days after exposure." He peaked over the partition. "Is this for you?"

Debra had never contemplated an alias before, not until that very moment. She wanted to be someone else, anyone else, even for an instant. "Yes," she said, avoiding eye contact. The affirmative word hung in her throat like a square pill.

CHAPTER 36

A warm wind swept the leaves into a whirlwind around Debra's ankles. It was 60 degrees, a rarity for November, and her last chance to dig up the rest of the dahlia bulbs and to mulch the roses. The warm weather, fleeting at best, had delayed the gales of November. A cold front was approaching from Canada, and the sudden drop in temperature was likely to produce thunderstorms by tomorrow, on Friday. At least she didn't have to worry about the electricity going off. Gus had rewired the entire circuit box. He must have known what he was doing—the house hadn't burned down.

After Gus had left though, Debra had noticed an extra switch, kind of like a light switch. She hadn't asked him to install it and neither had Greg, but there it was right next to the basement door. A switch to turn the sump pump on and off without having to unplug in the basement. A sump pump was an imperative now because when the creek rose; creek-water would back up into the basement right through the pipe that Greg had installed. So much for fixing the flooding problem. But this switch, this new switch perplexed her. Thinking back at it, she remembered how Gus had been talking to himself. At least she thought it was Gus's voice. There hadn't been anyone else there, just her and Gus and . . . . A chill ran down her back. No one had told Gus about Ed, not even about his accident. Debra instantly pictured Ed, the image of this policeman in the basement with water up to his knees, the plug in his hand. She tried to get that picture out of her head—him plugging it in—convulsing—electrocution—dying. Had Gus known? Is that why he put in the switch?

Friday came so quickly, and at 6 o'clock widespread thunderstorms were predicted to hit before midnight. LaGrange was often a target for storms that broke out over Lake Erie and pushed their way inland. The temperature had already fallen twenty degrees within the last hour. Debra wished Julie would call.

Greg had left, and Debra was wiping down the baseboards where he had sprayed ant poison. She heard the phone ring.

"Are we still on for tonight?" It was Julie.

"Julie! Hi! Sure! Come on over! I made a cake."

Sure enough a lopsided chocolate cake, still in the pan, was taunting Debra. Frosting would have to even it out. She stood on her toes, barely reaching the powdered sugar, and pulled the edge of it from the top shelf. The bag, closed with just a clothespin, slipped out of her fingers and exploded on the floor. Julie got there just in time to see Debra sweeping it up.

"How bad do you want frosting?" Debra looked into her dustpan, poking at powdered sugar where she picked out a hair.

"I think I'd rather have a drink," Julie announced, taking coconut rum and pineapple sherbet out of a paper bag. "Got a blender?"

"You always know just what to say," Debra said, pretending to be coy. "Would you like some popcorn, too?"

After they had settled, they were sitting in the living room with the television on. They drank just enough to feel relaxed.

"You're wearing your necklace," Debra said.

"It makes me feel like I'm a part of something."

"It's pretty."

"I'm sorry I carried on like I did. I've been meaning to tell you why I didn't call you those first few days. My doctor put me on Valium. I took it because I couldn't stop crying. All I could do was sleep. I didn't call anyone, I couldn't. You got me out for a jog the day after I stopped taking it. Then he prescribed Xanax. I took one a couple of days ago but I'm not going to take it anymore. I don't like the way it makes me feel.

"Ask him about Elavil. It doesn't knock you out, but it'll stop compulsive thoughts from going over and over in your mind."

"Have you taken it?" Julie asked.

"No. My mom did though," Debra said. "My mother is mentally ill . . ."

"Really . . . ." Julie sat straight up.

"She's in an institution."

"How come you never mentioned it?"

"I don't talk about it. I never know how someone's going to react. My mom killed my dad." Debra stopped here. She waited for a reaction, but none came. "She almost killed me, too, a few times. It sounds so bizarre, I don't think people believe me. I can't tell you how many times I was taken away from her and put in another foster home. They would play with my mom's medication and she would seem okay for a while, and they would give me back. Then she would start drinking again and would stop taking the pills because she couldn't do both, and it would start all over again." Debra was visibly shaking now. She'd never said this much out loud, and stopped herself from saying more.

"Oh Deb. I'm so sorry. I had no idea. It must have been horrible."

"It's past tense now. I don't think about it." Debra said, wanting to change the mood.

"I can't even imagine how hard that must have been for you to deal with."

"I got through it. Look at me. I'm married. I've got this nice house . . ." She laughed nervously, not an out loud laugh, a two-syllable laugh. Julie reacted with the same nervous laugh.

"How did you get to be so normal?" Julie asked.

Debra paused. To her 'normal' was more like a trick that she'd learned to master. How was she going to answer that? She would pull out her eyelashes. She would bite her fingernails and cuticles till her fingers bled. She'd had her share of panic attacks, too. Being as close to normal as she would ever be, she said the only thing that made any sense, "I truly believe, by the grace of God." It was time to change the subject. "You haven't told me. What's going on with Kyle?"

"Let's just say, for one night, he doesn't exist. I want to hear more about you. How did you meet Greg?"

"On a blind date; we went with another couple to Hinckley Hills, spent most of the afternoon climbing the cliffs. It was fun until we took a boat ride. After that I decided to never go out with him again."

"Well I know you married him. What happened?"

"We rented a rowboat, just the two of us." Debra hesitated, giving the look of a teenager who was about to share a secret. "I've never told this to anyone." She sipped her drink, and sat on the edge of the couch to pantomime. "Greg was rowing and sitting like, you know, like guys do . . . with his legs . . . out. He didn't realize that he had ripped a hole, a big one, up in the seam of his pants when we were climbing the ledges. It was the longest boat ride I ever had," she said, her two-syllable laugh infectious. "To this day I've never said a word to him."

"You never told him . . . never?" Julie laughed a girlish laugh.

"No, and I never will."

Rain hit hard against the house, the wind whistled through the drafty windows and the rustling bushes tap-tap-tapped on the porch outside. A tinny tap-clang resonated from somewhere outside, and a floorboard creaked from somewhere upstairs.

"What was that?" Julie asked, beaming with a fun-house kind of excitement. "This house really is creepy."

Debra turned the television down so Julie could hear the full effect. Strangely enough the sounds seemed more amusing than scary. Stranger still, the house seemed to have a pleasant effect on Julie, and the house seemed equally pleasant by having her here.

"I've been thinking . . . about those letters," Julie said. "From the way they're written, they sound like something a businessman would write, someone with a higher education, not someone who stalks women in grocery stores. They sound like they're from a weirdo, not a deviant. I'm starting to think there's no connection between the letters and that guy."

"Didn't you say the detective was supposed to compare the handwriting?"

"Lieutenant Barger. You've talked to him. Right?"

"I did. It wasn't bad. It was the first time that someone from the legal system hasn't made me feel like I was the criminal. He actually seemed concerned."

"I thought he would have called me by now."

"Whatever he tells you has to be undisputable. That's probably why it's taking so long."

It was 11 o'clock and Greg came home just in time to hear the thunderstorm warnings on the news. By then they could hear thunder from a distance, the wind blowing harder, and branches hitting the house.

Julie had walked over earlier, but now the thunder and lightning were getting closer, louder.

Heavy rain pelted the four-paned windows.

"I'll drive you home." Debra got her car keys.

Julie looked out the window. "Sounds good to me." The tree limbs flailed in the force of the wind. Lightning flashed. It thundered.

"Would you rather stay here until the storm is over?"

"No, I'll be fine," Julie answered, returning to a somber face.

They ran to the car and Debra backed out of the driveway, windshield wipers swishing madly. Pulling onto the road, she could hardly see because of the heavy rain. Hailstones, the size of pebbles, hit the car, first one ping, then two. Then an all-out hailstorm dropped from the sky and pounded the car.

"I'll turn around in your driveway and get you closer to the door," Debra told Julie, pulling into her driveway.

"I'm going to wait for it to let up some. I've never seen it like this."

They huddled in the car, watching the hail pile on the road. Lightning extended fingers across the sky, cracking thunder. In a lull between lightning strikes, the sound of hail didn't seem so loud any more. Then lightning flashed again, feathering out this time. This time it exploded in a thunderous clap and struck Debra's farmhouse, engulfing the lightning rod.

"My house! Did you see that? It hit my house!"

"Go!"

Debra hit the gas pedal hard, spinning the wheels, throwing

gravel. The hail finally stopped when she turned onto the road. Through the blinding rain, lightning flashed again, momentarily unveiling Greg's silhouette. He was climbing onto the roof.

"I don't see any fire." Julie squinted, looking through the watermarked window.

"Can you see Greg?" Debra asked, watching the road.

"No."

They pulled into Debra's garage and made their way to the kitchen. Debra opened the kitchen door hesitantly to see if it was safe to go inside. She smelled smoke, not thick smoke like the fire she'd survived, but lingering smoke like a fire that had been drenched. Debra quickly rummaged through a cupboard, pulled out a box of baking soda, and headed toward the stairs.

"Do you think it's safe?" Julie asked, holding her back by her elbow. "Don't you think you should call the fire department?"

"It would take too long to get here. I think it's manageable." Debra pulled away gingerly. "There can't be a fire, not anymore. The rain would have put it out." She marched up the stairs with Julie right behind her. Cinders were melting the rug at the top of the stairs so Debra doused it with baking soda. Rain was coming in through the roof, from the hallway to unused part of the house. She pushed the door open to an unused room where she could see the second staircase. A heat register in the center of the floor didn't conduct heat, per se. The thirty by thirty inch grate, which was right above the bathroom, was meant for heat to rise between the two floors. She had thrown a rubber mat over it to conserve heat. Rainwater was dripping through that, too.

"Greg!" Debra yelled through a watermelon size hole in the

ceiling. She could hear the branches of the old catalpa tree caught up in the gusts of wind, the scraping sounds they made on the roof, the house, the windows. She could see the lightning rod, an orange steamy glow. The carpet was getting wetter by the minute, and so was the bathroom below.

"Deb?" Greg yelled from the living room, running up the stairs, dripping wet.

"You should have seen it. The entire room turned blue." Greg shook off his baseball cap. "It sounded like a bomb went off. It went through the whole house and blew a hole right though the wall downstairs, above the front door."

"I thought the lightning rod was supposed to prevent lightning from hitting the house," Debra said.

"It does, as long as the metal cable grounds it, but that was broken." Greg looked up at the hole in the ceiling and back at Debra. "I don't get it. That cable was fine a week ago. It'll hold for the night. I wound it together with a couple of wire coat hangers and made a temporary ground. I've got to throw a tarp up there."

"You're going back on the roof?" Debra said with a please-don't sort of look.

"Get some buckets. A tarp's not leak-proof, not as long as this keeps up." Greg hurried down the stairs and back outside.

Debra grabbed a pile of towels from the bathroom and handed them to Julie. "Can you take these for me to sop up some of the water? I'm going to get a garbage can to catch the rain. I'll be right back."

When the towels and catch-buckets were all in place, Greg finally came inside. All of them had gotten wet, none of them as bad as Greg. Debra handed him a towel and gave one to Julie.

"Well, it was time to get a new roof, anyway." He seemed to make light of it, but Debra picked up on his sarcasm. That house had swallowed their every last cent, and always seemed to beg for more.

"I never saw anything like that," Greg said, still toweling off. "The whole room turned blue."

"I'm glad I wasn't here by myself when that happened," Debra said. "I don't know what I would have done."

Julie wasn't paying attention. She seemed fixated on the blackened hole above the front door. "Look at that. Does that look like . . .?"

Greg glanced up half-wittingly. "Like what?" he asked, stepping out of his wet shoes. Debra looked hard at the charred formation.

"Deb, do you see it?" Julie took a couple steps back, eyeing the hole.

Debra concentrated. The shape of the hole wasn't round at all. It was half-round on the right side. "It looks like . . . a half of a heart. Doesn't it?" Debra spoke, half-whispering. "Just like your pendant, Julie."

Greg had been towel-drying his hair and peaked out from under it. "You guys are funny. I'm going to bed." He kissed Debra and turned towards the stairs.

CHAPTER 37

Debra had no idea what to expect when she had answered the door. The person pounding was yelling, "Game warden! Open up! Game warden!" He neither looked nor acted like a professional. A heavy chain looped in and out of his jean pockets, and a faded denim jacket hugged what looked like a muscular frame. His shoulder-length hair half-covered a cobra tattoo on his neck, a cigarette dangled from his mouth. And a tattoo baring a ring of skulls wrapped his wrist like a vulgar bracelet at his tattered sleeve.

"You got infected cats?" He flipped out some sort of I.D. and instantly shoved it back in his pocket. "I'm supposed to take 'em out of here. Where do I go?" He looked over his shoulder, his back to the road, and hocked a wad of snot from the back of his throat and spit in the direction of the bushes. Debra knew he'd missed. She could see where it had landed on the sunken porch, and quickly looked away.

"They're back by the barn. I'll get my coat." Debra was just about to close the door when he caught it, acting like he was going to come inside.

"I'll meet you in back," she said, abruptly closing the door, instinctively leaning into it. He was absolutely not coming inside. Debra had instantly decided, she didn't like this man, his West Virginian drawl, and his dirty fingernails.

She brought the bag of cat food outside to lure the cats. The unlikely game warden was waiting on the deck with burlap bags and some sort of a pole that was outfitted with some sort of leash. She felt a shortness of breath . . . the reality of what they were about to do next sank in her chest. The extinction of all of these cats, what else could she do to get the fast spreading ringworm under control? There had to be more than twenty cats including kittens and the most recent drop-offs. She'd been spraying Kitty Callie twice a day with a fungicide and had made clean straw bed for her, only to be contaminated again by infected cats. There was no consoling herself; they had to be put down or they would suffer terribly. The sores were spreading quickly, and mucus matted their eyes. She had wanted to catch them all and make them better. She'd tried. Oh how she'd tried. The only consolation was at least they would die humanely.

Debra rattled the bag of cat food as she called out, "Here kitty, kitty. Here kitty, kitty." She poured out a smattering into an old aluminum pie plate. She may as well have poured poison.

"We inherited these cats when we moved in. I couldn't tell you how many generations these cats go back that have never been tamed."

The cats waited for her to back away from the generic cat food before they gathered around it. They growled like wild animals as they ate. Most of which had never let Debra get close. "You can't even pet them. They'll back away."

The game warden put on leather gloves. He placed himself a good distance behind a gray tomcat, extended the pole, and slowly looped the pole's retractable leash around the cat's neck. He jerked it fast and swung the cat up. The cat hissed and wailed, growling spitting, baring claws. The warden scooped it into a burlap sack and tied it closed. Debra wanted to slap the bag out of his hand. She wanted to tell him to leave and never come back. She had tried as hard as she could to corner just one more cat, just long enough to spray him, just long enough to save him. The same three-second recording spun in her head. These cats had to die. These cats had to die. Debra swallowed hard, her face ashen.

"Go inside," he said to Debra. "You don't need to see this."

"Wait. The calico is tame." Debra picked up the calico.

"Hey. I'm supposed to take all of them. Put it in the bag," he snapped, holding a sack open.

"No. It took me all summer long to tame her. I've been treating her for fungus."

"Fine, if you want to get disease and shit all over you. Just don't get that shit near me; I'm not gonna catch any Baganga plague."

Debra hurried to the garage, holding tight onto Kitty Callie, and locked her inside. But when she came back she saw this person slam a squirming burlap sack into the trunk of his car, a rusted Ford Mercury, on top of a layer of thick black plastic. She saw, too, evidence of empty beer bottles, oil soaked rags, and splats that looked like dried blood. She saw the handle of a hunting knife, a dirty towel wrapped around the blade. And right at the edge of the trunk, right where it latched, she saw a golf club. What was he doing with that? He didn't look like a man who golfed.

"You don't have to be so mean," she said with a cold stare. "Aren't you supposed to have cages? What happened to the game warden truck?"

He leaned both hands on the bumper, shoulders slumped, and without even looking at her, he spoke in a threatening tone. "I told you to go inside. I don't need some righteous do-gooder telling me how to do my job. If you have to pick at something," he faced her, "pick your panties out of your ass." He raised his voice, "and leave me alone."

Debra stood there, stunned at first. Now she was fuming. She marched inside without saying a word. If she had learned anything from her mother, she learned to tread lightly in the presence of insanity. She grabbed the Yellow Pages and looked up the telephone number for animal control. Whoever this man was, he didn't belong here. But when she called, a recording said the department was closed for the weekend. Debra made her way back outside to catch a glimpse of the warden's nametag with the full intention of reporting him on Monday. Halfway through the doorway, she stopped, wondering if she should call the sheriff. This man was rough and crude and even had a knife in his trunk . . . . Was any of that against the law? She put the idea on hold and went outside. Wailing cat cries came from inside the trunk.

Debra couldn't see a name anywhere on his jacket. "I didn't catch your name," she said.

"It's Bruce." He was hiding something behind his back.

She looked over at the trunk and saw five more burlap bag captives, but only a couple of them were moving. She could see what Bruce was trying to hide now, a golf club.

"What did you do?"

"I told you. You don't need to be out here. I suggest you get your china doll ass back in the house, and let me do my job."

"Bruce," she repeated his name to herself in a whisper, and stormed back inside. She thought hard about what to do next. Call the sheriff? An animal rights activist? By the time she would have looked up the numbers and called them, and sat there on hold . . . they were so far away . . . . By the time the sheriff would have gotten there, Bruce would have captured, tortured and killed all the cats and would be long gone.

If she had learned anything from her mother, anything at all, she learned in the presence of insanity, you fade out of the picture and come back with a gun. She retrieved her mother's rifle and stormed back outside to politely tell him to leave. This time she saw him whap a burlap sack with his golf club.

"Stop right now and leave." She planted the rifle butt in her shoulder and lined up the sites, aiming right at Bruce. "Get off my property now." Clutching the rifle, the wooden stock against her cheek, she took her rightful place as her mother's daughter, shaking quaking inside, not because she was so scared, but because it felt so right.

He stood, glaring at her, squinty-like. "What are you, crazy?"

"I come from a long line of crazy." She cocked the rifle.

"I don't take no shit from no one, bitch. Go ahead. Pull the trigger."

She fired a shot at his feet in the dirt.

"Damn you!"

"I called the sheriff. You better leave before he gets here."

"You're a liar. You're the one he'd arrest. You're the one who's threatening me with a rifle."

"I have the right to bear arms. This is my property. Leave!" She cocked the rifle again.

He stood firm. "You don't have the balls to do that again."

She pulled the trigger again. Another shot rang out, flinging dirt and grass at his feet. Her knees shook so badly she thought they would give out.

"Fine," he shouted, slamming his trunk, closing it. "But I'll have the Board of Health here on Monday. I'll make sure of that." He opened his car door. "I'm pissed now, bitch. You don't know who you're messin' with."

By Monday morning, Debra was frantic from worrying all weekend long. Scenes of Bruce, swinging the golf club, hitting a burlap sack, had skipped like a broken record in her head over and over again.

Surely firing a rifle on her own property fell into some sort of gray area—no harm, no foul—no intent to kill. Maybe she really was within her rights. She wasn't going to mention any of that when she called the Department of Wildlife. Maybe they wouldn't either. Still, she knew exactly what she would say if they would ask—that she was a woman here all alone. Not another house for miles. That she didn't know what else to do. That she wasn't going to shoot him. She just wanted to protect herself.

She finally got a dispatcher on the phone and initiated her complaint.

". . . Bruce only fills in on weekends. We have had complaints about him before, but he's harmless, I assure you," the director told her.

"He was unnecessarily cruel to those animals. Do you know what he was using? He . . . ."

The official interrupted Debra. "What you might think is cruel has to be done to capture the animal in the most efficient way possible."

"You can't be serious. He . . . ."

"Can you hold?" There was a click on the line and then she heard violin music. Debra sat down. Five minutes went by, then six. The director came back on the line. "Did he threaten you in any way?"

217

The question seemed to catch her off guard. "No," Debra said quietly. She was the one who had threatened him. "But he swore at me and . . . ." She felt her face getting red. If the dispatcher could have seen her, she would have known that Debra hadn't been completely honest. It wasn't exactly a lie but Debra couldn't be dishonest at all without it showing in her face.

"I'm scheduling Henry Carmen to come on Wednesday to get the rest of the cats. He's our official county game warden. I'm sure you won't have a problem with him," the dispatcher said sarcastically. "You can take up any issues you have with him."

"But . . ."

"I'll put you over to his voice mail."

Listening to more music, she got a feeling that Bruce hadn't said anything about the rifle. Why wouldn't he have said something? She heard a click and then a dial tone. Frustration mounting, she would wait until Wednesday when the real game warden would come.

CHAPTER 38

Julie entered a small room that smelled of mold and stale Pine Sol. The whitewashed walls seemed to close in around her, closer and closer, until it seemed as though they were sucking the air right out of her lungs.

Flanked by two guards, Kyle came in the room, wearing handcuffs. An armed guard prompted Kyle to sit, then stood by the door. Was this the new reality of what her life had become? She closed her eyes, praying that somehow when she opened them again, that she'd wake up from this nightmare. She looked up. The cold eyes of reality stared back at her, the cold eyes of a murderer. Kyle.

Bail was more money than she'd ever dreamed, more than she could ever pay and the trial date wasn't set for another four months. The stagnant room with only a table and two wooden chairs was the only suite they would be sharing, maybe for the next four months, maybe for the next forty years, maybe until he was sentenced to death.

"Hi," Julie said above a whisper. "How are you?"

Kyle sat quietly at the table, as if she hadn't said anything at all.

She waited in hollow silence. "What's going to happen now?" Julie searched his eyes. "How are you going to plead?"

Saying nothing, his head down, he looked at his hands, examining each finger over and over again.

"Kyle, talk to me. I'm your wife."

After a long silence, Julie slowly stood up. "Call your boys. They're worried about you." She inched toward the door. Beyond the point of being lightheaded, she thought that she might pass out. "I'll give the number to the guard."

"I didn't do it," Kyle said abruptly. "Someone else killed that guy, some ghoul. I could never do what he did to that man. I'm not kidding. This whole thing was a coincidence."

"Who are you trying to fool? I was there. I saw how mad you were. It wasn't a coincidence, you threatened to kill him. He's dead. You told the detective that you had a girlfriend. Why would you say that? A last ditch alibi?"

"Julie . . . . Listen to me. I didn't kill anyone. I know you don't want to hear this, but I was with another woman that night. You have to know, she means nothing to me. But I was with her the night that man was killed. She said her husband would kill her if he knew. I can't . . . ."

"I don't believe you. I don't believe any of this."

"Why are you so stupid? You believe me because I tell you to." Kyle shouted, pounding his fists on the table. The guard stepped forward, and Kyle sat still.

Julie could feel the blood rushing from her face. The room spun into a dizzying spinning carnival ride; she thought she was going to vomit.

"Has it sunk in yet? . . . Julie. Are you listening to me?"

A sudden ringing in her ears, Julie watched his mouth move without hearing his words. What was she doing in a marriage like this? He'd never loved her. Why did she think he could? She stared at nothing on a blank wall, unblinking. He was rewriting what really happened. Act two, scene one, casting her as the lead. Maybe he needed her to play along in order to fool everyone else.

"I won't lie for you." she said softy, steadily.

"I'm not asking you to lie. I'm asking you to believe me. The lawyer says that he can't convince a jury that I'm innocent if I can't convince you that I'm innocent. And I am. You're going to sit in that courtroom every day. And that jury has to be sympathetic to you. You can't be forced to testify against me. But that doesn't stop the prosecution from calling you as a witness, and that doesn't stop you from voluntarily testifying. You have to believe me. I didn't do it."

"What do you think? That you can write that on the chalkboard a hundred times and it'll make it true? You know as well as I do . . . you killed that man."

"You still don't get it. You're not as smart as I thought you were. What good are you?"

"I don't mean anything to you. Do I? I'm just the woman you were forced to marry. You don't think about how I was forced to marry you. Here's the real truth, you raped me eighteen years ago. I was only fifteen. Now I'm supposed to pretend that you are this great husband?"

"I don't know where you come up with this shit. You're selfish. Do you know that? This isn't about you. It's about me. I'm the one sitting in jail, not you. And I'm the one they're gonna execute for something I didn't do. So if you want to go and take this personal, go ahead. Just get out."

That never-ending Pine Sol smell had given Julie a headache. She stood up holding onto the table.

All these years . . . "You never loved me," she said, steadily moving toward the door. "I don't know why I stayed."

"Come on, you know how I get," Kyle said. "Come on Julie. Don't be so sensitive. I need you."

"I don't care. That's my new mantra—I don't care. It feels good just to say it. A truck plowed over our mailbox, I don't care. Your lawyer is going to cost more than our house, I don't care. You're never coming home again, not ever." She smiled a contented looking smile. "I don't care."

"Let me out," she said to the guard.

Julie walked past prison security and down the long corridor convinced that she was never coming back. Passing a drinking fountain, she stopped and waited for a drink where a young woman was bent over, slurping water. The woman wore a tight satin red dress, and her black lace slip stuck out from below the hem. The woman stood up and wiped the water from her mouth with the back of her hand, tugging, clumsily, at her slender waist, on the half-slip as she tried to pull it up. She chewed bubble gum, loudly. Her bright red lips exaggerated every chew.

When she saw Julie, she grinned like she didn't care who had seen her shifting her slip. And then, in a bold statement, she pulled it down to her ankles in plain view of anyone who might have been watching. "I hate wearing this stupid thing," she said to Julie, as she flipped it from her ankles, past her black spiked heels, seemingly unembarrassed. She wadded it up and crammed it in her tiger-striped purse.

Somewhat entertained, Julie instinctively glanced around to see if anyone else had seen it, too. "Yeah, they can be a pain," she said, taking her turn at the drinking fountain.

"You seeing someone here?" the woman asked.

Julie paused to politely respond, and couldn't help but notice the woman's appearance. Her youthful face had the features of a Barbie doll, a tad too much makeup. Her orangey-blond hair was in an off-center ponytail and the back of her hairline had been shaved two inches up the base of her neck.

"No, I'm not." Julie lied. A conversation with a stranger was the last thing she wanted.

"I was going to see someone, but they won't let me in. I'm not supposed to tell them my real name," the woman said. "It's Dee. My real name is Dorothy. You know, like The Wizard of Oz Dorothy. I like Dee better . . . ."

Julie nodded her head, waiting for the opportunity to walk away. "It was nice meeting you. Good luck," she said.

Dee rambled on, "How come you're here if you haven't got no one to see? I wouldn't come here if I didn't have to. I hate this place. You know what I mean? Do you work here or something?"

On the verge of being rude, she watched her lips move. She just wanted to be alone.

"Are you okay? You want another drink of water or something?"

"I've had a lot on my mind."

"Anyways, like I was saying, I came to see Kyle . . . I never could pronounce his last name. He's been in the news. He's innocent though. I know he is."

The only thing flashing in Julie's mind now was this woman's face. She looked so young.

"I shouldn't be here. I made up a fake name. But they wanted to see my I.D."

Julie played out a scenario in her head. Was this Kyle's lover? What were the chances? There had to be more than one person here who was named Kyle.

"So anyways, nice talking to you," Dee turned to leave.

"Nice to meet you," Julie politely answered, leaving the temptress behind. She stopped at the front desk on her way out. "Excuse me, officer. That young woman I passed in the hall, the one with the orangey hair, who was she here to see?"

"Sorry, ma'am. I can't give out that information."

Lost in thought, Julie stepped just outside the main entrance onto the marble steps, buttoning her coat. Freezing wind, icy sleet and snow stung her face, and whisked her dark curls. The drizzle had frozen on the slippery steps, now wet with snow. She slid on the first step and caught her balance. But just three steps from the bottom she slipped on the ice, and fell, landing on her knees at the bottom of the stoop. "Shit!" Her knees bled through her torn nylons.

"Are you all right?" A man, wearing a police uniform, took hold of her elbow and grabbed her around the waist, holding her tight as he helped her up. A dimple in his square chin, the man smiled, Dudley Do Right style.

"Thank you, officer. These steps are icy." Snow fell in swaths of white. Drawn into his eyes, almost hypnotized by this simple act of kindness, Julie sputtered, "I'll be fine. You wouldn't happen to have a tissue, would you?"

"Let me help you back inside. We'll get you cleaned up," he said, lifting her almost off her feet, holding her, tightly, around the waist.

This warm body against hers, she'd never been this physically close to any man except Kyle. She slipped again, but he didn't let her fall.

"These shoes have no tread at all. I wouldn't have worn them if I'd known we were in for freezing snow."

The policeman escorted her back inside and yelled to a fellow officer, "Get some salt on those steps, Bert. They're getting dangerous."

He took her to the officer's break room and told her to sit. There, he moistened a cloth and dabbed carefully at her knee, his hand steadying her leg, caressing her thigh. Julie sat perfectly still, completely submitting to his touch, taking wonder with his every move. It wasn't like Julie to accept help from a stranger. But she couldn't ever remember being touched like this.

After the policeman bandaged her knees, he sat next to her closely on the wooden bench. "You look like you could use a friend." He seemed genuinely concerned. "I saw you on the stairs before you fell. You looked so sad. It can't be all that bad. Can it?"

Julie pulled away from him and quickly stood up. "I'm fine now; I'll be all right. Thank you. I really have to go," she said. Such an array of feelings during the course of the day, sadness, abandonment, panic, amusement and now . . . what was this feeling? He was a stranger, what gave him the right to wake up this corner of her heart?

"I remember you. You came in last week. I hope everything's alright." He reached into his pocket and presented a card. "Call me if you ever need a cop. I'm always here." He shook her hand. "I'm Jack, be careful on those stairs."

CHAPTER 39

As she drove home in rush hour traffic, each swoosh of the windshield wipers clumped more snow on Julie's wiper blades. A snow sludge mix was now her view. Traffic moved slowly on the slick streets. At a red light, she rolled down her window and tried to lift the moving wiper blade and snap it back down, but she couldn't grab it before the light turned green. She finally pulled over and cleared the windshield with her bare hands.

Julie finally got home just before nightfall. Shaking off the snow inside the foyer she slipped off her coat and shoes. Then she took off her torn stockings, and scouting for some slippers she stepped into the kitchen in her bare feet. She was looking forward to changing into something big and bulky and warm.

But just as she rounded the corner, she saw a figure in the shadows. He was sitting at her dining table, sipping from a mug. She couldn't see his face.

"I thought you'd never get here, Juliet," a man's voice came from the shadows.

"Sam?" she asked, hoping it was. Sam was one of the few people who knew where to find the key to her house.

"No, but you can call me Sam if it makes you happy." The stranger slowly stood up. He had smudged his face with charcoal and was wearing tight-fitting black gloves.

"How did you get in my house?"

He came closer. A gleam of light bounced off a hunting knife in his hand.

Julie backed up to the wall and slid against it in the direction of the phone next to the stairs, her heart beating furiously.

"This is my favorite part. Go ahead. Pick up the phone. Try to call someone."

Julie picked up the phone. There was no dial tone. "Take whatever you want," Julie pleaded. "There's money in my purse, at least two hundred dollars." Julie gripped the phone in her hand like a weapon, hiding it behind her back

He came toward her, holding his hand out to her as if she would willingly take it.

Without even thinking, she bolted up the stairs just out of his reach, and flung a picture that was on the wall at him, her heart pounding. He chased her up the stairs. She tore family pictures off of the wall every step of the way, hurling them at him. Just as she reached the last stair step, he grabbed her ankle. She kicked him hard in the face. He fell backwards but just for an instant. Finally in her bedroom, she slammed the door shut and locked it.

He slammed his fist on the bedroom door. "I don't think I like you. You don't play nice."

"Who are you? Take what you want and leave!"

"You know what I want. Don't act like you don't. You were all over the news, broadcasting about your husband in jail. I bet I know how you like it, too."

She heard him jiggle something in the keyhole, probably what he had used to break into the house. She pushed a heavy dresser against the door, and backed away, suddenly remembering that she had a fire rescue ladder somewhere. But where?

"I bet you like to be tied up. I bet you like to be whipped. Don't you?" His voice was deep, taunting.

She pulled out the bottom dresser drawer, frantically looking for the ladder. It wasn't there. She heard the doorknob click and knew he'd unlocked the door. Julie flung every box inside her closet to the floor, dumping them upside down—still no ladder. She heard the dresser scrape the floor as the door inched open. He reached his arm through the gap in the door. It looked like he was leaning into the door, pushing it with his shoulder. She could see where his glove and sleeve had exposed his skin. A tattooed ring of skulls around his wrist seemed to be part of a bigger tattoo.

Julie opened the window; it was a long drop down from her second-story bedroom. The dresser scraped the floor as it moved. He was trying to wedge his body through. She took hold of her wedding picture, framed in heavy crystal and hit him hard in the face.

"You bitch! I'm going to cut your eyes out and make you eat them."

Ransacking every corner, ripping through every shoebox, she finally found the ladder. Frantic, she shook it out of the box, watching him all the while, and hooked it onto the open window's sill. She hoisted herself through the window, and climbed out faster than she should have, touching her bare feet to the flimsy ladder. Her foot slipped. The brick wall felt cold against her body. The ladder swung. Hanging onto the ledge by her fingers, she heard the dresser move again. Blindly, feeling for the cold metal bar with her toes, she regained her footing.

"They're going to find your body parts in every room of this house bitch," he said, his voice unwavering.

She slowly lowered herself, step by step, to the bottom of the ladder. Swaying in the wind, teetering on the last rung, she saw that it was five feet short from touching the ground. The wind blowing up her skirt, she let herself fall backward in the snow. She heard the dresser tumble and she saw him in the window, but just briefly. He had to be coming outside.

Her legs as bare as her feet, she fumbled to stand and ran to the road, every step more painful than the last. Crossing the road, taking glimpses back, she saw him. He was outside, crazy mad, stabbing at nothing below the ladder, kicking up snow where she had landed. Then he saw her. She knew he saw her. He was after her again.

It was dark now. She stumbled on the edge of the road, slipping on ice but caught herself before she fell. She crossed the ditch and slid again, falling down this time. She could still see him. He hadn't crossed the road yet. A string of cars had stopped him. She pulled herself up, her eyes on Debra's house. The telephone wires, the catalpa tree, the mailbox, crystallized in frozen drips. Julie made her way through Debra's white lawn, up Debra's quarry-stone steps, and barged through the door, shaking uncontrollably. "He . . . he's after me," she yelled, locking the door.

"Who's after you?"

"He's outside. He broke into my house."

"Okay, calm heads. Lock up the garage. You do that and I'll get the rifle." Debra headed upstairs. "Then we'll call the sheriff."

Julie hurriedly locked the door between the garage and the utility room. She locked the kitchen door, too. The card was still in her pocket the officer had given her. She dialed the number frantically.

"Precinct 46. How can I direct your call?" a dispatcher answered.

"A man broke into my house. He's got a knife. Please. Send

someone now. Officer Jack Wilson gave me this number."

"What is your address?"

"Hold on." Julie sifted through Debra's mail. "57795 Adams Road."

"Are you in the house now?"

"I'm at a neighbor's house, Debra Hamilton. He's outside. I know he is."

"We'll send our first available officer," the woman answered, in what seemed like a canned line. Then she hung up. Julie knew it would be a long time before anyone would come. It could be hours before a cop would show up—unless a patrol car happened to be near the county line.

Debra came back with her rifle. "I don't have any more bullets. Did you close up the garage?"

"I locked the kitchen door and that other door."

"No . . . they're broken." Debra blazed through the kitchen and to the garage. Julie followed her as far as the kitchen, she couldn't feel her feet anymore. Greg's loafers were by the door. She stepped into them and clomped out to the garage where the garage door was still wide open. Debra had hit the garage door button on the wall and the oversized door had started its slow decent.

"Come on! Come on!" Debra pleaded, clutching the barrel of her rifle.

In the dark, they could see the figure of a man. He was coming around the corner towards the semi-open garage door, from the direction of the front porch like he had already been there, like he might have tried to open that door first. The oversized garage door seemed to move in slow motion.

"Come on, come on!"

Julie scavenged Greg's workbench where she found a spray can of hornet killer, and took her place next to Debra. The garage door needed four more feet in order to close. They saw him fall on the ice— a short reprieve. He got right up.

"Come on! Close!" Debra pretended to cock the rifle, squatted down and aimed, trying to scare him. But he didn't seem to care.

The door closed another foot . . . three more feet to go. There he was right at the door, now in a running stoop to get under it. But the door suddenly slammed shut. He pounded on it, his fist shaking the whole thing.

The garage door had never done that before, just drop with three feet left. Julie could see that Debra was shaking. "I think we should blockade the doors inside. He's got some sort of tool that he used to pick my lock." They went back inside with their makeshift artillery. Debra blocked the kitchen door by hooking the back of a tilted chair under the doorknob. Julie blocked the front door the same way; she was so cold that her teeth were chattering.

"I think that'll hold. You need some dry clothes. Come on upstairs."

"I can't feel my feet anymore. I could use some socks, maybe some sweat pants and a spare robe?" Julie followed Debra up to her bedroom. "Where's Greg? I saw his truck outside," Julie asked, her body shaking.

"He left with his brother. I don't think he'll be home for a while." Debra rummaged through the closet and handed her a robe. "Was there anything familiar about the man who broke in?"

"No, I've never seen him before. Did you get a look at him?"

"It was too dark. I couldn't see his face."

"He said he saw me on the news." Julie tied the robe and brushed a wet curl away from her eyes.

"Do you think he's still out there?"

"I know he is. He's got to be on drugs or something."

Debra pulled back the window curtain and they peered outside, trying to see through the snowstorm against the darkness.

A man's face looked right back at her. He bashed the window with a hammer.

Both of them screamed. Both of them grabbed each other.

"He's got one of Greg's ladders!" Debra said.

"Help me," Julie said, leaning against one of Debra's heavy dressers. The two of them pushed it against the window. "How long do you think before he can get through one of the windows?"

"I . . . I don't know. He'd have to break through four panes of glass, the wood in between, a screen, plastic . . . Those windows have been painted shut a million times over." Debra said, leaving the bedroom with a handful of clothes. "Did the police say how long it would take to get here?" She closed the bedroom door tightly, and the two of them went downstairs.

"You forget. This isn't the city. We'll be lucky if they get here at all. What are our chances of getting to the car?" Julie asked at the bottom of the steps, pulling on a pair of sweat pants.

"Not good," Debra said, "my car's in the driveway. Greg has an order of supplies where my car usually is."

Julie put on a pair of thick socks. They heard more breaking glass from upstairs. Then they heard Greg's ladder clanging against the house outside.

"Did you hear that?" Debra said quietly. "It sounded like the ladder fell."

The wind outside rustled through the branches, playing its tune through the windows. They sat together, Debra with the rifle, Julie with the hornet spray, listening, and waiting, each of them afraid to speak. A train whistled, long and deliberate, from the distance. Five minutes went by, ten minutes, fifteen. The house grew eerily quiet.

"Did you see how he kept coming?" Debra whispered. "I was aiming right at him."

Julie whispered, "Did you see that? Something through the window?" Neither one of them moved. A sudden pounding came from the front door. They got up together. But neither of them could see who it was through the windows. Whoever it was, pounded again.

"Who's there?" Debra yelled. They heard a man's voice saying something through the door but couldn't make it out. His voice seemed to have an official tone.

Debra turned the doorknob before Julie could stop her.

CHAPTER 40

Two officers stood where a surge of wind burst the door open. Snow dusted the two women, the hornet spray and the rifle. Julie with Greg's slippers and Greg's checkered housecoat; and Debra with her innocent little girl face, her unloaded twenty-two. The snow reflected the patrol car's red and blue flashing lights against the night.

"Jack? . . . Officer Wilson?" Julie said, surprised, relieved, and puzzled by him being the one who responded.

Debra leaned into Julie. "You know him?" she whispered.

"Just barely," Julie whispered back, glancing briefly at Jack. "He gave me his card earlier today."

"There was a report of a prowler at this address," Jack said, letting the storm door close behind him.

"He broke in . . . not here . . . across the street." Julie stuttered. Relief hadn't hit, not yet, only the realization of what had just happened. Shaking as though she were freezing, Julie fought with her words to make coherent sentences. Suddenly very still, Julie looked as though every expression had been wiped from her face, every thought, every emotion.

Debra stepped in. "The man was trying to kill her. She got away by climbing out of her bedroom window about thirty minutes ago. He chased her all the way here."

Julie took a breath, lifted her chin, and composed herself. Even though her voice was shaking, she could answer questions in detail now. She described the hunting knife, the eerie tattoos. Jack's partner called for backup while Julie talked; then he searched the premises.

"Have you ever seen this man before?" Jack asked.

"No. Never."

"Have you?" He turned to Debra.

"I don't think so. I couldn't get a good look at him in the dark. But there was something familiar about him. I just can't say for sure what it was."

Jack jotted down some notes. "Let's get a look at your house . . . . Mrs. Zumminger?"

"It's Zourenger, just call me Julie." Julie was just about to leave with him when she turned to Debra. "Deb, is it okay if I come back and spend the night? I would go over to Marie's but I don't want any of this to upset her."

"You can stay as long as you like. I'll make up a place for you to sleep."

Still wearing the housecoat and slippers, Julie went with Jack to his car where he invited her to sit up front. Scooting into the passenger seat, him holding the door for her, she watched his every movement as he climbed into the driver's side. Oddly enough, it felt reminiscent of a date. What was wrong with her that she was interpreting ordinary gestures to be some sort of flirting? He was just doing his job.

He looked down at Julie's knees where one of them was bleeding through her sweat pants. "You're not having a good day, are you?"

She said the first thing that popped into her head, "I haven't had a good day in such a long time that I think they're avoiding me."

When they got to Julie's house and got out of the car, she opened the useless aluminum frame that was once the storm door. The other door was unlocked and gaped open.

"I've never seen anything quite like this. Not only did he break

235

the glass but he picked out every last piece," Jack said, sliding his foot in the snow, seemingly looking for broken glass. Julie stepped inside.

"That was already broken—my husband. I cleaned up the glass right afterwards."

"You're going to have to buy a new doorknob." Jack kept trying to lock the door but it wouldn't work. "I would get some dead-bolts, too. Show me where you saw him first."

Julie led him inside the foyer. "He was in the dining room. I don't know how long he'd been there." She walked him through the kitchen to the dining room. "He was sitting at that table. I tried to use the phone by the stairs but he must have cut the phone line."

"Is that the mug he was holding?"

"Yes."

"This should have a set of prints if he wasn't wearing gloves."

"He was wearing gloves, but I saw a tattoo on his wrist, creepy skulls all the way around. I couldn't tell for sure, but I think his whole arm must have been tattooed."

Jack was writing in his notebook.

"You probably want me to go down at the station with a full description. Can I do that tomorrow?"

"That won't be necessary. I'm writing it down. Was there anything else about him?"

"I can't tell you what he looked like. He blackened his face with something. It looked like it could have been charcoal. Will you excuse me for a minute? The window upstairs is open," Julie said, headed toward the stairs

"I'll go with you."

He followed Julie closely up the stairs. When they got to the top of the stairs her bedroom door was open just enough to squeeze through, around the toppled dresser. Julie made her way inside and went directly to the window. She pulled in the flimsy ladder and closed the window, keeping her back to him.

"He made quite a mess up here," Jack said.

"No. I did that when I was looking for this ladder," She said. All at once all the chain of events that lead to this flashed through her mind. From that first letter to Kyle sitting in jail for something he may not have done. Anguish enveloped her, deep down to the pit of her stomach. Tears followed, involuntary as a beating heart.

"Julie?"

"Yes," she answered, her face toward the window, wiping her eyes on her sleeve.

"Is this the crystal picture frame you said you hit him with? I'm going to take this with me to check for traces of blood."

"Go ahead. Take anything that will give you clues." She pulled her hair to one side, trying to keep her face hidden, staring at a loose board in the floor. Completely aware of his stillness across the room, she felt his eyes on her, his long gaze penetrating the back of her neck. Frozen to that very spot, she was grateful that she met Jack, grateful for feeling safe with him which was surprising in itself.

"I'll just be downstairs," he said, leaving the room.

Julie sat down on her bed as though she were shackled to it—the crying itself her jailer.

CHAPTER 41

Two weeks earlier . . . .

Bruce had managed to get out of work an hour early. Northbound, he was sitting in traffic at a red light on Pearl Road at the Fulton Bridge intersection. He heard tires screeching and horns blowing that seemed to be coming from the new Kroger's grocery store. It must have been opening day for the store. There were banners on every corner and more traffic today than usual. The wind blew the last of the falling leaves across the road and onto the curb, and sifted snow over his rusted Ford Mercury.

He was on his way home from where he worked rotating shifts at Cambridge Nut & Bolt on weekdays. He substituted as a game warden on weekends when no one else wanted to, which was fine with him. No one would get in his way. His wife worked nights at The Crimson Bar. Between the two of them, they made just enough to pay the bills, and once in a while, to buy cocaine. One way or the other, there were only two hours in the day when their paths would cross. Maybe today, because he was coming home early, maybe today he would find out who she was cheating with.

Waiting for a break in the oncoming traffic for his chance to make a right turn on red, he saw cars starting to slow down which meant that the light was going to change. A westbound Pontiac Bonneville sped up—it must have just made the green light. A white cargo van sped up—it must have just made the yellow light. The light turned green in Bruce's lane. He accelerated, as did the cars behind him.

But a Chevy Cavalier was coming fast, definitely against the red light. Bruce slammed on his brakes. The driver behind him slammed on his brakes and the driver after that. A procession of cars hit— bumpers, fenders, bumpers, fenders. All except his car. The Cavalier careened through the intersection against the light. A car across the street swerved off the road and hit a mailbox. Bruce accelerated again, watching the chaos he was leaving behind from his rear view mirror. He couldn't see the westbound maniacs anymore because he was going north.

The midday traffic hadn't kept him from getting home early. Bruce parked on the road in front of his cluster home and saw that his wife, Dee, was still home. Her Malibu was in the driveway. The garage door was open. He went inside the garage, opened his tool chest, and hid the hunting knife that he'd covered up in his coat. Just then he heard the garage phone ring, and quietly picked it up. He heard Dee say 'Hello'.

He heard a man's voice say, "I need to see you tonight. Julie's really done it this time. She's going around teasing perfect strangers in the grocery store now. She's just asking for trouble, flaunting herself in public like she's a hooker or something. Some poor bastard was going to take her up on it this time. She even conned my neighbor into sneaking over to this guy's house and getting his address, for crying out loud. She doesn't know what she's doing. She's going to get herself raped. I lost it this time," the voice on the other end of the phone said.

"How can you stand it?" Dee answered.

Bruce clenched his teeth, holding the receiver away so no one could hear how heavily he was breathing. He'd known for days that his wife had been cheating on him. Seething in revenge, Bruce had kept it to himself. All he could think of was killing the bastard who was screwing his wife. Hell-bent on finding out whose voice it was, Bruce knew that if he listened long enough, he was bound to hear something useful—a name, a place. Even a street would be enough for him to see where she might have been parking her car.

"She's got me so upset I can't think straight. It turns out that the man who was following her lives right down the road from us in Brentwood Pines on Jaycox. I even went over there."

"How did you know which house was his?" Dee asked.

"Julie had it written down. It was a blue house, the only one on the whole street. I knocked on his door, and it's a good thing he didn't answer it. I was so mad I could have beat him senseless."

"For god's sake! I can't believe you went to his house. He could have had you arrested."

"Meet me tonight. I've got to see you," Kyle said. "The place we always go."

"Wait. Kyle. I've got a lot to tell you. I'm leaving Bruce today before he comes home. My car is all packed. I'm moving in with my mother. Once I'm out of here, you can tell Julie about us. We can finally be together."

Bruce couldn't take it anymore. He hung up the phone. He barged inside. "Where are you?" he yelled, slamming the door. Searching the kitchen, the bathroom, throwing everything within his reach along the way, he found her in the bedroom. He pulled the quilt off the bed and then the sheets, throwing them to the floor. "Do you think I'm stupid?" The mattress was next; he threw it against the wall, hoisting up the end of it. The diary was laying on the box springs. He threw it at her. "You whoring piece of shit," he yelled. "You want to leave? Then get the hell out." He twisted her arm, dragging her. She screamed, clamoring to get away. His arms imprisoned her as she tried to kick him. He jerked her fast and slapped her hard. Finally dragging her out to her Malibu parked in the driveway. "What did you think? I wouldn't know?"

Dee whimpered, holding her arm as if it were broken, sprawled out on the cement, up against the car. The neighbor next door stopped washing his car and turned off the water. He stepped up to the property border without saying a word, acting like he would jump in to defend her.

"Are you fucking her, too?" Bruce yelled to the neighbor. "This narcissist ungrateful bitch?"

The neighbor took a step back. "I don't want no trouble Bruce. Don't make me call the cops."

Bruce's eyes on Dee, he backed away. "Don't ever come back here," he said, "or I'll . . . ." He stopped himself from saying more.

Dee pulled herself up. She opened her car door, her bracelets jangling. Watching him all along, she picked up a small cylinder of pepper spray from inside the driver's door. "You broke the deal," she said. "You said you'd have your own band by now. You kicked Ken out of the group. He was your best drummer."

"Shut up."

"Then you kicked Adam out. You just couldn't stand to have someone better at the guitar than you." She got inside her car. "You should have known this was going to happen. You said I was going to sing. You broke the deal."

"I said shut up. Leave already. I can't stand to look at you," Bruce said, his voice monotone. Dee backed the car out of the driveway and drove away.

Bruce stormed back to the bedroom and threw her entire collection of ceramic rabbits at the bedroom mirror, cursing, swearing he was going to kill her. He pulled out the drawers, threw them against the walls, and ripped apart the clothes she'd left behind. He flipped the mattress again landing it halfway on the floor and halfway on the box springs. There he sat with his face in his hands and cried. After a while he wiped his nose in the palm of his hand and on a pillow, and looked around the room at what he'd done. But as he started to leave the room, he saw the diary still on the floor, and picked it up. Flipping through the pages, he saw Kyle's name over and over again, but he couldn't see a last name anywhere. He flipped a page and saw a name. "Julie," he said the name out loud. Then something else in the diary caught his eye.

'. . . Brentwood Pines, down the road from Kyle.'

He stared at the words, 'Brentwood Pines.' It was that place, that development on Adams Road, an hour's drive. He remembered what he'd heard when he was listening to Dee on the phone. "Jaycox," he said out loud. "Blue house."

Bruce went to the garage and sharpened his hunting knife. He scavenged the drawers for a nail file.

"I'll fix him. I'll fix him good."

CHAPTER 42

Debra didn't want to be alone that night, not after that man had tried to break in. But Greg was going to leave anyway. The Co-Stan Homeowners Association was considering his bid to remodel their recreational center, and they only met once a month, which happened to be tonight. Greg had already installed deadbolt locks on the kitchen door and on the front door. And he had boarded up the broken windows upstairs.

Julie wouldn't be company either, seeing as Greg had installed deadbolt locks at her house, too. She would be home, cleaning up, and waiting for the telephone company to reconnect her telephone wires.

Putting dinner on the table, Debra tried to console herself by repeating what she had told Julie; someone would have to break through four panes of glass, the wood in between, a screen, and plastic in order to get in.

Greg seemed to be in a playful mood, whirling a kitchen towel, cowboy-like. Debra had bent down, her hands in oven mitts, gripping a hot tray. "That was nice of you to install new locks for Julie." She took a tray of baked chicken out of the oven.

He snapped the towel on her fanny.

"Stop," she said, standing straight up, shooting him a dirty look.

"Can I do this?" He tweaked her nose.

Debra let the tray drop on the stovetop, too late to smack his hand. "I hate it when you do that," she said, her voice stern, her expression harsh. "Why do you do that?"

"Cause you're so cute." He scooped her up in a bear hug, kissing her nose. Her hands were pinned at her sides.

"Let go!" she yelled, digging her fingers into the part of his arm she could reach, overwhelmed by anger, beyond aggravation.

Greg let go, looking stunned. "Why did you do that? That hurt." He rubbed his arm. "I was just playing with you. Look what you did."

She took a gander at his arm, at the purplish fingernail marks she'd made. She wouldn't feel bad. At least, she wouldn't let on that she did. "Wow, so this is what happens when you stop biting your nails," she said, saccharin sweet. "I've never had fingernails before. Let's see if I can do that again."

Greg whirled the towel.

"Don't."

"I have to leave pretty soon. You're not worried about me being gone, are you? I shouldn't be long."

How could she answer that and be convincing? He needed this job. They needed this job. She said, "No."

"Why don't you come with me?" He draped the towel over her shoulder.

"I'll be fine . . . really. I need to vacuum anyway," she said, letting him pick at a chicken breast with his fingers. "I finally got brave enough to bring the vacuum cleaner inside and clean it out. I'm telling you though, if one ant had crawled out of that bag . . . ."

Debra tuned the radio to station, 104.5. Tina Turner's *Private Dancer* was playing. One of her favorite songs to clean by. Singing along, caught up in the rhythm, she sprayed Lemon Pledge on the coffee table, soaking up enough in a rag to dust the end tables, too.

She moved on to the bookcase, and she heard the water pump

come on in the basement. This particular noise had taken some time to get used to. Likened to that of a tractor engine, it strained passed the point of humming. It was hard to say how old it was, but the Griswold Pump Company had stopped making this model in 1959. The pump only turned on when someone was using water, but because of a slow leak, it would turn on in short intervals. She listened for it to shut off like it usually did.

Close to the basement stairs, plugging in the vacuum cleaner, she heard the hot water heater come on, too. Not thinking about it, she vacuumed, watching the Hoover make patterns in the area rug. She got as far as the dining room chairs and turned off the vacuum to move the chairs out of the way. The water pump and the hot water heater should have turned off by now, but she could still hear them.

She turned off the radio and stood still, listening, trying to figure out what to do, and ended up by the basement door. At the top of the basement stairs in the opened doorway, she looked down into the darkness to where the light bulb's pull-chain couldn't be seen— thinking all along that a light switch on top of the stairs would have been nice.

Greg had showed her how to reset the pump so the motor wouldn't burn up. Why did this have to happen now? Going into the basement was bad enough during the day. She'd never gone there at night. Never enter the dungeon after dark . . . that was her crimson rule. The basement door creaked its familiar squawk as she opened it. Steam rose from the bowels of the basement—an odd occurrence. She stepped down into the darkness, commanding herself . . . breathe in . . . breathe out . . . breathe in . . . . Feeling each step beneath her foot in the dark, she knew not to touch the quarry-stone walls. At the bottom of the stairs, in the dark, she pulled the chain to turn on the light. Something was hissing. Now she could see it, an eruption, a fountain. A hole in the hot water tank.

Six feet high and three feet wide, the tank hummed, nonstop, burning oil. Fuel oil was four hundred dollars every delivery. She'd have to cut off the water to conserve fuel oil, and to conserve water from their shallow well. Something smelled like burnt rubber, probably the pump's motor. Without knowing which valve, she turned the one on the bottom of the hot water tank. Cold water splashed on her feet. She let out a yelp. The pump churned louder. She undid the turn. There were four valves and knobs, and any one of them might turn off the pilot light, or increase the pressure, or heaven only knows what. She decided to leave them alone, that the main water source would be the best way to go. Greg had showed her where that was, a valve under the steps along the wall, all by itself.

Her feet wet, her socks sloshing in her shoes amid the roaring motors, she crept under the darkened staircase, a place where webs were barely visible. She felt them brush against her face and arms, clinging, crawling, newly hatched spiders, hundreds of them. She screamed, smacking them out of her hair, off her face, running in place, running upstairs; she scrambled for a towel; and swiped them off. Back in the dungeon she flicked the towel across the webs while a continuous stream of water flowed across the basement floor to the natural drain.

Debra took a firm hold on the main water valve and tried to turn it, even just a little. It wouldn't budge. She squatted down, trying with everything that she had. She even tried to turn it the other way. It still wouldn't move. Frustration turned to anger, her face burning, anger turned to rage.

"You stupid son of a bitch" She screamed, she stomped her foot, punched the air, and took hold of it again. "Turn!" she yelled down on her knees, still trying to force it. "I hate this. I hate this damn . . ." She belted out a soul-cleansing gut-wrenching scream.

Standing there, all screamed out, she tried to think of someone to call. By the time Greg would get home, the motor would have burned up. The fuel oil would have diminished. And the shallow well would have been pumped dry. Maybe Julie would know what to do.

It hadn't been long when Julie showed up with a vice grip and a hammer.

"I'm curious to see how you're going to do this," Debra said, guiding her toward the basement. Opening the basement door, the hinges creaked their usual anti-song.

Julie nudged Debra on the way down the steps amid the misty fog, amid that earthworm and burnt rubber smell. "You should spray WD-40 on those hinges."

"I'll try anything that'll stop that noise."

"This is so creepy," Julie said, edging past the web-meshed quarry-stone walls. When they reached the bottom, Debra circled behind the steps, and flicked the towel again where the webs had been, shining a flashlight to see the rest. "I haven't cleaned down here in a while, and hardly ever behind these steps. The valve is right there."

Julie stooped behind the steps into a bog-like haze, and wedged the vice grip on the valve and hit it with the hammer. The valve snapped free and turned off the water. Debra shined the flashlight on the new circuit breaker box—there were twenty-four switches where fuses had been. "Which one do you think it is?" She switched the first one. The light went out. The pump was still running. "Not that one." She switched it back.

"Let me see." Julie mouthed numbers, counting down from the top with her finger. "This one." She flicked a switch. Nothing happened. She flicked it back. "Let's try this one." She flicked another switch and the pump shut off. Then the hot water heater shut off by itself.

The sound of trickling water, pooling in the low places of the uneven floor, formulated its own kind of quiet.

"I'll help you sweep the water to the drain. Do you have an extra broom?"

"Broom? Oh . . . yeah, broom . . . . No, Julie, you don't have to do that."

"Get the broom. I'm not leaving you down here alone."

Debra handed over her broom and took the mop that she'd brought down earlier. Encompassed by wet quarry-stone walls, a dripping ceiling, the steam whirled with every movement.

"I wouldn't want to do my laundry down here. Why don't you tell Greg to bring your washer and dryer upstairs?"

"The only other place to put them is the utility room. But it's not heated. The water lines will freeze out there."

"Oh. I didn't tell you, Lieutenant Barger called today."

"What did he say?"

"The handwriting matched. The man in the white van did write those letters. But he wasn't married like he said he was. He didn't even have kids. He made it all up. Probably so I would think he was harmless."

"Do you think he lied about being in the lounge, too? Did 'he' follow us to the car that night?"

"I wasn't sure before because the lounge was so dark, and the parking lot lights made his face all shadowy. But now that I've had time to think about it, I'm pretty sure it was the same man. All those expensive cars in the parking lot, I remember a white van that looked out of place."

"I remember it, too. But I thought it was there for deliveries." Debra wrung the mop out over the washing machine.

"The restaurant doesn't make deliveries. I know. I worked there. It was 'his'. But he made such an ass out of himself that night. I think he was too humiliated to admit he was there. That's when the letters got raunchy. I don't know why I didn't put it together."

Debra had only been half listening. "I'm so glad you're here."

"I don't mind coming over. You should have called me sooner." Julie continued, "Do you know what else Barger said? I thought I'd ask him if he had any leads on the break-in at my house while I had him on the phone. And get this, he hasn't even heard about it. I'm starting to wonder what kind of a station they're running down there." Julie stopped for a moment, scanning the haunted-like aura. The ceiling dripped a fat drop of water in Julie's hair. "I don't know how you can stand it down here," she said, swiping drips off the ceiling where a frost-covered window suddenly drew her attention. "Deb . . . come here," she said, looking up at that window. "What do you make of that?"

A shiver took hold of Debra as she looked in the window; a rose in full bloom pressed against the glass from the outside next to an overturned tiny leaf. The pair must have taken refuge in the warmth of the glass, apart from its dormant bush. Debra felt herself suddenly getting light-headed. The quarry-stone walls seemed to crowd in around the window, around the rose. The pull-chain light bulb bounced off the mist and glistened off Julie's pendant.

Her hand to her mouth, her face completely white, Debra turned toward the stairs. "I'm not feeling so good." She ran up the stairs, holding her mouth. Julie was right behind her. The door was already open when they made it to the top. Debra stepped through the doorway first and then Julie. The light bulb in the corridor flickered off.

A man was standing there perfectly still, his black silhouette etched in the light.

The smell of sweet honey—Debra fainted on the spot. Unblinking, her body fell as though time and space moved in slow motion. Here she laid as if she were paralyzed. Someone was screaming, maybe Julie.

'Is this it?' Debra thought to herself. 'Is this how it was for her mother? Seeing things that aren't really there, hearing screams that no one screamed.' She saw the shadow of a man back away slowly.

Julie's glance held Debra's, but only for a moment. When Debra looked again, the man had disappeared somehow into the light behind him. Lying in a heap on the floor, Debra couldn't speak. She couldn't move. How could she have fainted and still be conscious?

"We have to go, we have to go," Julie spit out the words whispering all along, clumsily lifting Debra by the shoulders. "Come on, come on, we have to get out of here." Julie was dragging her inches at a time.

"Did you see that?" Debra whispered back. "Did you see him, too?"

"Try to stand."

Their hushed whispers seemed to shout through the stillness. Debra stood, woozy, perplexed about how she'd gone down. They were halfway through the corridor. "Where is he?" she asked, watching for him, hanging onto Julie, who was rushing her, trying to make her move faster.

They were in the living room now, the central room, the biggest room in the house where the front door and a window overlooked the porch, where the dining room doorway shared a wall with the corridor they'd just come from, where the bathroom, stairway, and a door to the other part of the house were. The arched doorway to the kitchen to their left was the farthest room.

"We have to take your car. My purse is upstairs," Debra said quietly, struggling to get strength in her legs, still slowing them down.

"My coat's on a kitchen chair. My keys are in the pocket."

They were halfway through the living room. A door slammed from upstairs.

"Almost there," Julie said, headed toward the kitchen, tightening her hold on Debra.

Inside the kitchen, Debra took a labored step, a numbing sensation behind her eyes, throwing her off balance, confusing her feet. She tripped, and when she tried to catch herself from falling, she took Julie down. They both fell into the table and chairs. Debra wrenched her back—her chin hit a chair. Julie hit her head against the corner of the table. The two scrambled to their feet. Debra grabbed Julie's coat from an overturned chair, and they hurried outside as fast as they could limp. Julie was holding her head, staggering, fishing through her coat pocket for the keys.

"I'll drive," Debra said. "You don't look so good."

"Do you think you can? You don't look so good either."

"I'll be fine."

Julie handed over her keys and took the passenger's seat.

Debra got in, finally feeling her feet. She turned the key, slipped the gear in reverse, and stepped on the pedal. At the end of the driveway, they watched the old house for signs of life. He was there in the upstairs window, his black silhouette. Julie squeezed the juice out of Debra's hand.

Back light drew the outline of a faceless man. A round torso. A short crew cut.

"That's not the man from last night," Debra said, sure of it.

"I've still got Jack's card. I'll call him."

"Did you lock the dead bolt at your house?"

". . . I thought I was coming right back."

"There's a phone booth at the Sunoco station. I'll call the sheriff from there. We'll wait in the car until someone comes."

Twenty minutes later Jack and another officer arrived at the parking lot where the two women had been waiting. Jack approached the car, shining a flashlight in Debra's face. She rolled down the window.

"Debra Hamilton?" He leaned in.

"Yes," she answered, thrown off because Jack didn't seem to recognize her.

"I have a report here that says you reported an intruder."

Julie scooted into Debra, to say her piece. "Someone's in the house. We barely got out."

"Oh hi, Julie. I didn't see you there." He spoke differently,

252

happily, a silly wink in his eye. Debra didn't like it. She didn't like him, this Jack person, a policeman, so friendly to Julie, winking, flirting. What was he thinking?

"Officer . . ." Debra said, an edge of disdain in her voice.

"We checked the outer premises of your house and found nothing suspicious. The house is locked. Do you have a key? We'll see whose inside."

"It can't be locked. I didn't have time because of everything going on. We literally ran out of the house and left." Debra told him.

"He must have locked himself inside when he saw our patrol car. Give me the key." Jack commanded.

She handed it over. "This is for the deadbolt. It's the only lock that works." She watched him walk from her car to his, him turning around and eyeing Julie with that goofy look of his. There was something about him that Debra didn't trust. "It doesn't make sense. You need that key to lock it and unlock it." Debra said to Julie.

"It's been at least an hour. Let's hope whoever it was is gone."

Debra drove behind the cop car, following him to her house. Silence overtook them—for Debra, deliberate. She knew that Jack wouldn't find anyone. She and Julie had been in the basement . . . water everywhere . . . motors running . . . where Ed had died— electrocuted to death. Jack wasn't going to find anyone. Deep down inside something whispered, It had to be Ed.

Greg would have to believe her now.

CHAPTER 43

The Homeowner Association said that it was between Greg and another contractor; that they would let him know. He left the meeting, worried that he might not get the job. Greg wouldn't lower his price. Building materials had gone up because of Hurricane Diana, which hit the east coast. Resources were shifting to North and South Carolina, raising prices all around, grounding the nation's recession. The other contractor, some fly-by-night scab, bid so low that he could have flipped burgers and made the same amount.

Driving a long stretch down Route 82, he heard something thumping under his truck. But his mind was still on the job that he might or might not get. He wasn't going to lower his price for the sake of getting the job. He wasn't in this just to break even. He felt his ears getting hot, anger brewing. Hurricane season wasn't over yet. What if materials went up again? He would end up paying for the privilege to work. He thought about work that Mr. Brubom wanted him to do, dangerous work. It paid well. A high, steep, roofing job with a twelve/twelve pitch, a roof covered in moss, nestled in trees. Three layers of shingles had to come off. It needed new wood underneath, and a chimney rebuilt. Greg had used the last of his cash to pay for fixing his six-year old truck, a 1978 GMC Sierra. If he didn't get the Homeowner's job, he would have to call Mr. Brubom.

The thumping was getting louder.

Greg slowed down. The thumping slowed down. He sped up. The thumping sped up. He felt his veins pulsing. He'd spent six hundred and forty-two dollars on new brakes and rotors, and whatever else the mechanic had said it needed.

The thumping stopped. The truck lurched and stopped. When he gave it the gas, the engine revved, but the truck wouldn't move. He had chosen that mechanic because he was a friend of his brother's. Greg got outside and looked under the truck. The drive shaft was lying on the ground.

"Shit! Shit! Shit!" He kicked the tires with every 'shit', and slammed the truck door. "For crying out loud!" He kicked that, too. And kicking the gravel every other step, he started walking down a lonely road, lined with pasture fencing.

The stiff, leather, work boots he had on hadn't been broken in, even if they had been, they weren't meant for walking. He hadn't walked far when blisters stung the back of his heels. After seven miles, they hurt so bad that he could hardly walk. The final stretch down his driveway, he checked his pocket for his keys. Then he realized that he must have left them in the truck. He went up to the garage's side-door and looked inside the window. The garage was dark but he could see the car. The door was locked. Debra would never hear him knocking from out here. He went to the front door, which was locked, too, and knocked loudly. "Deb," he yelled. "Deb, it's me. Open the door." This was taking too long. He took a credit card from his wallet and slid it down the doorway frame, trying to catch the lock. That didn't work. He went to the garage's side door and tried it again. A police cruiser sped up the driveway, red and blue lights, lighting the night.

An officer jumped out of the cruiser. "Police officer, put your hands in the air!" he shouted charging toward Greg. Another officer jumped out.

"I live here." Greg casually walked towards him, showing him his hands, still holding his credit card.

The officer, still on the move, drew his gun. "Hands in the air!"

Greg threw his hands over his head. "You're making a mistake. I live here!" he yelled.

The officer tackled him and shoved him hard, to the ground. Greg tried to explain.

"Shut up." He stomped his boot in Greg's back, twisted his arm, and handcuffed him.

"Damn it! I live here." Greg yelled, flattened out on his stomach, face in the snow. "Listen to me."

The officer kneed Greg's back, searching him like a common thief. The wind had taken Greg's baseball cap and parked it on Julie's car that was idling at the end of the driveway.

Julie and Debra had followed the police car to Debra's house, and were watching the whole thing from inside the car when Jack's partner came up to them.

"This guy says he lives here. Maybe you should take a look."

Debra got out of the car. She saw Greg's baseball cap. "Greg?"

"Quit stalling, Deb! Tell him I live here!"

"Officer, that's my husband."

Jack let him go.

"What the hell do you think you're doing?" Greg yelled at Jack, his muscular hands clenched into fists. Every breath steaming in the cold night, his clothes wet with snow and mud, his muscles tensed. "Is this how you help someone who's locked out of their house?"

"Your wife reported an intruder." Jack unlocked the handcuffs. "Just doing my job, sir"

Greg clenched his jaw, not saying another word, glaring at Jack.

"I'll be going now. You folks have a good evening." He handed back Debra's keys, smacking them into her hand, looking amused, and got in his car. Debra hated Jack just then. He shouldn't have treated Greg like that. Any fool could have seen that Greg was being cooperative.

Debra watched Julie back out of the driveway. The police car backed out, too. She watched it follow Julie, hating Jack even more. 'What did he think he was doing?'

Greg and Debra went inside without saying a word. The only sound was Greg slamming the door.

"What happened to your truck?" Debra asked softly.

"It broke down," he said without raising his voice, carefully taking off his boots.

"Don't you want to know what happened?"

"I already know. You reported an intruder." His face was an indescribable shade of red. His muscles were bulging with tension. "I don't want to talk about it . . . not right now. I need some time to settle down. Okay?" He took off his socks. Blisters were broken and bleeding.

She swallowed, her throat dry, her ears ringing. When did she become afraid of him? She froze where she stood by the refrigerator, afraid to move, fixing her gaze on a chipped bud vase where the chip had been turned to the wall. She could picture Greg hauling off and hitting her—like her stepfather had, like her mother had. She had to be perfectly still.

He must have seen it in her eyes. "Aren't I allowed to ever get mad? Nobody's happy all the time," he said in a calm pretense.

Still water pooled in her green eyes—fixed on the bud vase.

Greg adjusted his baseball cap. "I'm not mad at you. You didn't do anything wrong. Why are you like this?"

She blinked and the water wasn't still anymore. It streamed down her cheek. She didn't move.

"Come here." He drew her into his arms and held her there. She didn't want to cry and she tried not to. She was scared and tired and just wanted him to hold her. To love her . . . to never get mad. She knew how to cry without making a sound, but she couldn't do it without trembling.

"It's okay," he said, holding her tight, stroking her hair. "Don't worry so much."

"Can I stay here just a little while?" She lifted her head to look up at him, at his face in need of a shave. Her eyes red and wet with tears.

He kissed her nose, "You can stay here as long as you want," and drew her close again, and held her. "Everything will be alright . . ."

CHAPTER 44

When Julie went home, Jack and his partner checked the premises there, and because she hadn't bolted the door, Jack wanted to check inside. She let them in, avoiding glances, keeping her words to a minimum. She didn't like what Jack had done to Greg, and she didn't want to be in the same room with him. Hiding out in the kitchen, she opened a bottle of wine. And leaning against the kitchen sink, she poured it into the first thing she could find, a tin measuring cup. It felt warm on her throat, warm all the way down.

"There's nothing here to indicate an intruder." Jack's voice from behind startled her. She coughed down a gulp.

"Thank you for coming over," she said, corking the bottle, her back to him. He approached the sink where she was. He was standing so close behind her that she sensed him smelling her hair. She turned around. Wanting to say, 'leave', wanting to say 'stay'. Face to face with him, a sudden rush of embarrassment rose up to her temples. She hoped he hadn't caught her, impulsively, breathing him in. The scent, his scent, was like a drug, a euphoric, dream-like nuance. 'What was so sensual about this hardened man? What the hell's wrong with me?' She curled around and led him to the door, telling herself, 'He's just a man, like any other man.'

"I'm officially off duty in about five minutes. I don't mind sticking around for a while."

With every small gesture, she unwittingly seemed to pull him in.

Julie hesitated for a moment. "That won't be necessary. It's been a long night. I just want to get some sleep." She opened the door for him to leave, looking at anything but him, being anything but friendly.

"Have I done something to offend you?"

"I didn't like the way you treated my neighbor. He wasn't a threat. You should have seen that."

"That's just it. I've seen a lot. A perpetrator will say anything to not get caught. They'll do anything. I had no way of knowing that he was telling the truth. He could have been carrying a weapon. I can't take the chance when I'm face to face with a suspect. And I can't say I'm sorry about it either. My life depends on it. Your life depends on it . . . ."

Feigning interest by nodding her head, Julie made no comment, thinking all along that this man was a natural at turning things around so he wouldn't have to take responsibility . . . just like Kyle, justifying bad behavior. She interrupted him. "I have to ask you. What happened to the evidence you took from here, the mug, the picture frame? You took my statement. Lieutenant Barger says he never got it."

"The lab must be behind. Barger should have gotten that by now. I'll check into it. Let me give you my number at home. If anything comes up, anything at all, call me. I don't live that far from here." He lingered there, writing down his phone number, and finally handed it to her and extended his hand for a handshake. She obliged, taking his hand in hers. The spark was gone, and no amount of handsome could bring it back. His handshake, strong, dominating, sickened her now. She thanked him again, said good-bye, and closed the door.

CHAPTER 45

It was just after midnight. Planted on the edge of his bed in nothing but his underwear, Bruce was smoking a cigarette. Tattooed on his chest, the grim reaper rippled with his muscles. A viper curled at the grim reaper's feet, and a tattoo on his abdomen said, 'Dee' 'Till death us do part'. He picked up a picture of Dee, busted the glass, and ripped out her face. Then he set fire to it, holding it in his fingers until the only thing left was a miniscule corner. He stuck out his tongue and lapped up the last of the fire.

The broken pieces of her entire ceramic rabbit collection had been swept to the corners of the bedroom so Bruce could walk barefoot without cutting his feet. Her dresser drawers had been spewed at the walls so many times that they were broken apart. Her unwanted panties and bras, and socks, her useless collection of yarn and buttons and bobby pins, and other bit-piece junk littered the floor from one end to another. He looked at the clock, burning with hate. She got off at two-thirty, a barmaid job at the Crimson Bar, almost two hours from now. He wanted to kill her. He wanted to strangle her to death. He wanted to watch her choke and gasp for breath. He wanted to watch her die. Bruce stood up with intention. Glancing at the drapes, eyeing the nylon curtain cord, he picked up the hunting knife strategically placed beside him on an overturned nightstand. He lengthened the cord just long enough to do the job and cut it down. Then he opened a black shoe polish tin, smudged his face, and looking in a mirror, marked his forehead with a pentagram. He picked up the hunting knife and ran his finger along the surface of the blade, purposely cutting his finger. He licked the blood. Dee's would taste so much sweeter.

He went to the kitchen and tore out the junk drawer where he had tossed the bolts from underneath Greg's truck, and dumped the drawer on the counter. Bolts and nails and screws, pens and pencils, scribbled phone numbers on wadded paper, every key they had ever owned— the key to Dee's Chevy Malibu.

Bruce dressed in black right down to a hooded sweatshirt, and drove to an office building a block away from The Crimson Bar. He parked his car in back where no one would see it and took off his shoes. Without making a sound in his stocking feet, he dodged between buildings, shrouded in darkness—every thought, hating Dee. The parking lot was deserted. He unlocked her Chevy Malibu and slipped inside in the back seat where he waited, hidden on the floor, perfectly still, the cord wrapped around his fist, the hunting knife in its leather case. The car smelled like week-old beer, like an ashtray on wheels, like hairspray. Ten minutes went by, then five minutes more. Cramped on the floor, he shifted his weight and kneeled on an aerosol can. Some kind of air freshener sprayed until he could get off the thing. Hateful breaths fogged the inside of the car windows.

Where the hell was she? He wiped off a spot on the window, big enough to see with one eye. What the fuck was taking so long? He crouched low in an awkward position, practicing the jerk of the cord. He fingered his shirt pocket for a bag of cocaine, a reward for when she was dead. Carefully lifting the zip-lock bag, he checked the seal, and put it back.

He heard voices, and sunk as close to the floor as he possibly could. He waited. Deathly still. No one came to the car. He stayed put, playing her death in his head, losing track of time.

"I'll see you tomorrow." Dee approached the car, got inside, and fished in her purse for the keys. She'd never been afraid of deserted parking lots, badly lit walkways, or being alone. Bravery had nothing to do with it. She was just stupid enough to believe that nothing would ever happen to her. From what she had told Bruce, she thought the things that her mother had warned her about only happened to somebody else.

Dee started the car to let the engine warm up, to clear the foggy windows, and lit a cigarette.

Bruce waited. He couldn't do it here. Dee had said good-bye to someone. Someone else must have been in the parking lot. There would be a witness. He dared not peek out of the window again, not without someone seeing him.

The car started to move. It would be a long ride to her mother's house, at least a half an hour. He wrapped the cord around each hand, tight, leaving enough room for her neck. She stopped for a red light. He crept up behind her, slowly, silently. Another car stopped at the light next to Dee's car. He slid down on the floor. He would wait for however long it took. Watching her die would be worth waiting for. The lull of the motor, the sound of rain drops, her humming to the song on the radio. Before he knew it he had fallen asleep. He abruptly awoke when she slammed the car door.

He sat up with the nylon cord still clenched in his fists. "Fuck me."

The night was still, not a soul around. Bruce calculated his steps to the back of the house. He remembered a key hidden under the mat, and let himself inside. Still in his stocking feet, he followed the hallway that led to where Dee had slept before when she'd gone home

263

to Mama. He saw the light in the bathroom and heard her brushing her teeth. He snuck to her room, slid under her bed and waited, anticipating how her body would feel, how she would squirm. Within a few minutes, Bruce could see her bare feet as she came inside. He saw the door close.

Dee undressed. She threw her blouse on a chair and then her bra. He could see her naked in the mirror. She always slept naked. He watched her turn off the light and heard the box springs give.

He rose up from under the bed, and smashed his hand against her mouth, forcing her under his body. Sitting on top of her, he pinned her arms down with his knees. She tried to scream, she tried to bite, thrashing, bouncing in the mattress. A yelp seeped out. He smashed down on her mouth and nose, trying to keep her still, waiting to see if she'd woken her mom. Nobody came down the hallway. Nobody opened the door. Nobody had heard her. He slipped the cord over her head, under her chin, around her neck. She clawed and squirmed beneath him, bumping, grinding. He jerked the cord hard. Her body heaving as she struggled to breathe, he kept kissing her, whispering, "So long bitch," until she didn't move anymore.

He withdrew his hunting knife. Aroused beyond his wildest dreams, he satisfied erotica's most sinful act.

Juliet would die next, that prick's wife. He knew how he would do it now. But he'd take his time with Debra Hamilton, an evening he would never forget. Husband Hamilton would be out of the picture, maybe dead, his truck in a heap, after what Bruce had done.

CHAPTER 46

Debra stood in the upstairs window, arms folded, looking out. It had rained during the night and the snow was almost gone. Everything looked dead from up there, the barren trees, the twigs that were once her flowers. That man had stood on this very spot, looking out this very window, whoever he was, whatever he was—like she was doing now. The outline of his body stuck in her head—his presence, him standing so close. That slip in time, her falling in slow motion, that sweet honey smell. "There are no such things as ghosts," she said out loud.

She opened Greg's sock drawer where he kept a coin collection in a canning jar. No one had taken that, or anything else. It didn't make sense, to break into someone's house and not take anything. None of it made sense, he could have killed her if he'd wanted to. He could have killed Julie, too.

The water pump kicked on. She jumped, startled. The chaos in the basement last night was all because of a loose fitting. The water pipe and the outtake valve on top of the hot water heater was easily fixed.

Greg would have stayed home that morning if it hadn't been for his truck. He would have come home that afternoon if it hadn't been for Mr. Brubom whose brother had some sort of leak. Brubom was a good customer, and Brubom was paying cash. Greg couldn't say no. But he did say that they would go out for a nice dinner. They were going to see the movie, 'Amadeus' after that.

Greg called at ten after three. "I don't know when I'll be home.

It took me all this time to tear off the section where the leak was, and the wood underneath is rotted. This thing had three layers of shingles and four inch nails. Now it needs new sheathing. What a bunch of rotten luck. We won't even be able to see a movie."

"Oh," she said quietly, repeating in her head what she wanted to believe, 'There're no such things as ghosts.'

"I'd let it wait till Monday, but it's supposed to rain again tonight. Call Julie. See what she's doing. I don't want you there alone."

"How are you going to work in the dark?"

"This guy hooked up a spotlight."

"Oh."

"Don't make any supper. His wife's cooking cabbage and noodles. I can smell them. She feels bad because I have to stay here so long. I'll bring some home."

"Don't worry about it. Julie is coming over at 4:30 to jog. I'll see what she's doing tonight. Maybe we'll go out for dinner or order something."

"Don't forget to bolt the doors . . . love you."

"Me, too."

Debra tore the wrapper off a new box of .22 caliber bullets, loaded the long-barrel Marlin rifle, and set it in the corner of the living room behind an old umbrella stand. She could shoot a man as well as she could a ghost. This wouldn't stop her from being afraid. She knew herself too well for that. But she wasn't going to give into fear. Not anymore.

She felt a headache coming on.

CHAPTER 47

Identical twins, each vying for their own identity. Nate came dressed in Levi jeans and a blue button-up shirt. Jeff came dressed in cargo pants and a pinstriped polo. The two stepped up to a window with a glass partition where a woman in police uniform was talking on the phone with her back to them.

"Excuse me," Nate said, tapping the window, his heart beating so. He had defied his mother to get here today. Here in this ominous courthouse, this place where prisoners bided their time waiting for trial. This place where 'pigs' lived and breathed to harass guys like him.

The woman swiveled her chair around with 'what the hell do you want' on her face. Purple fingernails, purple lips, unfit for this kind of work.

"We're Kyle Zourenger's sons. We're here to see him."

"Hold on," she said to whoever was on the phone. "Visiting hours are over," her curt answer.

"But this is our only chance."

"Then you should have been here between one and three." She swiveled back again, the phone to her ear.

"Ma'am? Can you give him the message that we were here?"

"Come back between one and three," she said over her shoulder.

The two college students, duffle bags in hand, had hitched a ride with another student who'd come home for his sister's wedding. They were supposed to ride back with him again on Sunday night.

Standing by a pay phone outside the courthouse, Nate dug deep in his jean pockets, and pulled out a wadded up dollar bill, three pennies and a nickel. "What have you got?" His army jacket was half-buttoned, his hair tousled in the wind.

"Where's the phone card?" Jeff's windbreaker rippled, caught up in a gust.

"I forgot it."

An RTA bus whizzed by throwing road slush leaving behind the smell of diesel exhaust.

Jeff dug in his pockets and pulled out three one-dollar bills, a quarter, and a dime. "It's long distance. This is all I've got."

"Give me the dime. I'll call collect." Nate fed the dime into the coin slot. "Do you think mom's got any food?" The only thing they'd eaten all day was a donut. Not five dollars between them. All the trouble they'd gone to, cutting classes, bartering for a ride, starving all day, and not to mention that their mother would be pissed. All that and they still couldn't see their dad.

"I'd settle for peanut butter and jelly about now."

"Bus fifty-seven goes to North Olmsted. She can pick us up there . . . what time do you think?"

"Tell her we'll just call her when we get there."

". . . . no one's answering the phone."

"Call Grams."

Nate recycled the dime and dialed. They'd only known Marie as Grams, and Sam as Gramps.

He heard Marie answer the phone, feeling sick inside. "Hello . . . ."

The operator interrupted his hello. "I have a collect call from . . . ." This was his cue to say his name.

"... Nate."

"Will you accept charges?" the operator prompted Marie.

"Yes."

"Grams? I'm sorry I had to call collect. We're in Elyria. If we take a bus to North Olmsted, can you pick us up? Mom's not answering the phone."

"Nate. Are you all right? Why are you in Elyria?"

"We tried to see Dad, but visiting hours are over, and when we called Mom, no one answered the phone. I'm sorry to have to ask you, but we don't have enough money for a cab."

"Of course. I'll pick you up in front of The May Company. What time, Honey?"

"In about an hour. I'll call when we get there, but I'll just let it ring twice and hang up. So don't answer the phone unless it rings three times or more. Is that okay?"

CHAPTER 48

Debra had a terrible headache. She downed two aspirins, intending to lie down just long enough for the aspirins to stop her head from throbbing. Greg wouldn't be home for a very long time, not until well after dark. Julie was supposed to come over at four thirty, just over an hour from now. Debra checked the doors to make sure they were locked, and lay down on the couch with an afghan blanket pulled up over her shoulders.

She closed her eyes and her breathing slowed, transcending between sleep and wakefulness. Then her muscles relaxed. Her subconscious sped up, and she began to dream.

Debra dreamt she was in the garage. It was dark. She could see the figure of a man who was coming around the corner fast, towards the opened garage door. She dreamt she'd hit the button to close the door and the oversized slab started its slow descent. Clutching her rifle, its stock in her shoulder, her finger on the trigger, she opened her mouth to yell, to hurry that damned slowpoke door, but she couldn't make a sound. The oversized door lumbered in slow motion. The earth seemed to shift underneath her feet. The man was running faster, faster. The door ceased to move at all.

'Wake up, wake up, wake up,' she said to her sleeping self, sweating, shaking. He was getting so close so fast. Shaking uncontrollably, she lined him up in her sites. She squeezed the trigger. Her body twitched. She'd shot him dead. Stepping into misty darkness to where he lay, she lowered her rifle, watching him for signs of life.

Him, lying at her feet, he grabbed both her ankles at once and took her down.

Muted screams were captive in her spit—gravel scraping her skin—her shoulder hit first, then her head. In the glare of a knife, she sucked in a breath and drew back her fist.

Wake up, wake up, wake up!

Suddenly Debra was in her twelve-year-old self, sitting in church, wearing her then favorite yellow dress decorated with white flowers. Her patent leather shoes, her white ankle socks, and white cotton gloves, taking her to a forgotten time. Mrs. O'Shell was playing, *Sweet Hour of Prayer* on the church organ. People were sitting in pews in front, and sitting in pews behind. This church had given her refuge, Mrs. O'Shell's church. Everyone stood up and sang.

"Sweet hour of prayer! Sweet hour of prayer! That calls me from a world of care . . ."

Her mother was coming down the aisle now, young and beautiful, her hair dark and flowing. She scooted in next to Debra, beaming with something that looked like love. She touched Debra's brow, her fingers smoothing a worry line. "Pray Debra. Pray real hard," she said in her ear. Her mom faced forward now, and sang *Sweet Hour of Prayer*.

The singing stopped. Her mom disappeared. The pew disappeared. Someone was carrying her out of the church. She smelled that sweet honey smell. Cradled in a policeman's arms, the warmth of his body, the sweet smell of his breath. Even though she couldn't see the dimensions of his face, she knew it was Ed, or at least her version of him.

She awoke, disoriented, wrapped in the afghan in the back seat

271

of her car, still in her stocking feet, her rifle next to her. The car doors were locked. How did she get here? Her socks were dry. Her hair wet with sweat, she saw that part-time game warden Bruce in her yard. Coming from a wooded area where the old barn was, he seemed to be heading toward the deck. She could tell that he hadn't seen her. How easy it would have been to shoot him from here.

She stepped out of the car in her stocking feet. The cold-wet sent a shocking chill through her body, her afghan slipping off her shoulders. Dreary gray canvassed the sky as far as the eye could see. "Hey!" Debra yelled, placing one foot after another, her own time-stamps in the mud and snow. "What are you doing here? Damn you," she cursed in the heat of the moment, cradling her rifle.

"I need to use your phone," he said, his tone sounding normal, kindly. But there wasn't anything normal about Bruce, and he definitely wasn't kind.

She could see blood in his hair. "What have you done to yourself?" she asked, her words quick, her steps quicker.

"I hit a deer down the road . . . put my car in the ditch." He finger-tip-combed his bloody hairline. "Look at that," he said, seeing his own blood. "I must have hit my head. I really need that phone."

"You said you came from down the road. You hit a deer. Then why did I see you coming out of the woods?"

". . . I had to piss. What do you think? Can't you see I'm hurt?"

Still haunted by slipstream dreams, looking as stern as her youthful face allowed. She hated this man. She hated his tattoos, his ragged jean jacket, his long hair; she hated everything about him. "There's a phone booth a couple of miles down the road just west of here," she said, opening the door, her back to him. Without missing a beat, she went inside. But as she tried to close the door, Bruce quick-wedged his foot inside.

"Problem is my truck is stuck in a ditch a couple miles in the opposite direction. I've been walking for a long time, and . . ." Bruce snort-sniffed, hocking a wad that he must have swallowed. "Come on . . . I really need a phone."

Shit. Debra didn't want him anywhere near the other side of the door. Okay, he was presumably harmless; at least that's what the County Department of Wildlife had said.

". . . fine." She relented, letting him come inside.

Bruce took off his muddy shoes and carried them with him, following her inside. Debra showed him to the phone inside the kitchen, and watched his every move, leaving just once to change her socks and put on some slippers. In the kitchen, she flitted through the mail, never letting go of the rifle.

The phone to his ear, he turned his back to her. "Madison, Bruce Madison . . . yes. I need a tow on Adams Road just south of Route 303 . . . ." He stood erect, his legs apart, knees locked, balling up the telephone cord in his fist.

Debra took a frustrated breath and huffed it out.

"I get it. Okay? They put me on hold." Bruce seemed agitated.

Then the doorbell rang. Debra hesitated to answer the front door. This door in the living room was the only door with a doorbell. She glared at him, conveying the message, 'hurry up.' The doorbell rang again. She stepped backward to the arched doorway between the kitchen and the vast living room, hoping to see who ever it was through the far off Victorian window that faced the porch. The bell rang for the third time. She hesitantly left Bruce, and hurried through the living room.

Hiding her rifle behind the umbrella stand, she opened the door and then the screen door where a postal carrier was waiting. From here, she could only see a swatch of Bruce's faded jean jacket.

"Would you mind coming inside?" she asked the carrier, holding open the door, not wanting to go outside because she wouldn't be able to see Bruce.

"This will just take a minute." The postal carrier held out a package and a clipboard for her to take, coaxing her onto the porch. "I just need a signature."

She stepped out onto the porch, holding the screen door open with her foot, and tossed the package inside.

The postman dropped the pen. "That's the kind of day I've been having." He bent over to pick it up, rolling it clumsily with every touch. The pen rolled off the porch. "I've got another one here somewhere." He unzipped his jacket and fingered his shirt pocket.

Debra shifted one foot in the door, trying to see Bruce, even a stitch of his clothing.

"Sign right here."

She scribbled her name.

The postman tore the perforated receipt the same awkward way that he'd dropped the pen. "How did you like all that snow we had the other day? Must have had six inches."

She nodded her head, anxious, "Yes. You have a nice day, too. Thank you," she pelted polite words, abruptly shutting the door, hurrying back to the kitchen.

Bruce was gone. It was four-thirty, and Julie pulled in the driveway right on schedule, passing the postal carrier on her way.

Debra was already at the door, locking it when Julie came up to it.

"I brought some WD-40." Julie seemed to be her old cheerful self. "I dug it out of Kyle's truck."

"What is that?"

"Oil in a can. You're going to like this." Julie set it down on the kitchen counter. "You're not ready yet?"

"Let me get my shoes." Debra opened the closet and dropped to her knees rummaging through a bunch of mismatched shoes to find them.

"What's in the package?" Julie picked up the package that was still on the floor, from when Debra had kicked it inside. "It says, The Co-Stan Homeowners Association. That's a big outfit."

"Is that who it's from? I didn't even look at it." Debra forgot all about finding her shoes, and grabbed a letter opener from a kitchen drawer. "I shouldn't have left this on the floor." She took the package from Julie, and cut it open. "The contract. Greg got the job. You can't imagine how much we wanted this." She handled the pages with care, taking them out of the box. Underneath, in the bottom of the box, she saw a check for ten-thousand dollars, with a note that said, 'Please accept this check as a down payment. We have another project when this one is finished, if you are interested.' Debra put everything back the way it had come. "Greg has worked so hard for this. I can't believe I just tossed it aside," and placed it in the back of the closet for safekeeping.

"What was it doing on the floor?"

"That game warden was here when the delivery man came." Debra found one of her shoes. "He was in the kitchen using the phone, and I was trying to keep an eye on him from the front door."

"You let him inside?"

"Not for long. One minute he was here and the next minute he was gone." Debra found the other shoe.

"It still makes me mad, what he did to those cats. Did anyone ever do anything about that?"

"Not as far as I know. If it was up to me, I would throw him in jail," Debra tied shoes, trying to hurry, wanting to leave right away, so they wouldn't come back to a dark house.

"I wouldn't have let him inside. There's a lot of sick people out there. Another woman was raped and killed in Parma this time. I just heard it on the news. They said her name was Dee Something. I don't know why, but that name sounds familiar . . . . I'm so glad that Greg put dead bolts on my doors."

"That's quite a ways from here. I would think that whoever killed her wouldn't come out this far." Debra buttoned her coat. "I hope they catch him." She tucked her hair under a stocking cap. "With everything that's been going on, it scares me to think, that could have been one of us." She locked the dead bolt as they left. "I had this crazy dream . . . ."

Upstairs in Debra's bedroom, Bruce watched them walk to the end of the driveway and onto the road. He sniffed a pinch of cocaine, and after the initial high subsided, he opened the dirty clothes hamper that was nestled next to the dresser and found Debra's panties. Smelling her sweet scent was a high all in itself.

CHAPTER 49

Debra felt the warmth coming back to her feet, her leather tennis shoes splashing through the sidewalk slush. The once orange mums she'd jogged by all month were drooping heavily to the ground, brown around the edges. Some of the houses showed signs of Thanksgiving, which was next week. She hadn't gone over the dream with Julie, not in its entirety. Right now she couldn't help but wonder where Bruce had gone, probably back to his broken down car. Mad at herself for letting him in, she wished that she had seen him leave. She could have locked him out for good and all. He had to have left . . . of course he left. They said he was harmless. That's what they'd said . . .

Julie clawed at the inside of her wrist, scratching it. "This itches so bad. Is this what I think it is?" She took off her glove, jogging all the while, and showed Debra three ugly welts, each the size of a dime, red bumpy, oozing.

"You've got it pretty bad." I wish I would have known the cats were sick. I can see it starting on your neck, too. Have you been using the fungicide?" Debra said, feeling terribly guilty.

"I've been spraying the kitten." Julie kept clawing at her wrist. "I never thought to spray myself. It didn't show up until last night, and I thought it was something else."

"Don't scratch. It'll spread." Debra scooped a handful of snow that hadn't melted yet. "Hold this on it. Ice really helps. You need to buy some Tinactin." Debra said in puffy breaths, jogging again, fast and quick. "Hey. Do you want to have dinner together? How 'bout Chinese?"

"Chinese . . . I know a new place so desperate for business, they'll deliver anywhere. We'll look up Won Chow when we get back," Julie said, the two of them jogging together, breathing heavily in the cold. The smell of wood burning from someone's fireplace; the rhythm of their feet hitting the wet sidewalk; the sound of Julie's breaths—each in their own right, enchanting, in these last hours of daylight.

At Debra's house, after an hour-long jog, they called Won Chow. Debra wasn't thinking about Bruce anymore, at least that's what she'd told herself. Julie sprayed the basement door's hinges with oil, and swung it open and closed to make sure the squeak was gone. Then she sprayed the bathroom door.

"Do you want me to spray the doors upstairs?"

"May as well. How much is left?"

Julie shook the spray-can. "Must be a new can. I think it's full."

Just then, floorboards creaked from up above.

Julie threw a hushed glance at Debra "You locked the doors, right?"

"There's no one up there, this house creaks for no reason at all." Debra walked over to the umbrella stand and retrieved the rifle.

"Then what's that for?"

"A little persuasion for 'no reason at all.'"

On their way upstairs, with every footstep, the stairs creaked their nostalgic song. Julie ran her finger along an extension cord that was tacked to the wood molding along the stairway.

"What's the extension cord for?" Julie asked, following Debra, going up another step. Three steps from reaching the top.

"There's no electricity up here. Greg wired that up to a light switch in our bedroom."

Finally at the top of the stairs, Debra faced the long narrow hallway that was lined with doors. "Which room do you want to see first? We don't have much time. It'll be dark soon. There's no light in these rooms."

Something tinny tapped against a window to the uneven rhythm of the breeze outside. Julie followed Debra to the furthest door down the hall, and turned the glass doorknob. A net of cobwebs swayed with the motion of the opening door. The hinges creaked a solitary voice. Duty-bound, Julie sprayed them with oil. Going inside, floorboards creaked beneath their footsteps. Scant beams of light filtered through the windows into translucent hues on the unfinished walls, on the vintage furniture. It was getting darker.

"This is so creepy," Julie said, running her finger over a cracked wall.

"Wait till you see the next room."

Bruce heard them talking. He eased open the bedroom door slightly to see through a small crack, the hunting knife in his hand. Behind the bedroom door, waiting, listening, he shifted his weight back a step.

Another floorboard creaked. Perfectly still, the two women exchanged glances.

Eyes wide, Julie mouthed, "Did you hear that?"

Debra mouthed back, "Yes." She was glad that Julie had heard it. She was glad that it was creepy and scary and all the things she'd tried to convey. Panicked and glad and scared and happy . . . she didn't have the crazy gene. Above all things, she didn't have that.

"Let's go to my house." Words came in whispers.

"What about the Chinese food?"

"We'll wait for it in the car."

Bruce opened the door a little more, trying to squeeze out of Debra's bedroom. He could see the rifle. That damned rifle. Opening the door a little further, the hinges creaked. He plastered his body against the wall, waiting for a few seconds. Then he took a step forward. The floorboard creaked.

The sound of a door convinced Debra and Julie to leave. The sound of the footstep ordered them to run. They met up with Bruce by her bedroom door. He took off, two steps at a time down the stairs.

"Stop!" Debra cocked the rifle. "Stop right now!"

Bruce jumped down three more steps.

Debra fired a shot over his head, trying to scare him into stopping. But he didn't stop. She fired again. Bruce fell down the rest of the stairs, his feet out from under him. His body hit the floor just short of the bathroom door. He didn't move, not even a little.

"You got him," Julie said, skimming past Debra, making her way to Bruce's body.

Debra's dream came back in a blur, the vision of her shooting him, of him grabbing her ankles, of him taking her down. "No. Don't." She quick grabbed Julie's arm.

Debra aimed at him, close range. "I just put two bullet holes in my new drywall because of you. Go ahead. Lie there. Just don't pretend you're shot. I didn't even come close."

Sprawled out, the knife's handle in his opened hand, its cutting edge against the floor. His eyes were closed. The cut on his forehead, the reason he'd used her phone, was bleeding. A wicked smile crested his lips, and he opened his eyes. "Enough foreplay," he said, rolling, grabbing for her ankles. Debra quick-stepped backwards. And shot him, aiming to graze his arm. Bruce sprang to the bathroom without an utterance of pain, and slammed the door shut. She heard the lock catch.

"Good," Debra yelled through the door. "Lock yourself in."

"It's him." Julie said to Debra. "There's no mistaking those tattoos. He's the one who broke into my house that night. I'll call the sheriff."

"Tell them we can't wait for someone to just happen by. Tell them I've killed a man, if you have to. If they don't get here soon, that might be the truth."

Julie called the sheriff's department from the kitchen, and came back a few minutes later. For reasons unknown, she still had the oil spray can.

"It didn't matter what I said. There's a multiple-car accident on Route 71 and the dispatcher said the department's short of officers today."

"I hate to ask this, but what about that cop, Jack?"

"His number's at home. I was this close to throwing it away," Julie said. "I wish I could call the detective who was on Kyle's case, Lieutenant Barger. He's the only one I trust. But he only takes homicide cases."

Bruce made an awful racket inside the bathroom—metal on metal. It sounded as if he was bashing the plumbing in there. Debra tried to think of what could make a sound like that. "The ventilation grate," she said out loud. "He's trying to get out through the ceiling." The shaft was big enough for him to crawl through, to the upper floor above. "That comes out by the other staircase in the other part of the house. Those stairs lead to another kitchen and to another door that goes outside."

Without thinking, Debra bolted up the stairs, leaving Julie by the bathroom door. When Debra got to the room with the ventilation grate, she looked for something heavy to block it, and ended up going to her bedroom where he had pulled out her dresser drawers. Dragging two dresser drawers the length of the hall, she realized that she couldn't hear Bruce anymore.

Then she heard Julie scream.

Debra wildly raced down the hall, back to the stairs, and down to the living room, the rifle an appendage now. The bathroom door was open. Bruce was holding Julie in a chokehold, using her as a shield, his knife at her throat. He pressed his oil-glazed face against hers. WD-40, Julie must have sprayed him.

"Let go of her." Debra said softly, her face, her hands, sweating, pulsing. "I have no problem killing you."

"Go ahead. Pull the trigger. Let's see how far this knife can slice Juliet's throat before I go down." He tightened his grip on Julie, his face against hers, and sloppily licked her cheek.

The phone rang, adding to the height of tension. It rang again. His skull-tattooed wrist, his tight fisted grip, his knife's polished blade— all a part of the whole—all poised at Julie's throat. The phone rang again.

Her eyes on his, Debra could see his reflection, Julie's too, captured in the knife's steel blade. The rifle barrel seemed to melt in her sweat-laden hands. She could see the skulls, as many as there were, each one unique—all with her eyes on his.

The phone rang again, and the answering machine picked up the call.

Debra's recorded voice mechanically announced,

"This is Hamilton Carpentry. Please leave your name and number, and a short message, and someone will return your call. Thank you."

"If you're there, pick up the phone. This is Jeff. I saw my mom's car over there, and our house is locked. Is someone there? I'm at Grams with Nate. We're going to have a sandwich first, and then we'll be over to get the key. Bye."

Bruce displayed a sort of smile through his stone cold expression. "You know I have to kill you. Don't you?" he said to Julie, his mouth nuzzled to her ear. "I have to kill your prick sons, too. That husband of yours should never have messed with me."

"Why are you doing this?" Julie asked.

"Come on, don't be stupid. My whoring wife, your prick husband. Dee is dead. Just up and died in her sleep." He tightened his grip. "See what happens when you mess with me?"

CHAPTER 50

It was Jack's day off and he had been listening to the radio. He had just heard the news. 'Dee Madison, dead in her mother's home.' He checked his police scanner. An all-points bulletin was out for the prime suspect, Bruce Madison.

Jack had never wanted it to get this far. Disheveled, he'd been working outside in his back yard where he'd buried various cats over the years. The first on the scene for every complaint, so no one would find out about Bruce. Bruce, swearing each time that he'd never do it again. The fire-bush hedgerow had lost its leaves, and now he could see where a cat skeleton had eroded toward the surface. It was better to conceal a carcass at night, but the neighbor's dog had discovered the skeleton and had started to dig it up.

Twenty minutes of driving had felt like hours. His tires sent eroded gravel pinging beneath his car, driving so fast on Adams Road. All these days and weeks, months of destroying evidence.

Bruce had promised. This wasn't supposed to happen.

In his rattiest clothes, a worn out painter's pants and a stained Hard Rock t-shirt, Jack cut the wheel. The car's tail end hit a rut at the end of the driveway. Getting darker by the minute, he bounded to Julie's door, laid on the doorbell, and slammed his fist on the door. What if he'd already been here? Jack busted the lock with a police-issued tool.

It shouldn't have gotten this far.

He yelled her name through the house, searching every room. She wasn't downstairs. She wasn't upstairs. He had to warn her. He had to tell her what Bruce had done.

Just a few weeks ago when the new Kroger's grocery store had first opened, the traffic was heavy. The red lights conflicted and mega signs were too close to the road—a raucous day for a cop who just happened to be Jack. It was a day of too many fender benders, too many beeping horns, too many flaring tempers. A chaotic mess, all because some car had run a red light, some careless woman they'd never found. All those police reports, all those screaming yelling people. It was a day he couldn't easily forget, a day that required vodka to wash it out of his head.

Bruce was already there at the bar, sitting in a dark booth, his eyes dilated, his nostrils rimmed red. Jack apprehensively sat down across from him, vodka-tonic in hand. Diary-like pages were spewed on the table like used napkins, writing all over them. He could tell that Bruce was high.

"I'll kill her. I'll kill that fucking whore." Bruce flicked his cigarette lighter and started to set a handful of the pages on fire.

Jack stopped him, "What the hell's the matter with you?"

"She's done it this time. She's fucking some bastard." Bruce flicked a diary page across the table. "Read it. The bastard's Kyle . . . no last name, just Kyle. I fixed him. I fixed him good."

"What are you talking about?" Jack sat straight up, his jaw clenched. "Bruce, what did you do?"

"I killed him. I went there, and I killed him."

"Who did you kill? Tell me! Who did you kill?"

"Some guy in a blue house, somewhere on Jaycox. They'll never connect it to me." He flicked another page. "The bastard's got a wife,

Julie . . . Juliet. Like Romeo and Juliet. They both died you know. They have to die."

"Don't say shit like that . . . Look at me . . . You didn't kill anyone, and you're not going to, either. Got that?"

Bruce tipped back his head, looking at Jack. His black-brown eyes looked just like their father's, cold, heartless. Jack hated that man. But he didn't hate Bruce. Bruce hadn't always been like this. Bruce had been more like their mother, fine, and upstanding. He'd almost died in a car accident a few years back, and he would have, if that surgeon hadn't screwed metal plates to his skull.

"Tell me the truth. Tell me you didn't kill anyone."

"But I did. I slit his throat," Bruce said as if he was proud of it. "I'll kill that Kyle prick, too, and my whoring wife. And then I'll kill Juliet, the prick's whore."

"No. Listen to me. I can protect you if you stop here. Do you understand? You can't hurt anyone else. Bruce. Promise me."

"I'm not going to promise shit."

"Promise me right now, or I'll turn you in. You'll get the death penalty."

"Don't get all police-the-man on me. I was just talking."

"I didn't hear you promise." Jack took out his handcuffs. "I can read you your rights, right now."

"Okay, I promise. There, I said it."

Bruce's words resonated in Jack's head, that day and every day since. They'd kept him awake at night. They gave him nightmares on the chance he had fallen asleep. He was an accessory to the crime now. He had to make sure that Bruce didn't get caught.

That was weeks ago. Dee was dead now. Bruce had let the demon out. He wouldn't stop there. Jack drove down Adams Road, hoping to find Julie out for a jog. He drove past Brentwood Pines and saw Bruce's beat-up car, unattended, in the parking lot behind the recreation hall. He knew it. Bruce was here.

Jack raced back to Julie's house. He searched the house again, he searched the barn, calling her name all the while. No one was here.

Finally, standing by the road, feverish in thought, he saw the old house across the way, beyond the gravel road . . . .

Jack bolted across the road to Debra's house and saw Julie's car. Without making a sound, he looked inside the window from the front porch and saw them, the unlikely threesome frozen in place, each waiting for the other one to make a move. Knowing how easily Bruce could spook, he busted the garage door lock. Up a few steps, his hand barely touched the next doorknob and the door bobbed open to a utility room. He hustled through the utility room, through the kitchen, to where they were.

"Bruce, let her go," Jack spoke like he would have to a child.

Bruce said nothing.

"Listen to me, Bruce. I can help you, but you have to let her go." Jack inched closer to Bruce.

"Stay where you are," Bruce commanded. "You're just like the rest of them. All you care about is yourself. Just like Dee."

Jack stood motionless. Bruce tightened the chokehold around her throat, the knife touching her skin. Julie choked a cough, gasping for air.

Despite the knife at her throat, Julie itch-rubbed her ringworm-infected hand hard against her pants.

He jerked his hold around her waist. "That's it," Bruce said playfully. "Realign the knife. It's not close enough, is it?" A line of blood trickled where the knifepoint pierced her skin.

Debra chimed in. "She's got the ugly-itch."

"What are you talking about?" Bruce asked.

"You'll never know sleepless nights until you've got the ugly-itch. Look at what those cats did to me. Look at the scabs on my hands."

"What is that?" Bruce's gaze focused on the grotesque welts—ringworm drying up on Debra's hand. "You got that shit on you! Don't you? I told you not to touch those damn cats."

"I should have listened to you. Julie's got it too, but hers are more contagious you know. Hers are oozing." There was a chill in Debra's voice, looking at Julie, willing the transference of thought between them. "Show him, Julie."

Julie raised her hand to give him a look, and swiped the ugly on his face.

"You got that shit on me, bitch!" Bruce frantically swiped his face. Julie broke free.

"I'll kill you!" Bruce raised the hunting knife to Julie.

"One more move, and I'll shoot you dead!" Debra yelled. The knife stopped midair.

Jack moved closer to Debra, extending his hand, "I'll take over from here; give me the rifle."

"No. I'll hold him here. Handcuff him."

Jack drew closer, open handed. "Just give me the rifle."

"How did you know his name?" Debra asked Jack, her eyes never leaving Bruce.

Jack kept coming toward her, slowly, holding out his hand, dismissing her question. "I'm not playing around anymore. Hand over the weapon."

"How did you know his name was Bruce?"

"He's my brother, you stupid bitch," Bruce answered. "Tell them, Jack. Tell them you're not going to let anything happen to me."

The doorbell rang. Debra and Bruce held their gaze.

No one moved.

The doorbell rang again.

"Give me the rifle," Jack insisted with his hand still extended.

That incessant doorbell rang again. She wasn't going to look, not even for a second. Then she heard the familiar rattle of ladders, a sound that only she would know, Greg's truck, ladders atop. She glanced at the window for just a second. In that second, Bruce ambushed her, a backhand to her face. He swiped his knife, cutting her lip. It happened so fast. She screamed. She kicked. She fought over the rifle, hanging on to it with both hands. He swiped the knife again. She dodged the blade so close to her face, and in doing so, she fell backward, off her feet. Half on the stairs, half on the floor, holding her mouth, blood in her hand, she started to kick him again. Then, she realized he had taken the rifle. She had looked away for a second, only a second.

Bruce . . . Julie . . . Jack, three corners of a triangle. Bruce pivoted toward Julie and cocked the rifle.

"No! Don't!" Jack yelled, closing the triangle fast.

The shot rang out just as Jack plowed into Julie, toppling the two of them. Their bodies, entwined, splattered in blood, lay unmoving on the hardwood floor. Time hiccupped the scene over and over, but never divulged which one had taken the bullet.

Bruce held his stance, the rifle warm in his hands. The slow song of anguish played in his eyes, his black-brown eyes—unblinking in clear disbelief.

Jack rolled off Julie, holding his chest, whispering something that only she could have heard. Blood seeped between his fingers, pooling on his shirt. He closed his eyes. His head fell backward.

"No," Bruce uttered, looking paralyzed. His lips parted. He uttered 'no' again. His eyes glazed, blinking once. A third 'no' came out as a whisper. Reality hit. He sloppy-sobbed inside his lifted shoulder, still armed, a weapon in each hand.

Julie scooted in slow motion to where Debra was, and very carefully leaned into her, and whispered low, "Jack said, 'Bruce framed Kyle'."

Debra glanced out the window again through a blur of tears. Where was Greg?

Greg had just come home, minutes earlier. He'd had seen the delivery boy with the Chinese food, and had gone to the porch. But just as he'd lifted his wallet to pay the boy, he heard the shot from inside the house. The delivery boy was startled so badly that he threw the takeout straight up; takeout boxes landed one by one, splattering. The boy jumped off the porch and ran to his car. Then he was gone.

Alone on the porch, in the dark, Greg saw them through the window. He ducked down so they wouldn't see him. Making small movements, taking short glances, he saw a thug by the bathroom door with Debra's rifle. He saw Julie on the floor a few feet away. He saw the man who'd been shot next to her. The scene played out in proximity of the stairway where he saw Debra draped against the bottom step; her face bled through her fingers onto her blouse. He raged in quiet. He had to stay hidden. He had to get inside without anyone knowing.

Greg headed to the garage, picturing them, picturing Debra.

"Hi, Greg," Nate yelled, coming up the driveway with his brother.

"Hi, Greg." Jeff waved overhead.

Greg ran to them. "Go back. Call the sheriff. Tell them someone's been shot. Tell them we need an ambulance."

"What . . . ."

"Go!" Greg ordered, his rage building. Keeping his head, he headed to the garage again. He grabbed a heavy-duty pipe wrench. A flashlight, too, he went to the utility room, to the crawl-space. He lifted the plywood lid, and lowered himself inside. Adrenalin pumping, lying on his back in this narrow space of nesting spiders, he dare not make a sound. The ceiling barely three feet from the floor, he scooted inch by inch on the hard dirt until he made it to an opening on the basement wall. Climbing out of the crawl-space, into the basement, he could hear himself breathing; he could hear his own heartbeat. He crept up the stairs. At the top, he opened the door in slow motion in an all-out effort to prevent it from creaking. The door opened without a sound.

The thug blubbered incoherently, kneeling over the man he'd shot—the rifle under his arm, his back to Greg. It seemed that Julie had made her way to Debra next to the stairs, where the two sat Indian style, their arms linked. Greg crept up behind the thug. The floorboards that usually creaked were silent.

Debra's eyes darted between Bruce and Greg, and an ominous wrench. Then Bruce looked up. He saw Debra's face, the direction of her eyes; and from where he was kneeling, he stabbed Greg in the ribs. Debra screamed Greg's name, feeling the knife slice through his ribs, too. She stood up with a start, but Julie pulled her back down.

As if he couldn't believe it, Greg looked at the knife wound, at the blood. The wrench still in his hand, he fell to his knees. Bruce stabbed him again.

"Greg!" Debra screamed his name, unable to move because Julie was holding her down, bruising her arm to keep her in place. The wrench fell first. Then Greg. From the distance, there was an echo of sirens. The sirens grew louder, closer. Any minute now—they waited. But just as quickly as the sound came, it left, and passed right by the house, echoing back through a tunnel of sound until it diminished all together.

Bruce stood up. He wiped his snot. Securing the rifle to fire at will, he walked brisk paces over to Julie.

Debra prayed, "Our Father who art in heaven, hallowed be thy name . . ." The calm before imminent death. The mind goes to a place when deep in prayer. She knew this place—this dying calm. Her mother's face wafted in like a dream, her haunting words. 'Pray, Debra. Pray real hard.'

Bruce placed the tip of the barrel against Julie's temple.

"Dear Lord, look down upon us sinners. Spare us oh Lord . . . ." Debra prayed out loud. She prayed in earnest.

"Shut up!" Bruce yelled. Then he cocked the rifle.

". . . in Jesus name I pray . . . ."

Julie shut her eyes tight, her hand in Debra's, holding on for dear life. The room lit up, red and blue lights from outside, bouncing off the walls.

". . . please help us Lord. I pray. In Jesus name please help us Lord. I pray . . . ."

Out of nowhere, a police officer rushed in from the kitchen; his uniform, a freshly pressed navy blue, his hair, a scrubbed crew cut. "Police officer! Drop your weapon!" he shouted, his gun drawn.

Bruce turned the rifle on the officer and fired. The shot struck the clean-shaven officer and he fell backwards into a dark room. Almost instantly two more officers in gray shades of blue ran from the kitchen. Guns were drawn. Shots were fired. Debra shielded her face in her hands, jolted by every shot. And then she looked through her hands. A bullet hit Bruce under his eye. He dropped to his knees on her level, face to face. A bullet hit his forehead. He fell forward on Debra's lap. She didn't scream. She didn't move.

Almost as if she were vacant, as if she wasn't there, Debra sunk into herself like she had so many times as a child, frozen in place, staring at nothing; the aftermath of shock and surprise—like a great fall where you stay perfectly still, afraid to move, afraid you are broken.

Julie, crying in hysterics, shoved Bruce off Debra's lap. She hugged Debra tight, taking in the whole of her body.

"Call for an ambulance!" one of the officers shouted.

Debra's breathing was shallow, rapid. Julie pulled back. "Deb . . . Deb," she said shaking Debra's shoulders.

Debra didn't respond.

"I've got a pulse over here," One of the officers yelled.

Julie shouted at Debra, shaking her harder. "Deb. You're scaring me . . . Deb!"

Debra took in this fair Irish face, the laugh lines around these freckled eyes, this woman who was her friend. Reality clicked.

"Greg." Horror stricken all over again she bounded to Greg—ten feet away. He was barely breathing. "Greg. No. Greg," she said, holding his face in her trembling hands, sniffing back the tears.

Paramedics arrived in two groups of three, breaking up into two-man teams, gravitating to each of the critically wounded. A paramedic knelt down beside Greg.

Debra spoke up, her hair tear-plastered to her face, "He stabbed him . . . he stabbed him twice." Her lip was swollen, so swollen that it had stopped bleeding. Julie was close beside her.

A paramedic pressed his fingers into Greg's neck. "Systolic 80, pulsac 40," he said to his partner. He turned to Debra, "Are you family?"

"I'm his wife."

"He has a low pulse. We're going to give him some oxygen," he said, slipping a facemask over Greg's head. He pushed into Greg's breastplate and rubbed deep. "Sir. I need you to wake now. Sir. I need you to open your eyes for me." Another paramedic lined up a backboard next to Greg, and both of them eased Greg onto it. "He's not responding." They lifted the backboard to a gurney. Debra heard someone in the background pronounce Bruce dead. ". . . the time, seven twelve."

She took Greg's face in her hands, crying all the while. "Greg," she said. "Look at me. Come on honey. Please." She squeezed his hand. "Please," she cried, "Greg look at me."

Greg squeezed her fingers.

They were moving Jack outside on a gurney, a facemask, too. Things were happening so fast. Three men down, one dead, blood everywhere. The fifteen-by-twenty living room was a war zone.

The paramedic checked Greg's pulse again. "Pulse is strong."

Julie's eyes wandered the room, quizzical, like she was searching for someone. She was standing a foot away from Debra when one of the officers approached her.

"You should have a paramedic look at that," The policeman said, handing her an ice pack.

"What happened to the first officer? I don't see him anywhere." Julie said. "Did he make it?"

"What do you mean, ma'am? I was the first one here." The officer reached around her as he spoke, handing an ice pack to Debra, too.

An edge of agitation in her voice, Julie said, "No. The officer who came in before you did? I'd be dead if it weren't for him."

"I don't understand. It's just me and my partner."

"You've got to be kidding me. He was shot . . . right over there. Young, heavyset, he was the one wearing a dark blue uniform."

"You're mistaken. Our uniforms haven't been that color for a long time. You've been through a lot today."

Debra was still upset, but not so upset that she didn't hear the rhetoric going on between Julie and the officer, and interjected, "Yes, we have been through a lot today. But I saw him, too."

A paramedic interrupted them. "Officer Clark, I need you to sign off on this." The officer took the clipboard, "Excuse me," and tended to his duty across the room.

Julie trailed off to the darkened room where the young officer had taken her bullet, the closest room to the kitchen, which was the dining room.

The paramedics were strapping Greg to the gurney, packing him up. They'd said that he was stable. They'd said that it was possible for the knife to have missed his vital organs. Debra kissed him. "I'll be right back," she said, and went to find Julie.

Just inside the dark room, Julie concentrated on the floor where the officer had fallen, where the officer should have been. No one was there. No blood. No gun. Not even the cap he'd been wearing. But something shiny was lying on the floor in his place, a piece of jewelry. Julie knelt down. Her eyes fixated on it, she touched her own necklace, the half-heart that adorned her neck. Her hands shaking, she picked the golden trinket up from the floor.

Never taking her eyes off Julie, Debra turned on the light, holding an icepack on her lip.

Clutching the trinket she'd found in her fist, holding it to her heart, Julie heaved in throws of sorrow.

"Julie . . . what is it?" Debra knelt down next to her. "What is it?"

Julie placed what she'd found in Debra's hand. It was a half-broken heart . . . on the back, a rose and a tear.

"Only one person had the other half . . . ." A stream of tears befell the fine lines of Julie's face, ". . . my brother."

Debra lifted her eyes, and recited a single word, a name.

". . . Ed."

A cat cried outside the window. A whirlwind of spent leaves dispersed against the old windowpane. The sound, a lingering hush. She knew . . . Ed was gone.

CHAPTER 51

The next morning, Debra came home from Julie's house where she'd spent the night. Wearing clothes she had borrowed from Julie, she carried her blood-splattered clothes from the night before. There was a police issued car in her driveway, a black 1984 Maverick. On her way inside she saw where Jack had broken the locks. In her living room, an official-looking man was taking pictures.

"You must be Lieutenant Barger," Debra slurred just a little, stitches in her swollen lip. "I talked to you on the phone last night."

"Well hello. It's nice to meet you. You had quite a time here last night," he said, shaking her hand.

"It's nice to meet you, too," she said feeling self-conscious, looking rag-tailed in oversized clothes, her freshly washed hair still wet, smelling of Prell shampoo—real shampoo. "I'm just here to change clothes, and wash these things from last night." She stepped the rest of the way into the living room, a dried up version of the night before. "I heard that Jack Wilson made it through surgery last night. Someone called Julie this morning. I just came from there. From what I heard, Jack said that Kyle didn't kill the man on Jaycox. He said Bruce did it. He said he'd only found out yesterday, but I don't believe that. Jack didn't start coming around until that man was killed. I think he was protecting his brother the whole time."

"There will be an inquiry. Your friend Julie must be awfully relieved to know that her husband is coming home."

"So much has happened. It hasn't been a happy marriage, according to Julie. I think they might be getting a divorce."

"That's always sad news to hear. Now, the reason I'm here. I read the statement you gave last night. I'd like to ask you a few questions. If that's all right, I promise not to keep you."

"What would you like to know?"

"The rifle, it's not registered. Where did you get it?"

"My grandfather wanted me to have it. It was my mother's." Debra could feel her heart beating faster.

"Yes. Your mother is in Hamilton County Prison. That must have been rough for you."

"Sometimes." Debra's heart was beating so. He knew she was damaged. Was he looking at the bald spot in her eyelash line? Was he looking at her torn cuticles? She'd only come home to change, to wash her bloody clothes. She wanted to be at the hospital by nine. Her eyes darted between the clock and him. Did he think she was like her mother?

"That's all. Thank you." He folded up some sort of kit and carefully placed it in a leather case.

"That's all?"

He smiled a father-knows-best kind of smile. "That's all."

"I'll be in the basement. Let me know if you think of anything else," she said relieved. Wanting to start some laundry before she went to the hospital, expecting the basement door to open silently, like it had for Greg the night before, she swung it open. The hinges creaked louder than ever. She shivered just as she had so many times. A wolf spider ran across the floor. She took off her shoe and bashed it without shivering at all.

THE END

CPSIA information can be obtained
at www.ICGtesting.com
Printed in the USA
FFOW04n1034211015